THE PATH OF THE RAWL WIELDER

PETE BIEHL

First hardcover edition October 2021

Cover Art by Joseph Gruber
Map by Joseph Gruber

ISBN 978-1-7365286-0-0 (hardcover)
ISBN 978-1-7365286-1-7 (paperback)
ISBN 978-1-7365286-2-4 (ebook)

www.petebiehl.com

For Mercedes,
Who always pushes me to follow my dreams.

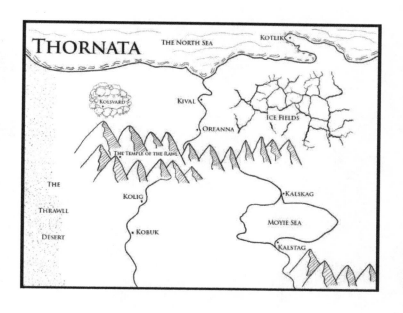

Chapter One

Adel stood at the bow of the ship, gazing out across the water in front of him. The barge wound its way steadily through the slow-moving waters of the Moyie River, drawing ever closer to the towering peaks of the Bonner Mountains. He was staring up at the snowcapped mountains with the same sense of awe that always seemed to strike him when he first caught sight of the stunning peaks. The stone giants had first come into view the afternoon before, and now they towered over him like a grown man standing over an ant. He had sailed this route perhaps a dozen times over the past four years, but the sight of the towering mountains never ceased to leave him amazed. Maybe it was merely the enormity of the stone giants that made him see how small and insignificant he truly was in the grand scheme of things.

Still young enough that many would consider him more of a boy than a man, Adel had served as a cabin boy on this barge for the better part of the last four years. To his knowledge, he had no family left in the world. His mother had taken ill and died without warning, and when she had, Adel had lost his home. Captain Boyd had known his mother for many years and took pity on the young boy. He had offered to take Adel on as a deckhand, even though he'd been a boy of twelve years at the time. It had been an act of charity, but Adel had proven to be more than worth the investment. The young man had met many other captains during the past four years, but had not met any man who he believed would have done the same thing. Adel would be eternally in debt to Captain Boyd, who gave him a place to live and food to eat, but also provided him with fair pay for his work. Furthermore, the job was work he was fortunate enough to enjoy doing.

He would clean the ship and was responsible for ensuring their cargo was not damaged while traveling to its buyer. He also chipped in with any other chores that needed doing, and over the past four years he had become well-versed in all of the ship's functions. Last fall, he had even learned to steer the large craft from the captain's box. He had never been able to comprehend the feeling of power he'd felt while maneuvering the immense vessel. One day, perhaps Adel would save enough money to purchase a barge of his own and sail it across the Empire. As a boy, he had dreamed about seeing places far and wide, places he had only heard of in stories. This job afforded him that opportunity at a young age. The fact that he earned as much coin as any grown man would for the same job spoke to the generous character of Captain Boyd.

Captain Boyd's barge made shipments on the waterways throughout the vast province of Thornata, one of the Empire's most enormous. It stretched across a broad expanse of the Empire's far northern coast, and as such, experienced the most brutal winter conditions of any of the ten provinces. This was their first spring shipment. The barge and its crew had spent the winter docked in the northern port city of Kival. Only a fool would try to run cargo on Thornata's rivers during the harsh winter months.

Adel had enjoyed the time onshore, although he had perhaps spent too much of his coin in the local taverns. He had spent most of his time observing the people from across the Empire that passed through Kival, which was Thornata's largest port. He had always been fascinated by people, particularly those from distant lands, and the long winter in Kival had afforded him the opportunity to learn much. The ice on the rivers had thawed a few weeks early this year, and so the barge was on the river several weeks earlier than usual. For this first voyage, they were carrying a large shipment of salted pork and beef to the southern city of Kalskag.

Adel had become so lost in thought while staring out at the beauty of the river and mountains before him that it came as a shock to hear his own name being called behind him. It was perhaps his greatest weakness, a tendency to become easily distracted. The habit of falling too deeply into his own thoughts was one he had long struggled to break. Reminding himself once again to be more mindful of his duties, he turned toward the voice.

"Adel! Adel! Daydreaming again, are we?" Captain Boyd was approaching, a big smile on his face.

A black-bearded giant of a man, Boyd ran a tight ship, but he was a good captain and treated his crew well. Unlike the men under the command of other captains, Boyd's men were all paid fairly, and their captain genuinely cared about their well-being. Conversations with sailors across the province had told Adel that Boyd was unusual in this regard. Many deckhands were treated as temporary employees, worked brutally until their bodies began to fail, then fired at the first sign of weakness. Few ships were fortunate to have the type of family environment Boyd had cultivated.

"My apologies, Captain. You know how they always draw me in, especially on the first trip of the year. What can I do, sir?" Adel asked ruefully, brushing his sandy-brown hair away from his eyes. He was slightly ashamed of his propensity for daydreaming, and getting caught in the act was always embarrassing. His captain and fellow sailors would occasionally tease him for it, but never with genuine malice. All appreciated his hard work on the barge, and he had truly become a part of their family despite the vast difference in age.

"I need you to go below decks and bring up the crossbows. Stagger them along each rail: port, starboard, and aft. Bring along at least a dozen bolts for each, please," Captain Boyd instructed, his muscular arm indicating the spots where he would like the weapons placed.

"Expecting trouble, sir?" Adel asked, immediately concerned. The crossbows were mainly kept on board as a precaution. They had rarely been brought on deck and had never been used in his four years on the ship.

"Not necessarily, but I want us to be prepared, just in case. When we were docked in Oreanna the other day, another captain told me Hoyt outlaws have been targeting the barges coming through the canyon ahead. The winter must have been hard on the bandit scum, but they'll not be taking our shipment so easily!" Captain Boyd explained, his gruff manner reassuring as always. Boyd was never fazed by anything. The seasoned captain always knew exactly how to command his vessel through any situation, a trait Adel admired. Decisiveness had always been a weakness, and it was a fault that he hoped enough time with the seasoned captain would help him correct.

"Yes, sir, I will have them up right away!" Adel replied, and set to his task without delay.

Knowing they would be entering the canyon within the hour, Adel wasted no time in hauling up the crossbows and bolts. The Hoyt were a group of outlaws who enjoyed preying on the weak and defenseless, but they would regret it if they tried to target this barge. Captain Boyd had served in the Imperial Navy many years before, and he knew how to defend his vessel from attackers.

As Adel was bringing up the weapons, the captain was speaking with his oarsmen, explaining the potential danger and assigning roles should the ship come under attack. That had not happened in the four years Adel had been onboard. His heart beating harder in his chest, Adel hurried to complete his task.

The mountains drew ever closer, and they entered the canyon as midmorning was setting in. There was still an early spring chill in the air, especially here, where the mountains provided a great deal of cover from the sun. Adel retreated to his bunk long enough to pull a wool jacket on over his standard leather shirt. As he climbed back on deck, Boyd called Adel into his captain's box, asking him to keep his eyes open for signs of danger. This did not fool Adel for a moment. The captain was no doubt wanting to keep him as safe as possible should an attack happen. The walls of the box would provide more cover than any other spot on the deck. Adel nervously fingered the hilt of a small dagger he carried in his belt, the sole weapon he owned.

He gazed intently at the rock walls to either side of the river, noting as he did so that it would be challenging to see bandits with the amount of thick green brush and loose boulders lining the jagged shores. Most of the snow on the lower cliffs had melted already, costing them the ability to easily spot people moving above. There were plenty of places for the Hoyt to hide, making him uneasy.

Hours went by, hours which were spent in silence by the entire crew, tense hours of feeling as though a hammer was about to fall, and they were the nail. Adel began to breathe more comfortably as they approached the southern end of the canyon, knowing the edge of the mountains and the open plains beyond were near. Once they were free of the mountains, there would be few places for the Hoyt to plot an ambush.

Moments after the thought passed through his head, the loud thump of an arrow striking the roof of the captain's box shook him back to a grim reality.

"Get to your stations!" Captain Boyd cried out, sending a handful of the oarsmen racing to retrieve their crossbows.

Adel moved to take the helm as Boyd had instructed him. He was to help steer the boat through danger while Boyd led the defense of the vessel. Boyd had stressed that under no circumstance was he to leave the safety of the captain's box.

The men began rowing harder and faster. More arrows were striking the barge now, coming in from both sides of the river. A crewman named Donil was positioned in front of the captain's box. Donil had just loosed a bolt and was reloading his crossbow when an arrow struck him in the leg. Adel cried out to the wounded man, urging him to crawl to the safety of the box. He was hit twice more before he could make a move, this time clean through his chest. He tumbled from the barge, pulled out of sight by the river before Adel could process what had happened.

There were more cries behind him; it was easy to hear that more of the crewmen were wounded, though how severely he dared not turn back to discover. He was terrified, but he could not let that fear take control of him now. The crew was counting on him to steer the barge to safety. If he allowed himself to become distracted, they could run right into a jagged rock, and such a catastrophe would mean the end for all of them.

The noises around him seemed to become one: the crashing waves of the river, the cries of the men around him, the thud of arrows striking the barge, Boyd screaming orders, and the twang of the crossbows as fire was returned toward their attackers.

The end of the canyon was close now; he could see it drawing near. Adel focused solely on the point where the river left the mountains, the point where the Hoyt would no longer be able to rain arrows down upon them from above. That spot was all he allowed himself to focus on; he was not even sure if there were any men still rowing at this point, or if the current was all that was carrying them downriver. He was in a trancelike state, focused solely on the river ahead, willing the current to carry them along faster. For reasons he could not explain, in his highly focused state, it felt as though the current was indeed picking up speed, carrying them away from their assailants. His trance was broken as Boyd crashed back into the captain's box, causing Adel to leap about a foot into the air.

"Well done, lad! We'll be clear of the canyon in a minute. I'm certain I put a bolt through at least one of those thieving scum. The current seemed to pick up a bit as we drew close to the end of the canyon. Sometimes the water is kind to us," the captain said, breathing heavily.

Within moments, they had broken free of the Bonners, the sounds of the pursuing arrows fading and then finally coming to a halt. The rolling foothills they now found themselves cruising through did not afford the same advantageous positions as the canyon had. Adel's head spun in every direction as though mounted on a swivel, but he saw no sign of any more Hoyt bandits. After several minutes of holding his breath, waiting for the next arrow to hit, he let out a sigh of relief. It was over. Adel found his torso was drenched with sweat, and he pulled off the wool jacket. The cool breeze was a relief, though he guessed the heat was not the primary reason for his prior discomfort.

Adel climbed out of the captain's box, and the sight that waited for him left him speechless. At first glance, there were at least four men dead on the deck, and more might have gone over the side like Donil. There must have been at least two hundred arrows buried in the wood of the barge; the Hoyt had wanted their cargo badly. How many bandits had been firing down on them? The sight was so sickening that he was hardly aware of Boyd speaking to him.

"The lads will see to the wounded. Adel, I need you to start pulling those blasted arrows out of our ship. Salvage as many of them as can be reused; we can sell them once we reach Kalskag. Worst-case, we may need to use them to return fire if those bastards have the guts to attack us again," Boyd ordered. Adel detected a hint of grief in his voice for the first time in four years. Adel knew his captain must be fraught with despair over the loss of his men, but he still gave off the aura of strength and confidence required of a commander in such a moment.

Adel set about his task at once, wrenching the black-feathered arrows from the barge. It was tedious work, and more strenuous than expected, as most of the arrows had penetrated deep into the wood. Around half were in good enough shape to fire again; the rest he set aside to burn the next time they were onshore. By the time he finished, the crew had managed to move all the wounded below decks. Of the twenty men who sailed on the barge, seven were dead and four more wounded, leaving only nine of them to continue guiding their cargo toward Kalskag. The ship could sail with as few as four men crewing it, but it would mean a lot more work for those who remained uninjured.

To make matters worse, nearly all of their crossbow bolts had been spent during the attack. If the Hoyt thought to attack again, they would be hard-pressed to defend themselves for a prolonged period. They had longbows available and now plenty of arrows at their disposal thanks to the Hoyt attack, but they lacked the range and accuracy of the crossbows. Adel did take some small comfort from the fact that the land to either side of them was becoming less rugged by the hour. They would soon be sailing through open plains and farmland. The Hoyt would not be able to rain arrows down on them from above as they had in the mountain canyon. Boyd was less optimistic, opining there were likely to be more of the Hoyt waiting up ahead.

"They wanted our cargo, no doubt about that. But they weren't about to take control of the vessel from those cliffs. They probably did not expect us to fight back as fiercely as we did. No doubt, they meant to kill as many of us as possible and make it nice and easy for their comrades up ahead to come aboard and make off with anything of value. I feel a great deal of pity for the fool who tries to board this vessel as long as I am still breathing," the captain growled, Adel noting that he had strapped his sword to his belt.

Boyd dismissed Adel, ordering him to go below and get some rest, shouting down the protests Adel immediately tried to mount. With few of them still able-bodied, the captain needed his crew as sharp and well-rested as possible. Forced to acknowledge that the events of the day had indeed exhausted him, Adel acquiesced and stepped out of the captain's box.

He shuffled down the stairs, his mind still racing to process what had happened during the attack. He had taken some comfort in the chores he'd been given earlier; the busywork had kept the image of Donil's lifeless body tumbling into the river out of his mind. Sitting awake in his bunk, there were no such distractions to keep him occupied. He had never seen such violence up close, and it unsettled him. He had seen his mother waste away from sickness, but to see the life cut from a man so suddenly brought about a range of emotions he had never felt before.

There was no denying the fact this line of work was getting more dangerous by the year, but Adel loved traveling on the barge and could not imagine doing anything else with his life. He had been to almost every major city in the province and hoped to one day sail to other provinces of the Empire as well. All the same, he did not think he could stand another incident like the Hoyt attack. Adel was not much of a fighter, and there was little hope he would ever become a formidable warrior. The gang of bandits had been growing bolder all throughout the previous year, though things were not likely to improve until the Thornatan Army was dispatched to stamp them out. That would be a challenge in its own right. The outlaws had grown in number and had been causing chaos all across the province. How could the army snuff out a group that made their living by spreading far and wide rather than gathering together?

Perhaps Boyd would wait for a while before taking them back north through the Bonners again; he was a man who cared deeply for the well-being of his crew, after all. There was plenty of work to be had moving shipments across the inland Moyie Sea from Kalskag to Kalstag. Besides, Boyd would need to find several new crewmen, which would take time as well. Yes, Boyd would keep them here in the south for a time. They would be much safer here.

If we can be safe anywhere, Adel thought blackly to himself. It was shocking how his entire view of the world could be corrupted in the blink of an eye. Anxiousness chewing away at him, he lay down on his bunk, but much-needed rest would prove to be elusive on that day.

Chapter Two

As he had feared would be the case, Adel was able to find little sleep and was awake again within hours. The nightmares had been too vivid to allow him a decent rest. Deciding he could not bear to watch Donil's lifeless body tumble from the barge in his mind one more time, he rose and got dressed. He climbed up onto the deck to find Captain Boyd at the helm. No doubt, the stubborn and protective man had not slept at all since the attack. A skeleton crew of two other men was on the deck; the captain must have ordered most of the crew to bed. The sun was just beginning to show itself on the eastern horizon, and the moon had not yet fallen entirely out of sight to the west. Adel offered to take the helm so the captain could get some sleep and was utterly unsurprised when Boyd shook his head.

"I don't need rest, lad. I need justice for those men I lost yesterday, but I'm not likely to get that anytime soon, am I? Until the Hoyt start bothering the nobles and the rich men, the duke won't do anything about them, will he? The lack of action is pathetic; it's as though the plight of the common people means nothing. So, how about a few pieces of bacon? Fetch a few for yourself too, and maybe a few bread rolls to go along with it. I wouldn't say no to something to drink either. If I can't sleep, I might as well have something to eat. We need to keep our strength up," Boyd replied wearily.

Adel climbed back down below decks, and within a few minutes had returned with a plate of bacon, bread, and two cups of cider. The captain wordlessly accepted the food and drink, and the pair stood in the box in silence, no doubt lost in feelings that were better left unshared. The food was hard to swallow, Adel finding he had no appetite despite not eating for almost an entire day. With every bite, the images of the day before raced through his head. Adel suspected their thoughts were not so different. It was Boyd who eventually broke the silence.

"I promised your mother I would keep you safe. I came pretty close to failing that promise yesterday, and I can't stop thinking about it. How are you holding up, my young friend?" the captain asked.

Adel hesitated, not wanting to say anything to upset the man who had been so good to him over the past few years. He knew the captain took the safety of his men seriously, and Adel even more so due to his young age. He thought of Boyd as a close friend, and the captain had been a father figure to him in many ways. Adel had never known his own father, but if he could choose one for himself, it would be the steady and reliable Captain Boyd. He knew if there was anyone he could confide in, it was the captain.

"I saw Donil die right in front of me during the attack. He got hit in the leg and then twice in the chest before he could crawl to cover. He fell off the barge, and there was nothing I could do about it. I never thought I would see such a thing, and it disturbed me in a way I didn't think was possible. A man I knew, who I'd sailed with for years, and he's gone in an instant. It doesn't make sense to me that something like that could happen. All I could think of last night was why it happened. I couldn't stop thinking about his lifeless body just tumbling into the water. It keeps playing over in my head, and I can't make it stop. He was here one second and gone the next, and it bothers me."

Adel paused. He had been fighting to keep his emotions as neutral as possible. He did not want to show any weakness to the captain; he needed to demonstrate his strength at a time like this. Boyd would never judge him, but he wanted to appear as dependable for the captain in this hour of need as possible.

"It happened because the Hoyt are greedy, lazy scum of the earth. They want the rewards of hard work without earning them for themselves," Boyd replied fiercely. The graphic description Adel had provided of his crewman's death was obviously troubling to him. He did not want to amplify his captain's pain, but his confusion demanded more questions.

"Yes, but how can they do that? How can they mercilessly end a person's life in an instant like that? We did nothing to harm them. What kind of people are willing to kill for robbery? Are our lives worth so little to them? They never even said a word to us," Adel said, trying and failing to envision a situation where he would be put into a mindset that would allow him to do such things.

"When I served in the Imperial Navy, I often wondered the same thing. Our chief mission was to run down pirates in the southern seas, way down in the Elven Isles. They would target merchant ships, often killing everyone on board so they could take whatever they pleased. Often, they did not even know what was on the ships before they attacked. Yet still, they would butcher every last crewman to get at it. There were times we came across vessels full of murdered men, and not a single item had been stolen. All those lives were snuffed out for no reason at all. The pirates didn't even take the cargo, even though they had been willing to murder so many to get their hands on it. In time, I realized some men are so selfish that they have no feeling for anyone but themselves. Their own comfort and pleasure are more important to them than the life of another person. For some of them, I think they get a thrill out of it, as sick as it sounds. The act of killing and marauding is enjoyable to them."

Adel fell silent, reflecting on what the captain had said. Could it be that simple? Was the world merely full of people who cared nothing for the lives of their fellow men? Was he surrounded by men who cared more about a cheap thrill than they did about the well-being of others? This was a depressing thought. Until that point, Adel had thought of people as generally good-hearted in nature. The idea that there could be so many callous, indifferent people in the world was nothing short of disgusting.

"I will tell you one thing," the captain said, interrupting Adel's thoughts. "If I ever cross paths with any of those Hoyt bastards again, I will show them exactly how much the men I lost meant to me. I swear I will hack the life right out of the next Hoyt who thinks he is going to take my vessel."

No sooner had the words left his mouth then the barge was turning around a bend in the river. The sight ahead of them left both men stunned. A chill ran down

Adel's spine. He had known this was possible, but his foresight did not make the sight any less horrifying. Small boats, at least two dozen of them, were lined up across the river ahead of them, blocking their path forward. Looking closely, Adel could see that the boats appeared to be connected by a long chain, and the ends of the chain were fastened to trees on each shoreline. There was no way around them; the river had been completely blockaded.

They were still far enough out that he could not see the men aboard the boats, but he had little doubt as to their identities. The Hoyt had found them again. Nobody else would go to the work of blockading the river. Captain Boyd swore loudly, then began crying out to the remainder of his crew, shouting for the men below decks to get to their stations. They were fast to respond; fortunately, it seemed sleep had eluded them as well.

He ordered all men to take up a crossbow or longbow and prepare to fire on the enemies ahead. Adel moved to take a position with them, but the captain's outstretched arm stopped him before he could take two steps. The captain's message was clear without saying a word: Adel was to stay in the box once again. He obeyed wordlessly, stepping to the helm; Boyd did not have time to argue with him. He hated leaving the others to do the fighting, but he would never disobey Captain Boyd, especially in a moment of crisis.

The current was bringing them closer to the Hoyt

at an alarming rate. Adel could see the barge would be within the range of their longbows within minutes. Once again, he could feel the fear set in, this time far more palpable than the day before, the images of his dead crewmates flashing through his mind. They were going to die, and there was nothing they could do about it. Had it not been for the chain, their barge could have possibly slammed through the line of smaller boats, but they could not break through the chain. The Hoyt would catch them like fish in a net. There were not enough healthy crewmen left to row the barge against the river's southbound current, not that it would matter much if they could. Even if there were enough men, they would end up right back in the same canyon where the previous attack had occurred, sheep for the slaughter once again.

The thought of what would happen if he was still alive when the Hoyt boarded the barge now began to creep into his mind. The Hoyt were not known for their mercy nor their kind treatment of those unfortunate enough to cross their path. He had heard stories of men who had been found, strung from trees by their ankles, and then burned alive. Another tale told of a ship full of men who'd had massive rocks tied around their necks and had then been thrown into the river to drown. The Hoyt did not just enjoy killing; they reveled in making the act as gruesome as possible.

I will not die in such a way, he thought, steeling himself for what lay ahead, preparing to fight them with everything he had. He was armed with nothing but the small dagger on his belt. He began to mentally prepare himself for the possibility of using it against an enemy in close quarters.

They were a few hundred yards away from their enemies now. The closer they drew to the Hoyt ships, the faster the current seemed to move. From Adel's perspective, time sped up right along with the current, the last moments of his life slipping away from him. He was absorbed so deeply in his fears that he jerked in surprise when one of the Hoyt began to shout.

"Good voyages to you, my friends! May I ask what you are carrying on your fine vessel?" The disarming voice was trying to convey friendship, but the effort to hide the underlying malice was quite unsuccessful.

"Cotton and wool, bound for Kalstag," Boyd lied. His voice was quivering slightly, though with fear or rage, Adel could not tell.

"That is quite interesting," the messenger called out. "There must be some terrible misunderstanding. You see, the dock records in Kival show that you cast off with a significant amount of salted meat and other foods. I must confess that my friends and I are quite hungry; this past winter was a harsh one for us. Could you perhaps find the kindness in your hearts to let us onboard to fill our bellies with some of your fine shipment? We will pay you quite generously for the inconvenience, of course!"

He is being quite nice for a man with a dozen boats

blocking our path, Adel thought.

"Is that a fact? And what amount are you willing to pay, exactly?" Boyd asked. His voice was calmer this time, the iron-clad resolve he had shown the entire time Adel had known him taking over. He was standing directly in front of the box, his hand tightly wrapped around his loaded crossbow. Adel knew Boyd was not buying the Hoyt's story any more than he was.

"Oh, it's quite straightforward. You will give us your cargo in exchange for the lives of the thirteen men left aboard your vessel. Is my count correct? Although I must say, I am growing rather impatient; it is rude of you to make us wait for an answer like this," the Hoyt replied.

Without further warning, a single arrow flew up into the air and then dropped toward them. Faster than anyone could react, it came flying in, striking one of the crewmen squarely in the head. He was dead before his body hit the deck, his crossbow clattering down with him. The rest of the men raised their crossbows in anger, but a sharp word from the captain stopped them in their tracks. Silence fell upon them for a moment, broken only by the distant chuckles of the Hoyt.

Adel stared down at the man's lifeless body, there one second and gone the next, just like Donil, all so a gang of thieves could steal from them. He had never been so angry in his life; he wished he were a great warrior like the captain. Boyd would, without a doubt, be able to take a few of the Hoyt down with him when they boarded, and Adel envied that. Maybe he would be able to get at least one of them with his dagger. The least he could do would be to rid the world of one thieving, murderous bandit. The Hoyt was shouting at them again from the blockade.

"Nasty business, it's quite unfortunate. You have my deepest condolences for your loss. You see, my friends, our patience has its limits. Now the price we are willing to pay for your goods is twelve lives. If you stall any longer, that number will continue to drop. We do hate to be kept waiting. It's rather rude of you. What do you say, Captain? Is your cargo worth more to you than the lives of your men?"

There was another moment of silence. Adel knew Boyd was considering his options, trying to decide if the Hoyt were genuine in their promise to let them go if he turned over their shipment. Adel did not doubt the captain would do so if he felt that it would save the lives of his crew. But the reputation the Hoyt had earned in Thornata suggested there was no reason to trust them to keep their word. Boyd seemed to have reached the same conclusion, and an expression of acceptance crossed his face as he bellowed his response.

"I will make you an offer, you Hoyt scum! Any man who wants to board my vessel will receive my sword through his neck as a toll. That will be payment for the lives they have already taken from my crew! What is your reply to that?" Captain Boyd cried out.

The reply was a volley of arrows that came flying in before Boyd had finished speaking. The deck of the barge erupted into chaos, the crewmen rushing for cover while trying to return fire. Boyd was shouting orders, but he was so close to the front of the captain's box that Adel couldn't understand a word. He ducked down low, trying to present as small of a target as possible. There was little need to steer the barge anymore. The river was close to a perfectly straight line making its way toward the blockade. A second volley followed the first, and then a third and a fourth after that. He could not see much, but men were dying around him; of that much, Adel was certain.

It was at that moment Adel felt angrier than he had ever been. Twenty good men, men who wanted nothing more than to make an honest living for themselves, were going to be dead because of these murderous thieves. They were going to die so the Hoyt could have a feast they hadn't earned. The Hoyt would murder them to feed their bloodthirsty gangs of bandits so they could go on to kill and steal again. The injustice of it was infuriating, and his fists clenched in rage.

They were within a hundred feet of the Hoyt boats now; the arrows were coming in from close range. Adel would never understand the feeling that urged him to step out of the safety of the captain's box. All he knew was that some force was compelling him to step out and face the Hoyt himself. At that moment, the world around him seemed to disappear. He did not hear Boyd screaming at him to get back in cover, did not notice the arrows flying in all around him. All he knew was that he was angry and needed to direct that anger at the people who deserved to receive it. The whole world was comprised of himself and the Hoyt bandits who sought to kill them. Nothing else mattered.

He reached the frontmost railing of the barge, though he was barely aware of where he was; his focus was solely on the Hoyt boats. He was about thirty feet away from the nearest Hoyt warrior, close enough to see his face, contorted with glee as he loosed yet another arrow, this one straight at Adel. The arrow flew straight until the last second when a sudden gust of wind blew it off course. At that moment, Adel could not spare any thought to how strange of an occurrence it was that the arrow had been blown off course so abruptly. All he knew was that he needed to focus his anger at the Hoyt.

The river beneath them was angry as well, powerful waves surging forward toward the Hoyt, slamming into their boats and knocking the men off-balance. Strange, the waters had been so calm moments earlier. The river was as enraged as he was. But that was insane; a river could not be angry. It was nothing more than an illusion in his head. But what if it wasn't? Without even understanding what he was trying to do, Adel focused on the Hoyt and silently spoke to the river, telling it what he wanted it to do. Later, he would think back on how crazy this thought was, but at the time, when their lives were in danger, it seemed the sanest idea that had ever occurred to him.

To his complete amazement, the water seemed to respond, surging toward the Hoyt boats harder than ever. A massive surge struck the boats, sending most of the Hoyt bandits into a state of total disarray. Could this really be happening? There was only one way to find out, and he focused his thoughts one more time. This time, the water rose from the river, forming a massive ball suspended in the air. It was a spectacular sight, one unlike anything Adel had ever witnessed before. With one last surge of concentration, Adel willed the ball of water to crash into the Hoyt boats, and so it did.

It struck with tremendous force. Thousands of gallons of water fell upon the Hoyt with the power of a small hurricane concentrated into a minuscule area. Most of the small wooden boats splintered into hundreds of pieces from the force of the impact, their crews washed away by the crushing strength of the water. The water hit with such power that it ripped the long chain free from the trees on the shore. The attack lasted only a few moments, but the destructive force was incredible and terrifying to behold.

As quickly as the attack had come, it was over. The barge was already moving through the spot where the blockade had been a few moments before. Adel was still standing at the front of the ship, perfectly still. His head turned as they passed through the remnants of the

Hoyt boats, taking in the driftwood that was all that remained of the Hoyt blockade.

Had that truly just happened, or was this some sort of hallucination formed by his dying brain? In the moment, he couldn't help but feel the latter was the more plausible explanation. Adel glanced down at his body, searching for any visible wounds, but he found none. But this could not possibly be real; it was impossible. He had never heard of anyone having the ability to do what he had just done.

Within seconds, a sense of extreme fatigue fell over Adel. He was still not sure what he had done, or even if he had actually done anything at all, but his strength was gone. His legs were no longer working, and he could feel them giving out on him. He collapsed to the deck, his arms so heavy that he was barely able to stop himself from hitting his head. He felt as though he had not slept for weeks, and the need for rest was overpowering him on the spot. He fought as hard as he could against the sensation, but his eyelids were drooping and he could not force them to stay open. The blackness overtook him before he could so much as move from his position. He slumped over sideways right there on the deck, leaving his companions every bit as confused as he was.

Chapter Three

Adel came awake to find his head spinning and his surroundings nothing more than a dizzying blur. He was unsure of where he was or what had happened. The only thing he knew with any degree of certainty was that his head was in horrible pain and he was struggling to move his limbs. His arms and legs all felt as though they were weighed down by bags full of rocks, and each movement he made was an incredible struggle. For the first few moments after his eyes opened, everything around him seemed to be swimming in circles. His senses came back slowly, and he became aware of Captain Boyd sitting nearby, his face coming into focus. He was still on the barge, lying comfortably in his own bunk. They must have carried him down here after he had broken them through the Hoyt blockade.

At that moment, it dawned on Adel how insane the thought truly was. It must have been a dream; he could not have single-handedly dispatched so many boats, so many men. A river following his orders? He must have struck his head in the commotion and had a strange dream. That was the only sane explanation for the insane memories that were coming back to him more vividly by the second. He looked at the captain, who appeared to have dozed off in his chair while watching over him. Boyd would have the answers he needed; he was confident of that. He cleared his throat loudly, bringing the captain awake with a startled grunt.

"Adel! You're finally awake! You had us all quite worried, lad," the big man said, smiling down at him.

"Captain, what happened?" Adel rasped, realizing his throat was parched as he attempted to speak. The captain rose, hurried to one of the water casks, and returned with a cup. Adel sipped it down, his throat too dry to allow him to drink normally. He must have been unconscious for quite a while.

"What happened? To be honest, Adel, I was hoping you could fill me in on that. We were done for; those bastards were filling this boat full of arrows. We were a few minutes away from being close enough for them to come aboard and finish us off. You could have told me you had a trick up your sleeve!" Captain Boyd exclaimed.

"You mean to tell me it was real? That I wasn't dreaming? That I somehow got us through the blockade?"

"Got us through it? Boy, you ripped that blockade to shreds! In all my days, I've never seen anything like it, boats reduced to driftwood in a matter of seconds. I would never have guessed you were a mage. You could have confided in me; I would have kept your secret."

Adel felt his confusion grow deeper by the second. He was no mage, of that much he was sure. He had spoken with several mages a few years ago while the barge was docked in the far northern city of Kotlik. He had asked them what it felt like to summon their magic; he had always been curious about how the process worked. All of them had given similar answers: it felt like slowly drawing power away from their own bodies. They had described creating fire or water at the tips of their fingers; he had not done this. His own experience had been entirely different. Their power came from within, while his felt as though it were tied to the environment around him. He had not created water from thin air, rather he had somehow managed to channel the river to respond to his need. There had been no slow, steady drain of his energy. He had experienced a sudden feeling of immense power, right up until the moment he had collapsed on the deck.

"I'm not a mage, Captain, and that is the truth. I

have no idea what happened. All I know is that I was so angry at what was happening, so angry at the Hoyt. Something compelled me to walk out onto the deck; it was like an instinct. I had no idea what I was doing. The only thing I knew was I wanted to stop them. For some reason, I just knew I could do it. I've never experienced anything like that in my life," Adel said. He struggled to find more words, feeling all the while as though this explanation was woefully inadequate. If he couldn't believe it himself, what would Boyd think?

Boyd gave him a long, hard look, and Adel knew the captain was trying to decide if his story was to be believed. Maybe Boyd thought he was a liar, that he had been hiding the truth about himself for all these years. When the captain failed to speak again for a few moments, Adel took the opportunity to ask a question. He dreaded the answer, but he had to know.

"How many of us are left?"

"We lost four more during the attack. Fortunately, most of our wounded are starting to recover. You were out cold for nearly two days, you know. We should reach Kalskag by midday tomorrow," Boyd replied, sighing heavily.

Four more men were dead, and Adel could not help but feel responsible. If he had stepped out of the box sooner, perhaps they could have been saved. Maybe this was all his fault, and Boyd was probably thinking the same thing. It was possible the captain would not even want him onboard the barge anymore. He wouldn't blame the captain for feeling that way. But where would he go, what would he do? The captain spoke up again, as though he had read Adel's mind.

"I have something I need to say to you, Adel. Thank you. Thank you for doing whatever it is you did. If you hadn't, all of my men would have been butchered back there, and me along with them. I've known you for many years now, and I've never known you to be a liar. So, if you tell me you don't know what happened back there, then that's all I need to hear. I believe you, and I want you to know that I will do everything I can to help you figure out exactly what that was," Boyd said reassuringly, the familiar smile back on his face once more.

Adel felt a rush of gratitude for the kindly captain, the closest thing to family he had left in this world. The man had shown him so many acts of kindness over the years, but this was perhaps the most meaningful. To have the faith and trust of the man he looked up to more than any other filled him with a deep sense of relief. Now that his fear of losing his home and job was relieved, his mind strayed back to the questions of exactly what had happened, though he knew he was unlikely to get answers until they arrived in Kalskag. For now, he might as well get back to being a productive member of the crew.

"I should get back to work, Captain. What do you need me to do?" Adel asked, his feet beginning to swing out of his bunk, fighting against his weariness.

"I need you to shut your hole and lie back down. Whatever it is that happened, it drained everything you had in you, and I don't need you working before you are ready. Stay here and rest. I'll bring you some food in a bit. Don't argue with your captain; I said you are to stay here and rest, and that's an order," Captain Boyd said sternly, one hand holding Adel effortlessly in place as he tried to rise in protest.

With that, the big captain climbed to his feet and started to walk toward the stairs but stopped and turned as Adel called out,

"Captain! Thank you, sir."

With a smile and a nod, Boyd turned and climbed back up to the deck.

Adel lay back in his bunk, though his sense of relief at the captain's acceptance was unable to completely relieve him of his newly mounting anxiety. Going back to work would have helped keep him distracted; instead, he was left alone with his thoughts. Now that he knew he had not been dreaming, he could not help but reflect on every last detail he could remember. The intensity of his rage and the river seemingly rising up to match it was stuck in his mind. How was it possible? He had heard of mages who were capable of incredible feats of power, but never had he heard of a man being able to control the power of a river. Such an act was beyond the capabilities of any man. Nobody could manipulate nature in such a way.

He took some heart from the fact they would be in Kalskag tomorrow, safe from the Hoyt within the protective confines of the city. The ragtag band of outlaws would never try anything in a large city like Kalskag; the Thornatan Army would not stand for it. Boyd knew a great many people in every city of Thornata, and he no doubt knew somebody in Kalskag who could explain what had happened to Adel on the river. He needed answers—of that much he was sure. He would not be able to rest until he had them.

No sooner had the thought passed through his mind than he found himself drifting back off to sleep, his body still not recovered from its exhausting ordeal. His overactive mind struggled against the darkness, but sleep won the battle swiftly, leaving his questions to be pondered another time.

***

On Captain Boyd's orders, Adel did not go back onto the deck of the barge until they entered the city of Kalskag the next afternoon. It was a sobering moment, seeing the severely depleted crew for the first time. A few of them spared him cautious glances, but none of them offered any words of greeting. This came as little surprise; Captain Boyd had warned him some of the men were frightened by what they had seen him do to the Hoyt. He tried not to let his face show how much the silence disturbed him. He hoped they would regain their comfort around him in due time.

Kalskag and its twin city of Kalstag were among Adel's favorites in the province. Sitting on opposite shores of the vast inland Moyie Sea, the nearly identical cities were the youngest of Thornata's major cities. The buildings here were built from stone and marble instead of the wooden structures more common in places like Kolig and Kobuk. They also rose far higher than those in the cities to the north or west. Some of these buildings rose as high as seventy or eighty feet, a sight Adel had been awestruck by the first time he had set eye on them. He had grown up near the city of Kobuk, an older, much less modern cluster of wooden buildings. Boyd had told him tales of cities in other provinces where the buildings seemed to reach all the way to the clouds, such as the dwarven city of Muog in the distant province of Qwitzite. Such a thing seemed impossible, and Adel suspected the captain must be embellishing such tales.

Boyd steered the barge to their assigned dock and ordered his crew to begin unloading their cargo and delivering it to the buyer. The wounded men were to go to a nearby healer to have their injuries examined and treated in any way necessary. Boyd would pay for their expenses upon his return. Then he beckoned for Adel to join him in the captain's box.

"All right, lad, you and I are going to pay a visit to

a friend of mine. He has traveled all across the Empire and has seen a great many unusual things. He is something of an expert on the oddities of the world, so to speak. There isn't much out there that he has not encountered at one time or another. We will find him in a tavern not too far from here. It's not in the friendliest part of the city, so I want you to stay close by and don't let your gaze stay on anyone for too long. People in this area are not known for hospitality, and they don't appreciate gawking strangers. We're not in this part of town looking for new friends. Understood?" he said as he secured his sword on his waist, a gesture that Adel did not fail to notice. Boyd rarely carried his sword onshore, leading Adel to heed his warning about the area they would be visiting.

Adel nodded in agreement, and they climbed off the barge and made their way across the dock and into the city proper. The streets closest to the docks were filled with merchants hawking their goods to travelers passing through on the river, but these soon gave way to alleys filled with taverns, inns, and gambling houses. The pair occasionally had to sidestep ragged looking people lying in the streets, though it was difficult to tell at times if they were homeless or merely overcome with intoxication. Adel had never frequented the taverns in this part of the city. In fact, he had never ventured here at all because of the area's rough reputation.

Boyd guided him toward a tavern called The

Purple Dinosaur. Immediately upon entering, Adel could see this establishment catered to the type of people he would prefer to avoid, if possible. A handful of green tables dotted the center of the room, and most were filled with patrons. The stench of ale and sweat was as strong as he had ever encountered, the pungent aroma bringing tears to his eyes. Looking around, it was hard to tell if the stench emanated from the patrons or had been ingrained over time in the horrendous, shaggy purple carpet. The patrons looked like a rough crowd, and Adel made it a point not to make eye contact with any of them, as his captain had advised. Boyd gave him a tap on the shoulder and motioned for him to follow. Adel did so without delay, eager to be out of the place as soon as possible.

The captain led Adel to a door in a far corner of the tavern and then through a narrow corridor. At the end of this corridor was a single door, which Boyd tapped on four times. There was the sound of a man on the other side of the door cursing, followed by impatient footsteps. The door flew open to reveal a diminutive elf with an irritated expression etched across his face. Upon recognizing Boyd, this stern expression gave way to a grin, splitting the old elf's face from ear to ear.

"Boyd! What's it been, my old friend, three years? Four? Get in here this instant! You never were one to bother with making appointments, were you? I wasn't expecting you, but you know you are always welcome here." The elf greeted the barge captain with a warm embrace.

Boyd and Adel followed the elf into what appeared to be an office. Loose bits of parchment were strewn all over the room and the small desk the elf moved to sit behind. Adel had seen a few elves in his life. However, they rarely came to Thornata, preferring the warmer tropical climates of the southern provinces, particularly the tropical Elven Isles that they called home. This fellow was quite small compared to the others Adel had seen, and far older. Most elves were similar to a human in physical size, albeit usually a bit leaner. Adel would guess the elf's age to be well into his seventies or eighties based on his thin streaks of receding white hair and the numerous age spots dotting his face.

"Brought a guest for me to entertain, have you? Well, any friend of yours is a friend of mine. How do you do, young man?" the elf greeted Adel, reaching over and shaking his hand with a grip surprisingly firm for a man so small and old.

"I'm sorry to say this isn't a social call. This is Adel; he is a deckhand on my barge. To be honest with you, he is the reason I have come to see you. Adel, this is Keeler. I know him from my time in the navy," Captain Boyd explained.

"What's the matter, Boyd? Not going to tell the boy the whole story?" the old man said with a laugh. Boyd began to reply, but Keeler cut him off before he could get two words out, launching into a story.

The Path of the Rawl Wielder

"Your captain here was in command of a ship that was running down pirates on the elven coasts in the far southern waters of the Empire. Beautiful islands and coastlines down there. If you've never been, make sure to get there before you die. These cold Thornatan winters have me longing for those days. Anyway, in those days, ships used green flags to signal when they were in distress. So, Boyd here sees a ship out in the water with a green flag flying and rushes to respond like the fine naval officer he is. The second his crew starts to board the vessel to investigate what was wrong, he realizes he's walked right into a pirate trap. So, the pirates take him and a few of his men captive while helping themselves to all the weaponry on Boyd's ship. Imperial High Command would have been quite displeased with him for that! He would have lost his command if my men and I hadn't stumbled across those pirates before the Imperial Navy did. Of course, that's assuming the pirates wouldn't have taken his head off first! That was a proper fight, and those pirates didn't know what hit them!" Keeler obviously took great joy from the telling of the story, his mouth split in a wide grin the entire time. Adel thought he even saw the elf wipe away a small tear of laughter as he finished talking.

Adel had a hard time imagining Captain Boyd being fooled so easily. The thought of the captain, who was now red with embarrassment, as a young man was a foreign concept to him. It was almost as foreign as the thought of this tiny elf doing battle with pirates. Keeler must be the type of man to embellish his stories. Boyd seemed to sense the skepticism.

"Oh, don't let this one's size fool you; he is something to behold with a sword in his hand. I would wager he is still one of the finer swordsmen in the Empire, despite his rather advanced age," Boyd explained with a small smirk at the end.

"Make another quip about my advanced age and you may just find out how fine my skills still are," Keeler chuckled. "They could use some practice, as a matter of fact, so don't tempt me. Very well, enough gossip and stories of days long gone. I'm sure you can see I have quite a bit of work to keep up with here. I swear, I'm not cut out for an honest day's work. I never worked this hard in my life. But of course, I'm sure you already knew that. Oh, to be out there on the open water again. I haven't had a proper fight in years. What can I do for you, Boyd?" Keeler asked.

Wasting no time, Boyd launched into an explanation of the events of the past several days. He told the elf about the initial attack by the Hoyt in the Bonner Mountains and then the blockade in the plains. When he came to Adel breaking the barge past the blockade, the boy expected the old elf to reply with skepticism, but to his surprise, Keeler listened intently to the entire tale. Once Boyd finished, Keeler looked toward Adel.

"Is this whole story true, Adel? This old sea dog

didn't put you up to pulling a joke on me, did he?" he asked.

"It's all true," Adel confirmed.

"Well, then I'll tell you exactly what you need to do. You need to go and visit the Children of the Rawl. I've heard tales like this several times over my many years, though such instances are uncommon. It always seems to happen when the person in question, in this case Adel here, is under some form of great duress. They all seem to lead back to the Children of the Rawl. Rumor is, they're a group of people who are capable of manipulating the earth and environment around them into doing their bidding, but not much else is known about them. What they do isn't magic, not in the traditional sense, at least, from what I understand. They are just attuned to the world around us to an extent that the rest of us could never imagine. They're a secretive group, and they rarely communicate with the outside world. Don't want word of their secret powers spreading too far, I suppose. Having seen quite a bit of the outside world myself, I can't say I blame them. It's a nasty place full of nasty people."

The promptness of the response left Adel speechless. Boyd had not been lying; Keeler had undoubtedly seen much of the world. Could these Children of the Rawl help him understand what had happened to him? He knew he had little choice but to find out. The mystery of what had happened on the river was not one he could live with without seeking an answer.

"Do you know where to find these Children of the Rawl?" he asked.

"No, nobody does except those who have crossed paths with them. Rumor is they are based right here in Thornata, but I haven't the faintest idea where. But you are in luck. I know a man who is in Kalstag at the moment and has been in their service for several years. I can tell you how to find him, and maybe you can persuade him to take you to them," Keeler replied.

Keeler proceeded to write down the name of the man they needed to find and where in Kalstag he could be found on one of the countless scraps of loose parchment that flooded the small office. Glancing at the back of the paper, Adel saw it had previously been used to record various gambling debts Keeler was owed. The elf did not know exactly what type of work the man did for the Children of the Rawl, but was sure he would know where they could be found. The pair was in the process of thanking Keeler for his assistance when the door of the office was blasted from its hinges. They spun to see five large men rush into the cramped office, their black clothing unmistakable. The Hoyt had found them again!

"We will make this simple for you, elf," the largest said, his mocking tone of voice at the last word unmistakable, sneering down at Keeler's small frame. "We're going to be taking the boy. Stand back, and we will allow you to live. If you try to resist us, we will burn your dump of a tavern to the ground with you inside it! What will it be?"

Everything seemed to freeze for a moment. The nearest Hoyt fighter was no more than three feet away. Adel had no weapon with which to defend himself other than a small dagger. Boyd carried a longsword, but would no doubt be killed before it cleared his scabbard. Keeler rose and waved his hands disarmingly, attempting to calm the situation. He shot the Hoyt a broad smile as though he were addressing a group of old friends.

"Relax, everyone! There is simply no need for such tension. You should go out to the tavern and buy yourselves a drink. I would offer you one on the house, but a man has to make a living, doesn't he? I'm sure hard-working men such as yourselves understand. If a day should ever come that I am intimidated by a mob of dull-witted Hoyt brutes, do be kind and toss me into the sea with a stone tied around my neck!" Keeler said, his voice innocently trying to smooth the insult as he hurled it at the Hoyt.

"That can be arranged," the Hoyt leader growled, clearly in no mood to be insulted. He waved a hand, and his men began advancing on Keeler. Boyd shifted in a futile attempt to block their path. Now all of the Hoyt were advancing on them, weapons in hand. The tiny room gave them no space to maneuver; they would surely be killed like fish in a barrel.

The Hoyt leader had taken no more than two

steps toward Adel before Keeler exploded into a whirlwind of motion. He stepped out from behind his desk, drawing a short-bladed scimitar from a hidden compartment near his waist. The Hoyt leader took a swing at the elf with his longsword, the blow so wild that Keeler did not even need to parry it. The tiny elf was within reach before the man could swing again, the scimitar opening his gut and then taking off his sword hand in what seemed to be a single fluid motion. The Hoyt leader hit the ground hard; he would be dead within moments. His companions stepped back for a moment, unsure of themselves before squaring off against the tiny elf.

"Oh dear, my friends, running would have been the wiser option," Keeler advised them.

Boyd seized Adel by the arm and dragged him behind Keeler's desk, trying to shield him from harm. Adel stuck his head back above the desk in time to see Keeler's scimitar open one of the Hoyt from waist to collarbone; he had never seen anybody move so fast! Then Boyd was dragging him back below the desk, leaving him to listen to the gruesome sounds of the brief but ferocious fight. Within moments, the sound of clattering metal and grunting fighters had stopped, leaving only the sound of Keeler, clicking his tongue in disappointment.

"Ducking under the desk, my old friend? You must believe I am well beyond my prime after all, Boyd! I will admit, that took longer than it would have in the old days, but as I said, it's been a long time since I had a good fight. I wanted it to last! The oafs could have at least given me the courtesy of a challenge if they were going to make me get out of my chair. At my age, I don't get up unless I think something is actually worth the effort. It's one of the pleasures of old age that you will discover for yourself if you are fortunate. What a pathetic display."

Boyd rose cautiously, allowing Adel to come up a moment later. He was stunned by the sight that met his eyes. Five Hoyt warriors were dead on the floor, more wounds on their bodies then he could begin to count. Keeler appeared to be entirely unharmed. If anything, his face bore an expression akin to boredom. Many of the scraps of parchment scattered across the room were steadily turning red from the blood of the fallen fighters. Looking down at the mess, Keeler clicked his tongue in annoyance again.

"Well, it seems the Hoyt are not pleased with what you did to them on the river. If I were you, I'd be getting out of Kalskag before more of them show up. They apparently know you are here and are angry enough to risk drawing the wrath of the army to get to you. Just look at this mess, all my paperwork ruined. I should have made it a more painful end for them," lamented Keeler.

"What about you? Aren't you in danger now?" Adel asked, pointing to the dead Hoyt on the floor, but Keeler merely chuckled in response.

"Any more of them who want to come and try to shake me up will meet the same fate as these beauties. In fact, once I clean up this mess, they will probably get it worse. Boyd, always good to see you, old friend. Now, you get this boy safely to Kalstag, you hear me?"

Boyd nodded and clasped Keeler's hand in farewell before leading Adel back out through the tavern and into the street. Their pace was much quicker this time. It was clear to Adel that Boyd was anxious to get back to the barge and out of Kalskag as soon as possible. If those Hoyt had found them, it was likely there were more nearby. When their companions did not return, they would be out looking for Adel.

Adel noticed Boyd glancing continually in every direction as they walked, his hand never straying far from the pommel of his sword. They walked in silence until Adel felt the urge to speak. The thoughts that came to his head in the silence were nothing he wanted to dwell on.

"Keeler must have been quite a soldier; I've never seen anyone who could fight like that."

"Soldier?" Boyd started laughing. "Lad, Keeler was no soldier. He was a pirate, just as nasty as the group that captured me, if not nastier. They were operating in his waters, so he came after them and happened to rescue me in the process, quite by accident. When he found me on their ship, I was shocked when he didn't kill or try to ransom me. Sailed me back to my crew and everything! He's an odd fellow, no doubt about it, but he's a good man underneath it all, or at least as good as any pirate can be. He has his own code of honor, not one like any other I've encountered, mind you, but a code nonetheless. He never killed the victims of his robberies. He saved his brutality for other pirates who had the audacity to get in his way. Eventually, he grew tired of the pirate's life and began traveling around the Empire, opening businesses like the shockingly classy tavern we just left. He must have a dozen of them by now, bought and paid for with his pirate booty, and making him more money than his life of crime ever did. I guarantee you he hates every second of it, though. He would love to be back out of the high seas, but he's too old for that life, even if he would never admit as much out loud."

Adel let Boyd's explanation sink in for a moment. The elf's demeanor had been more in line with what he would expect from a pirate, though he had not thought to piece that together during their meeting. It was a small surprise that Boyd would associate with a former criminal, even one who had saved his life, but he supposed they were lucky he did. The thought of more Hoyt trying to rough up the small elf gave him the slightest feeling of amusement. There would be fewer of the scum to trouble Thornata if they tried. Hopefully this acquaintance of Keeler's would be able to help him.

He was shaken out of his thoughts as they arrived back at the barge. The crew had returned from the healer and were awaiting instructions. Boyd gave the order to cast off at once. With the Hoyt already in the city, there was no time to wait for a cargo shipment to haul to Kalstag with them. They would make no money from the trip, but there was no help for it. Within minutes they were casting off from the dock and making their way toward the Moyie Sea with an empty barge and more questions than they'd had when they'd arrived in Kalskag. At least they had a person to contact who may be able to help them. Adel was confident this matter would be cleared up within a matter of days.

Chapter Four

A week after departing Kalskag, the small barge and what remained of its crew reached the southern coast of the Moyie Sea and entered the harbor of Kalstag. Kalstag bore many similarities to its twin city of Kalskag. Both had been built at roughly the same time, around three hundred years ago, and to the untrained eye appeared identical from a distance. The main difference was that Kalstag was the city closest to the southern border of the province of Thornata, and as such, saw a far more diverse array of visitors from other regions of the Empire. It was not uncommon to see elves, dwarves, and men from distant provinces roaming its streets.

Captain Boyd wasted no time in pulling the barge into the nearest available slip. Once they were docked, he asked Adel to wait on the barge while he made arrangements for their next shipment. Adel noted that this took a bit longer than usual, but eventually the captain returned and beckoned for Adel to join him. Adel assumed Boyd had taken longer due to wanting a shipment to take back with them to Kalskag. With the continued threat of the Hoyt north of the Moyie Sea, it was unlikely they would venture farther north in the near future; they may even spend the entire season in the southern reaches of the province. Without further delay, the pair made their way into the city together.

Keeler's contact was a man named Ola, and he was to be found at an inn overlooking the Moyie Sea on the northern edge of the city. Keeler had said that Ola moved around Thornata frequently, but the pirate was confident he could be found in Kalstag if they did not tarry in getting there. Boyd led the way through the city streets, and Adel did not fail to notice the way his eyes were continually scanning in every direction. He surmised that the captain was concerned the Hoyt might have tracked them here, a concern he shared, especially after what had happened at The Purple Dinosaur. Once again, the captain had retrieved his sword prior to leaving the barge.

Adel had reassured himself that the Hoyt had managed to track them down so easily in Kalskag because it was their logical next stop after the attack on the river. Still, the swiftness with which they had located them at the tavern was quite alarming. The Hoyt's network must be vaster than he had previously imagined. It was entirely possible they had been watched from the moment their barge docked in Kalskag. Even now, it was likely there were Hoyt spies following their every move.

Their voyage across the Moyie Sea had been uneventful, a fact for which Adel was immeasurably grateful. Boyd had not spoken to him much during the trip, other than to assign the occasional chore. Adel knew the events of recent days had taken a toll on his captain. Losing so many of his crew and being under constant fear of attack by the Hoyt were heavy burdens for Boyd to bear. He had even noticed a few streaks of gray in the captain's otherwise jet-black beard. The thought of everything they had endured together filled Adel with a rush of gratitude for the steadfast captain who remained by his side. He knew he owed the man a debt he could never repay.

"This is the place," the captain announced, sooner than Adel had anticipated.

Adel was surprised to find they had arrived at one of the newer looking inns in the city. His expectations had been formed by the seedy type of establishment in which they had met with Keeler. However, it appeared Ola preferred a cleaner, more comfortable setting, which drew no complaints from Adel. At least here he would not have to be wary of looking too long at the wrong person. Adel had not given a great deal of thought to the man they were coming to meet, thinking of him more as a means to an end. Now he could not help but wonder about the type of person he was about to meet. Was this another flamboyant former criminal like Keeler? He noticed Boyd was looking at him expectantly; Adel nodded his readiness to enter.

Boyd approached the innkeeper and asked where they could find a man named Ola. The man seemed surprised anyone would be asking, but nonetheless directed them to a room on the third floor. The pair made their way up the two flights of stairs to the third floor. They then made their way along the hallway to the room the innkeeper had indicated. Adel had never been inside an inn quite this nice before, and he allowed himself a few extra glances at the artwork that decorated the halls, but the captain seemed impatient to get on with business. He knocked on the door of the room the innkeeper had directed them to and it swung open within seconds, as though Ola had been expecting them.

"Welcome, welcome. It took you longer than I expected. Please, come in. I trust you made sure you were not followed on your way here?" the contact said in greeting.

Both Boyd and Adel stood in the hallway in shocked silence. Keeler had neglected to inform them that the man they were coming to see was an ogre. Ogres were a rare sight outside of the mountains of their homeland far to the south. They were exceptionally uncommon in the far northern province of Thornata. He stood well over six feet tall, perhaps even close to seven. His thick, dark skin was exactly like Adel had heard of in the tales; it even had the famous bluish color to it. There was a prolonged moment of silence as Ola stared back at them, seemingly not noticing the shock of the two men. At last, it seemed to dawn on him.

"Keeler didn't tell you I was an ogre, did he? No doubt he thought it would be terribly amusing to allow you to discover that fact on your own. It is precisely his idea of humor. Please, we need to hurry, time is short. The Hoyt are searching for you endlessly, and it will only be a matter of time until they track you here. They have many resources here in Kalstag, more than you might suspect." Ola opened the door wide to allow them to enter his room. The ogre's voice was rough, though he spoke with the words of a well-educated man.

Overcoming their initial surprise, the pair followed the ogre into his room. Motioning for them to be seated at the table, he latched the door securely behind them. Moving to the window, he glanced out at the street below before drawing the curtains closed. Adel now noticed that Ola was garbed in thick plate armor from his neck to his feet. Scanning the room, he saw the largest greatsword he had ever seen on the bed; it may very well be as long as Adel was tall. Whoever Ola was, he was obviously prepared for a fight. Seemingly realizing nobody else was about to start the conversation, Captain Boyd spoke up, breaking the awkward silence at last.

"Keeler seemed to think you could help Adel," he began before the ogre cut him off.

"I very much intend to try, Captain Boyd. Answer me this, boy. Was the incident with the Hoyt on the river the first time you have ever experienced anything like this? Or have there been other occurrences?" Ola asked.

"Yes, it was the first time. To be honest, I still don't fully understand what happened. Can you explain it to me?" Adel replied, struggling to maintain a steady voice as he addressed the intimidating ogre. Ola's voice and words were nothing short of polite, if somewhat abrupt, but the ogre's fierce countenance was particularly daunting.

"No, I am afraid I cannot, but it is crucial that we get you safely to the Children of the Rawl as soon as possible. The leader of the Hoyt is a man named Idanox; you may have heard of him. He was once well-known for his wealth. However, he has used his considerable resources to build the Hoyt. He is not a merciful man, and what you did to his men will make him quite angry. I have reason to believe he has heard of you and your exploits on the river. He is now searching for you with great interest. I can only assume that he either plans to eliminate you or attempt to sway you to join the Hoyt," Ola said.

The Path of the Rawl Wielder

He doesn't waste any time on formalities, this one, Adel thought. Still, he needed more information if he was going to be convinced to set off alone with an ogre about whom he knew nothing. Ola could not possibly expect him to do so. Perhaps a few probing questions would be enough to shed some light on Ola and reveal if he could be trusted.

"Tell me about yourself. Why should I trust you or these Children of the Rawl? How did you know we were coming to see you? It seemed as though you were expecting us."

"We can talk later. Time is of the essence, and we need to leave now. Every minute spent here is a minute the Hoyt could be using to close in on you," Ola replied, as blunt as ever. The ogre was now moving about the room, throwing his few belongings into a canvas sack.

So much for gleaning any information, Adel thought, frustrated by the ogre's evasive nature.

"You will answer his questions now, or he is going nowhere with you!" Captain Boyd interjected. Once again, Adel felt a rush of gratitude for his captain.

This interjection seemed to anger Ola, or at least his face contorted in an unpleasant manner that Adel assumed indicated anger, or perhaps annoyance. But the barge captain did not seem to care much about offending Ola. He had watched over Adel for these past four years, and it was clear he was not about to let him set off with some stranger who could not be bothered to address Adel with respect. The ogre glared at the captain for a moment, and then upon realizing Boyd was not going to back down, he sighed in resignation.

"As you know, my name is Ola. I have served the Children of the Rawl for many years now. I do so in payment of a debt I owe them. I do whatever they ask of me, although typically that involves searching for people like you, people who have demonstrated that they may possess the power of the Rawl. I do not know what I can say to win your trust. I can only stress that without the proper instruction, your power could prove to be perilous. It will be a danger both for yourself and for those around you," Ola explained, his voice rather monotonous, as though he was trying to convey his thoughts while using as few words as possible.

"Dangerous? How?" Adel asked, his curiosity heightened.

"You saw the destructive power you possess with your own eyes, Adel. The power of the Rawl can be used for so much more than destruction, but you need somebody who can train you properly in its use. The Children can do this; we must get you to them before you are discovered by the Hoyt. If they find you, and you are forced to use your powers to defend yourself again, you could inadvertently harm or kill innocents, or even yourself. You need to be taught to control your abilities properly. The consequences of failing to do so could prove to be catastrophic," Ola said.

The Path of the Rawl Wielder

"The Rawl, is that the name of my power? What is the Rawl?" Adel's curiosity was piqued.

This time there was a long pause. Ola seemed uncertain of how he should reply. Adel did not doubt that the ogre would prefer not to provide an answer at all. At last, he began to speak again, his words slow and uncertain.

"Please understand, the Children can explain this much better than I can. It is not a power I possess myself, so my information is secondhand. However, in most basic terms, the Rawl allows its wielder to manipulate the world around them. As you saw for yourself, you can shift the waters of a river, even utilize them as a weapon if necessary. You could potentially manipulate the wind or the sand of a desert. The possibilities are endless, but if you do not learn how to harness them safely, you will not survive. The danger is more pronounced now that the Hoyt know of your gift and are quite angry with you for using it against them. They are searching for you. They already located you once, in Keeler's tavern. They will do so again, in greater numbers, if we do not get out of Kalstag immediately. They will not give up easily," Ola explained.

Adel slumped back in his chair, uncertain of how he felt. His instincts told him that he could trust the information Ola was giving him was true. But even if it was, should he leave behind his life and travel to train with these Children? He glanced toward Boyd for guidance, but his companion seemed lost in thoughts of his own, not looking Adel in the eye. It was unlike Boyd to remain quiet at such a time.

It was at that moment it dawned on Adel that he had no choice in the matter. He could not stay on the barge anymore, not with the Hoyt hunting him. Boyd and his crew had suffered enough at the hands of the outlaw gang as it was, and he could not live with himself if he asked them to risk themselves further on his behalf. If the Hoyt attacked again, his power might resurface, and what if he could not control it? What if he accidentally killed Boyd or another crewmate? He knew the captain would never ask him to leave, would never even suggest such a thing. But this was not a burden Adel could lay on another's shoulders. There was no decision to be made at all; it had already been made for him. He could not stay on the barge, and he would not survive long on his own. Therefore, he must go with Ola and hope the Children of the Rawl could help him.

"Very well, I will come with you, Ola. Where will we find these Children of the Rawl?" Adel asked, his decision made much quicker than he had expected. He hoped it was the right one.

"They have lived for many years in the Temple of the Rawl. It is located above a valley deep within the Bonner Mountains, northeast of the city of Kolig. Once there, you will be quite safe from any threat that the Hoyt pose to you. Captain, would you be kind enough to ferry us across the Moyie Sea to Kalskag? From there, we will need to travel on foot across the plains," Ola said, turning his attention to Boyd.

Captain Boyd hesitated for a moment and then began to reply, but Adel cut him off. He had already decided that Boyd and his crew's involvement in this matter had ended. There was no point in extending it further for their convenience.

"No, Ola, we will leave on foot from here. I will not continue to risk the lives of Boyd and his crew with my continued presence. If the Hoyt are hunting me as you say they are, then anybody with me is in danger, and I will not allow that. Captain Boyd and his men have taken on enough risk on my behalf. Whatever lies ahead, I cannot ask them to face it with me."

The ogre looked as though he might argue the point, but decided against it and shrugged his acceptance. Boyd shot Adel a glance, and he could see the gratitude in the captain's eyes. He did not doubt Boyd would have done as the ogre had asked. He would want to keep Adel safe for as long as possible, but the time for allowing himself to be shielded was gone. It was time to take responsibility for himself. Captain Boyd had given him a chance at a good life. The rest was up to him.

"As you wish. Return to your barge and gather anything you'll need for this journey. I will come for you shortly; we must leave the city at once, so please do not delay. Be alert in the streets, for the Hoyt have spies everywhere," Ola said.

Nodding his consent, Adel rose and moved for the door. Boyd rushed to follow, perhaps surprised by how Adel was taking charge of the situation. Adel had concluded that it was time to take control of his own destiny. He could not ask Captain Boyd to protect him, could not hide and hope the Hoyt would not find him. He had to take action that would allow him to face the trials before him on his own. For now, the Children of the Rawl seemed to be his best chance of doing this.

The pair made their way back through the inn and out onto the streets of Kalstag. No words were exchanged while they walked. It was the end of a chapter of their lives. Boyd was undoubtedly hoping for a return to something akin to normalcy. Adel did not even fully understand what he was hoping to find. As long as he could keep Boyd and his crew out of danger, it would be enough.

They reached the city docks, and Adel knew his old life was coming to an end much sooner than he could have ever suspected. As they moved closer to the slip where the barge was docked, it felt as though his childhood was falling away from him. It was time for him to grow into the man he was born to be, even if he had never suspected that time would come so soon. In spite of this, he knew there was one more thing he must do before he walked away from the life he had known for these past four years, one last thing he must do in order to truly leave the boy behind. He stopped a few yards short of the barge and turned to his captain. There was something that needed to be said.

"Captain Boyd, I want to thank you for everything you have done for me. You have given me a home and treated me as though I was a member of your own family. I do not know what would have become of me after my mother's death, were it not for you. I will never forget that. I owe you a debt I will never be able to repay." Adel extended a hand to the grizzled barge captain, who seemed quite taken aback by the statement.

"Lad, you don't owe me a thing. You have earned everything I have ever given you a hundred times over. The only person you owe anything to is yourself. Go and discover yourself, Adel. Discover who you are meant to be in this life. I have treated you like family because I think of you like family, and I hope that we cross paths again before this life is over," Captain Boyd replied, clasping Adel's hand.

"As do I, Captain. Where is your next shipment heading? Hopefully not back through the Bonners; I wouldn't want you to cross paths with the Hoyt again so soon," Adel said, still concerned about what might befall the barge and what remained of its crew.

"No worries there, lad. I've arranged for our next shipment to take us south and out of Thornata for the time being. It's just too dangerous with the Hoyt operating here, and I won't risk more of my men's lives needlessly. We will sail south and explore more of the Empire. Hopefully we can pick up more crewmen along the way; we are going to need them. Our first stop is an Imperial fort about five hundred miles south of here, in the southern reaches of Verizia. It's a long journey, but it should prove to be quite an adventure!"

Adel felt a wave of envy wash over him; he had always wanted to explore the other provinces. But that was not his path, not now at least. He had an adventure of his own to embark on, and there was no time to waste. Climbing onto the barge, he hurried to his bunk and emptied his trunk of his possessions. He had a sizeable amount of gold he had saved over the last four years, as well as his knife and a ring his mother had given him when he was young. He slipped the ring onto his finger, pocketed the money, and belted the knife securely to his waist. Everything he owned could be carried comfortably in a small rucksack, which he slung over his shoulder as he made his way back onto the deck. It struck him as he stepped out of the cabin that he was probably saying goodbye to this barge for the last time.

He said his goodbyes to the rest of the crew in short order, not wanting to give himself the temptation of second thoughts. The men seemed distant, as though they were still uncertain around him after what he had done to the Hoyt. He could not blame them; he would have reacted the same if their positions had been reversed. The captain was waiting for him on the dock, and the two shared another handshake and a quick embrace. Beckoning to him, Boyd led him out of sight of the others, Adel noting that he had a large package wrapped in a blanket tucked under one arm.

"I have a few things for you. First, some gold, and don't you dare try to turn it away. It's the payment you rightfully earned by doing your job and a small bonus for saving my skin back on the river! So take it with no back talk. Now, this second thing is a gift, and again, I don't want to hear a word of protest," Boyd said, cutting Adel off before he could argue.

The captain unwrapped the large package he was holding, and Adel was shocked to see a magnificent sword. The blade was razor-sharp and had the shine of a weapon that had been cared for meticulously. The hilt and pommel were a perfect fit for his hand, wrapped in black leather that felt marvelous to the grip. The weapon was of the most excellent quality Adel had ever seen, yet also surprisingly lightweight for its size, allowing him to hold and move it with relative ease. The sword was housed in a sturdy leather sheath that could be easily attached to his belt.

"I have a feeling you'll need a better weapon than a dagger on your journey, so I want you to take that. It's mine from when I served in the navy, but I haven't used it in years. They don't make them like that anymore. I want it in hands where it can possibly do some good. I'll feel better knowing you have it. So you'll take it with you, and that's the end of the matter," Boyd explained, again leaving no room for protest.

At a loss for words, Adel nodded and clasped the captain's hand one last time. He quickly fastened the sheath to his belt. It would take time to grow accustomed to the feel of the weapon on his waist, but the captain was right, he was sure to need it at some point. He jumped at the sudden voice behind him.

"Are you ready to depart? Have you retrieved your belongings and said your goodbyes?"

Ola had arrived to guide him to the Children of the Rawl. He had his possessions, and his goodbyes were said. But was he ready? Adel was not satisfied that he was, nor was he sure if he ever would be. Yet he knew there was nothing to be gained by stalling further. He nodded his readiness and turned to nod a final farewell to his captain.

"Farewell, Adel. You were the finest cabin boy any captain could ever want. The next time we meet, you will have changed the world. I believe this to be true with all of my heart," the captain said before turning back toward his barge.

Adel looked at the barge for one last moment before turning to Ola and indicating he was ready to depart. The ogre gave him what appeared to be a smile and began to lead him away from the barge. It occurred to Adel that he was not only walking away from the dock and away from the city, he was also walking away from the only life he had known for the past four years. All of that was behind him now, and the only thing ahead was an uncertain future. Steeling himself to meet whatever it held in store for him, Adel walked toward it without looking back.

Chapter Five

For the better part of the next week, Adel and Ola made their way west and then north along the western shoreline of the Moyie Sea. Adel had always prided himself on how many places he had voyaged to aboard the barge, but he had never traveled this far from the major cities before and was stunned to find so many new and unfamiliar sights waiting for him. The sheer enormity and beauty of the countryside were astounding to him. The lands to the south and west of the Moyie Sea were mostly farmlands. Their crops fed most of the province, for the regions north of the Bonners were too hard and their winters too long and cold to sustain farms. While the fields looked mostly identical to

Adel, he enjoyed the trek, seeing the first signs of life creeping up through the early spring frost.

So onward they marched, the Moyie Sea on one side and seemingly endless fields of corn, potatoes, and soybeans on the other. By the end of the first day, Adel had come to the realization he was not traveling with the most talkative of companions, and this was even more obvious now, a full week later. Ola rarely spoke, other than to announce when they were departing or stopping for the day. Any attempts Adel made at conversation were met with the briefest acceptable answer the ogre could possibly provide. As soon as the reply was complete, the awkward silence would resume.

Still, Adel had enjoyed the opportunity to observe an ogre up close, no matter how little interest Ola showed in conversing with him. Most of the information he knew about them came from stories he had heard in taverns around Thornata. Most of these tales had depicted the ogres as mindless, war-hungry beasts who lived for the pleasure of their next kill. After this time spent with Ola, Adel had concluded that such stories were not true. True, Ola was a solitary example of an entire race, most of whom had secluded themselves deep in the Ogra Mountains far to the south, but he found it difficult to believe Ola could be the sole exception to a rule. Ola spoke eloquently and had manners far more civilized than most of the men Adel had encountered on docks and in taverns throughout Thornata's cities.

When they had stopped for the evening on the western shore of the Moyie Sea, Adel decided to attempt to engage the ogre in conversation once more. He felt perhaps if he kept trying, he could coax the ogre to open up to him. He had done so on every night of their journey since leaving Kalstag. Thus far, the strategy had not paid off, but Adel was patient, and he hoped his patience and persistence would pay off. Doing his best not to let the futility of his prior attempts discourage him, he posed his first question.

"How long do you think it will take us to reach the Temple of the Rawl?" he asked, trying to start with an easy question that he knew Ola would answer.

"Perhaps ten days if we have good weather and are not delayed. We will soon be heading into the foothills of the Bonners, and the trek will be more difficult as we climb uphill," was the ogre's brief response. Adel had not expected a lengthy reply but had merely been probing, hoping to make the ogre more comfortable speaking with him.

"How did you meet Keeler? Do you know he used to be a pirate? We were attacked by the Hoyt in his tavern, five of them, and he killed them all. I've never seen anything like it before. What sort of business do you do with him?" Adel tried, hoping Ola would be more open to talking about an outside party.

"I do not do much in the way of business with Keeler. I am aware of his past, though I do not judge him for it; a man's past is his own. But my work for the Children of the Rawl takes me many places. Having contacts in these places is useful, and Keeler has more connections than most. So I befriended him, and it has been a fruitful relationship," Ola said cryptically. It was enough, Adel decided, to lead him into the question that he had been dying to ask.

"Can you tell me more about the Children of the Rawl? Who are they? Where do they come from? What makes you think they can help me?" Adel asked, hoping he was not proceeding too quickly, fearful the ogre would retreat into his shell if he did.

"They can help you, rest assured of that. They possess a great deal of knowledge about the power you wield. The Children can show you how to use it in a safe manner. I do not know where they come from originally; they have all lived in the temple for as long as I have served them. As for who they are, you know what they are called. What else would you like to know?" Ola said, blunt and straight to the point as always.

Frustrated at the ogre's lack of helpfulness, Adel fell silent for a few minutes. Then a question occurred to him. He asked without thinking it through, though he did not have much hope at this point for an elaborate answer.

"Ola, why do you serve the Children?" he asked, wondering if his incessant questions would eventually anger the ogre.

There was another long moment of silence, a

moment so long that Adel began to suspect his companion was now ignoring him altogether. He stole a glance at Ola's face, though interpreting the ogre's expression was not a feat of which he was capable. The silence stretched long enough that it came as a slight surprise when the ogre finally started to speak.

"They did me a kindness many years ago. Perhaps one day I will tell you what that kindness was, but it is not important now. I expected that they would then demand my service in return, but they told me I did not owe them a thing. This was the first time in my life that I had encountered people who acted for others while expecting nothing in return. I found myself wanting to serve them, wanting to be of help to the people who had been of help to me. I believed that to do so would be serving a just and righteous cause. So now I serve them, and I do so happily."

Adel lay back and reflected a bit on what the ogre had told him. That had been the most Ola had spoken to him since they had left Kalstag, and the first words of any real weight. He wondered what kindness the Children had done for Ola, but decided he should not press the issue this night. Ola had made it clear enough no answer would be forthcoming, so there was no sense in pushing further. But he had gotten the ogre to open up, if ever so slightly. Perhaps going forward he would have an easier time of it. Besides, he was growing weary, and as he drifted off to sleep, he felt there would be plenty of time for answers later.

He woke with the rising sun in his eyes and the sound of voices in the air. He sat up to find Ola standing over him with his greatsword drawn, and was immediately filled with a sense of dread. Looking around, his worst fears were confirmed. No fewer than six Hoyt were approaching swiftly from the north, their black garb immediately recognizable. Wide awake now, he rose and drew the sword Captain Boyd had given him. He had never fought with a sword before, and the idea of experiencing such a thing for the first time while facing a Hoyt fighter was a terrifying proposition.

Oh well, he thought, *there's no help for that now.*

Ola motioned for him to take a few steps back. Adel was happy to comply, but he knew there was no way to avoid fighting this time. The fight was coming whether he was ready for it or not. All Adel could do was fight his hardest when it arrived and hope it would be enough to fend off the Hoyt. He examined the blade, finding that Boyd had kept it razor-sharp over the years. Breathing heavily, he held it out in front of him, trying his best to look like he knew what he was doing.

"Stay behind me; do not engage them unless you have no other option. No matter what, do not attempt to use your power, for the consequences could be catastrophic," the ogre instructed, never taking his eyes off the approaching attackers. They were closing in on them rapidly; they would be within speaking range within moments. Adel had barely opened his mouth to reply when one of the Hoyt interrupted him, shouting out in a voice that echoed across the empty fields around them.

"Well, what have we here, boys? I can't say I've ever seen an ogre before, and what a magnificent specimen he is," the Hoyt exclaimed loudly as they approached.

"I need a new pair of leather gloves for next winter. You think the skin we're gonna carve off his face would be a comfortable fit?" another joked, drawing a raucous round of sycophantic laughter from his companions.

"Looks pretty thick; you might have a hard time sewing it. Might have to tan it for a few weeks first," another Hoyt replied, again to a round of laughter.

A rather simple sense of humor, Adel thought in disgust. He had never in his life been a violent person, but he would be happy for the opportunity to stick his sword into one of these brutes.

"All right, ogre, here's the deal. We are here for the boy, not you. Turn around and start walking, and maybe you escape with your life, whatever that's worth to you. Or you can stand there and try to scare us with that big sword of yours and die, because your life sure isn't worth a damn thing to me!" the first Hoyt called out to Ola. "What's it going to be?"

There was a long moment of silence as the Hoyt waited for Ola's reply. As Adel had anticipated, based on his own experience with the ogre, no response was forthcoming.

At least it isn't just me he doesn't like to talk to, Adel thought, allowing himself the briefest moment of amusement. The ogre silently held his position, staring at the Hoyt with his fierce eyes, his sword held calmly in front of him. Realizing Ola was not going to respond, the Hoyt began to laugh.

"What's wrong, ogre? Are you too dim-witted to know how to speak? Or I wonder if you're too stupid to even understand what I am saying to you right now? Not surprising, as I always heard the ogres were a race of dumb brutes. I suppose I could point and grunt. Maybe he would understand that better, boys. Maybe once the Hoyt are done conquering Thornata, we will head south and butcher whatever is left of your savage disgrace of a people. Nothing of value would be lost, and your pelts might make nice coats for the winter!" the Hoyt shouted, taking delight in ridiculing the silent ogre. Adel glanced at his companion, but Ola made no move to indicate he was offended in the slightest.

The Hoyt looked as though he planned on continuing to taunt Ola; however, for a brief moment, the ogre became a blur of motion. The Hoyt fighter found himself unable to speak because a throwing knife was buried deep in his neck. The look of shock upon his face lasted only moments, and then he was collapsing to the grass, a pool of blood forming beneath him immediately.

The remaining Hoyt drew their weapons at once, no longer interested in playing their entertaining little game.

"Kill the ogre, and make sure it is slow and painful for him! Idanox wants the boy alive. Don't harm him any more than necessary," one of the Hoyt cried out, and they charged as one.

One of the men was much faster than the others, and he reached Ola first, crying out in rage and swinging wildly with a large poleaxe. Ola shifted his stance, angling his body to one side to avoid the swing of the long weapon, and then struck twice with his greatsword. The first strike caught the handle of the poleaxe, cleaving it in half. The second strike did the same to the man who had been wielding it, sending him to the ground in two pieces amidst a shower of blood.

The remaining four Hoyt seemed to slow their charge upon seeing their comrade cut down so effortlessly, but on they came, nevertheless. Instead of charging blindly as their companion had done, they began to spread out, trying to surround the mighty ogre. Two in front of him and one to each side, they began to feint and thrust from different directions, trying to breach the ogre's defenses. Ola was severely outnumbered, but his long arms and the massive greatsword gave him a decisive reach advantage over the men trying mercilessly to cut him down. Adel stared in amazement as Ola deflected every attack launched his way. The ogre moved with a grace and effortlessness that defied logic for a man so large. He was a blur of motion as Adel tried in vain to follow the movements of his sword.

Growing impatient, the man to his right ran at the ogre while his back was to him, hoping to drive his sword into Ola's back while he was distracted by his Hoyt comrades. Adel cried out in warning, and the ogre spun with inhuman speed. How could it be possible for someone so large to move so fast? His greatsword flashed forward in a killing thrust, catching the Hoyt in the gut and running him through all the way to the hilt.

Again, the remaining Hoyt sought to take advantage of the ogre's apparent disadvantage. Ola reacted faster than should have been possible. His greatsword still lodged in the Hoyt's gut, he swung it around to deflect the oncoming attacks, taking the body of his previous victim along with it. Adel stared in awe of Ola's tremendous strength and skill. His attackers backed away momentarily, apparently as awestruck by the power of the massive ogre as Adel was. Ola took this moment of distraction to the slide his sword free of the body of the Hoyt he had slain before resuming his defensive posture.

One of the Hoyt charged Ola in a desperate rush, his sword striking fast, but wildly. Ola expertly parried every single blow before at last countering with a strike of such force that it tore the other man's weapon from his hand. Before the man could think to flee, Ola's greatsword had cut him down, leaving him in a bloody pile on the ground. Two Hoyt remained now, and it was more apparent by the second they were regretting their decision to attack the ogre.

They attacked as one, trying to strike Ola on two sides at the same moment. Once again, the ogre displayed footwork that defied his large stature, easily stepping back and away from the attacks, the strikes hitting nothing but thin air. Now he struck back, the greatsword coming down once and then twice, each well placed strike cutting the life from one of his remaining foes. All six Hoyt dispatched, he calmly drew a cloth and began to wipe down his greatsword in silence. It took Adel's mind a moment to comprehend what it had witnessed; six attackers brutally defeated within a matter of seconds.

"Ola, how did you do that? Where did you learn to fight like that?" Adel cried out, unable to contain himself.

He was filled with a mix of awe at his companion's skill, fear that they had been found, and disgust at the sight of the six mangled Hoyt corpses. He did not pity the thugs in the slightest, but witnessing death in such an up close and violent manner was not something he felt he would ever grow accustomed to seeing. He took comfort that, unlike the men on the barge, these men had deserved exactly what they had received.

"I learned when I was younger. I have seen my fair share of battles in my life, more than I care to remember. With experience comes skill, if you are fortunate enough to survive the experience," Ola replied, vague as ever. Evidently, the thrill and excitement of a battle did not make him more inclined to be talkative.

Adel was still so awestruck that the ogre's typical short-worded answer did not bother him for once. What did bother him was the fact that he had been able to do nothing during the attack. He had been forced to stand back and hope Ola was capable of handling the Hoyt without his help. If any of those men had broken through the ogre's defense and reached him, he would have been unable to protect himself. What was the point of having this sword, Adel wondered as he sheathed it, if he did not know how to use it? The solution came to him at once, and he blurted it out without a second thought.

"Can you teach me how to fight?" he asked.

Ola had clearly not expected this question, and he seemed quite taken aback by the request. He stopped cleaning his blade and turned to face Adel. He hesitated for a long moment before responding, his words slow and uncertain.

"I am here to see you safely to the Children of the Rawl. If fighting is needed along the way, I will handle it," was the response.

"So your duty is to protect me, correct? What if something happens to you along the way? I would be left alone in the wilderness with no way to defend myself. If the Hoyt found me, I would not be able to stop them from taking me to Idanox. Apparently, he wants me alive, and I cannot imagine his reasons are good for me. It is your duty, therefore, to show me how to protect myself if needed. I don't know anything about these Children of the Rawl, but I can't imagine they would be pleased if I was injured or killed because you refused to teach me how to protect myself," Adel rebutted, quite pleased with his own reasoning.

Again, the ogre took his time responding. When he did, it was not the response Adel had been expecting. To his utter astonishment, the ogre began to laugh. Not a brief laugh, but a long, deep, full-bellied laugh that Adel would never have suspected the ogre capable of producing. Adel watched in amazement as Ola roared with laughter.

"Well, you certainly do have a way with words, young man. Very well, beginning tomorrow, we will train every evening. There is a village nearby; we can acquire sparring swords for our training sessions there. If you truly want to be taught, I will teach you, but you should know that I will not go easy on you. After all, this is a matter of survival, as you said," Ola replied, at last flashing him a rare smile.

"Good, I want to learn. I am tired of standing aside and allowing others to protect me," Adel said, realizing as he did how much he must sound like a whining child.

"You are too hard on yourself, Adel. If it were not for you, the Hoyt would have butchered your captain and his men on the river. You possess power far beyond anything I could ever do with a sword, and you are on your way to learn how to use it properly. Never forget that. Always know your own value. With that being said, I agree, you do need to know how to fight with a weapon. Such a skill could save your life. So, I shall teach you if that is your desire," Ola replied.

Again, the ogre had astonished Adel with his lengthy response. He was beginning to believe there was more underneath Ola's gruff exterior than the ogre had allowed him to see thus far. Ola was hesitant to share information about himself, which was understandable, but Adel resented this fact for the simple reason that he was entrusting his life to this man. Before he could reflect on this further, Ola was speaking again.

"We need to get moving again, Adel. I think it is best if we leave the shoreline of the sea from here; it makes it too easy for the Hoyt to track us. We will cut across the countryside toward the Bonners. We should make haste. Once Idanox discovers these men failed to capture you, he will no doubt send more, in greater numbers. There may already be more groups nearby if they suspect you are in this area. We have to reach the temple as soon as possible."

The mention of the ongoing threat from the Hoyt brought Adel back to his senses. Ola was right; they had to go quickly. Satisfied that his companion had agreed to teach him how to use his sword, he decided that would have to be good enough for now. Still, Adel was determined to learn more about the mysterious ogre before their journey was complete. Resigned to the fact that this would need to wait, he nodded his readiness. He followed Ola away from the shore and the mutilated bodies of their attackers. It was time to head onward toward the Children of the Rawl. At least he would no longer be a helpless boy for much longer.

Chapter Six

The blow was racing toward Adel's head so fast his eyes could hardly follow it. The movement of his sword to deflect it was more instinctual than it was premeditated, though the effect was the same. The attack glanced away harmlessly, though the force of the impact reverberated throughout his entire body. Another strike was coming toward him before he could even begin to devise a counterattack, this one a thrust aimed straight for his gut. It would be impossible to parry this blow with his sword; his foe had forced his sword too far outside of his frame. Instead, he used his feet, stepping to the side and evading the attack by inches. His opponent was now the one caught in a compromised position, fully committed to a thrust that had failed to find its mark. Now was the time to press against his opponent's disadvantage and take the offensive.

He launched his attack, shifting all of his weight to his back foot to propel himself forward with greater speed. His first strike cut down toward his opponent's neck, but his foe was far too skilled to be overcome by such a simple maneuver, his feet moving with inhuman speed, carrying him out of the path of the attack.

No problem, Adel told himself, moving fluidly from one attack into the next, determined to end the fight before his foe could regain the offensive. He strung his strikes together, one after another. He moved, not with the grace of an experienced swordsman, but rather with that of a skilled novice. He pressed forward, determined to finish off his opponent.

Such a feat would not be accomplished with ease. Adel's opponent was exceptionally skilled, dancing away from or parrying every offensive strike launched in his direction. It was no use, no matter how fast Adel struck, no matter how unpredictable he attempted to be, he could not breach his opponent's defenses. Frustrated, he feinted to the left, drawing his foe's defenses to that side before pulling back and swinging from the right with all of his might. His opponent's blade inexplicably snapped into position to deflect his, striking with shocking force and then twisting his sword from his hand before he could blink, let alone launch another attack. Adel was left defenseless, his sword lying in the dirt a few feet away.

"That is enough for tonight," Ola announced.

Adel was sweating heavily, his tunic soaked through entirely, and his eyes were stinging from the salty perspiration now dripping into them. He was frustrated that he had been unable to land a single strike once again. He was disappointed as well that for the fifth consecutive day, Ola had been able to end their training session by disarming him at will. It was a rather demoralizing feeling to watch his sword fall to the dirt whenever the ogre decided the lesson was over. How was Ola able to move so fast? He would never have suspected a man of that size could move with such ease.

He stalked over to the spot where his training sword had landed, retrieving it and returning it to his pack. Ola had acquired a pair of blunted swords from a village they had passed a few hours after the Hoyt attack, and they had trained every evening since. Each lesson had been a frenzied whirlwind of pain and exhaustion, Adel struggling the entire time to keep up with his companion. Fortunately, the Hoyt had not appeared again, and Adel had not been forced to put his training to practical use. He was increasingly grateful for this after each lesson. He moved to take a seat, his limbs aching from the strain of the session.

"You are improving, Adel. Every day you are better than you were the last. You should be proud," Ola commented, apparently aware of his young trainee's frustration.

"Yet I still can't even come close to striking you. It sure doesn't feel like I've made much progress," Adel replied, attempting and failing to hide the bitterness in his voice.

"You have been training for a mere five days, young one," Ola chuckled. "It took me many years of training and practical use for my skills to reach the level they are at now. If you thought you would be able to beat me after a few short sessions, I find that assumption rather insulting. Fighting is not a skill that can be mastered overnight, any more than shooting a bow or forging weapons. It is a craft that can only be learned through hard work, dedication, and most importantly of all, experience. To get as good as I am, you will need to see more fights than you would care to, that much I can promise you."

Ola was right, and Adel knew it, but that did not stop him from thinking he should be better by now. One positive that had come from their training was the fact that his traveling companion was more talkative after each session. The once stoic ogre was now seemingly eager to engage in discussion about the practice. The talks had made these past few days of walking closer and closer to the foothills of the Bonner Mountains more bearable. Having a companion willing to engage in conversation made quite the difference in the enjoyment of the journey, even if his interest was in discussing a single subject. It was still a vast improvement over the silent nights of their early days together.

"That was a clever feint you attempted at the end. It may very well have succeeded against a less experienced opponent. And your defenses have improved drastically. Remember our first session? I put so many welts on you that I wasn't sure you would be able to walk the next day! Don't sell yourself short," Ola continued, heaping much-needed praise on the young man.

This was true, Adel admitted to himself. Their first few sessions had been a thoroughly unpleasant experience, the ogre landing blow after blow with his blunted blade. The bruises and welts were adding up so quickly that Adel had found himself questioning his request for sword training. However, the pain had apparently been a useful teaching aid, for he had improved every day and was now able to avoid or parry most of Ola's attacks. Beyond that, his body was stronger than ever, no doubt a result of clashing with the mighty ogre every night. He would never be able to match his companion's brute strength, but he was by far in the best shape of his life. He doubted many men were fortunate enough to have a training partner like Ola to beat them into shape.

"Just remember this, Adel. Don't get frustrated when you fail to strike me. Every miss is a lesson, and every lesson makes you better than you were before you tried. Every bruise you suffer is an even more valuable lesson," Ola continued, sharing wisdom Adel would never have thought to find in an ogre a week earlier.

Many misconceptions about the race had been revealed in their time together, something for which Adel was thankful. His time with the ogre made him feel like a wiser man than he had been before he met Ola. He was not a beastlike, bloodthirsty savage as tales told in taverns across Thornata would have one believe. He was an intelligent and thoughtful man, not so different from any other man, other than in appearance.

"Thank you, Ola. I do try not to get so frustrated. I just can't help but feel like a Hoyt fighter would make short work of me in a real fight. I swore to myself when I agreed to leave the barge and come with you that I was done allowing others to shield me, that I had to take charge of my own life and my own safety. Helplessness is the most frustrating feeling I've ever felt. I'd never felt that way until the Hoyt opened fire on our barge, but I am already tired of it," Adel explained, wondering if Ola could sympathize with his feelings.

"I understand, lad. But don't underestimate yourself. I think you could hold your own against one of those blundering oafs. For the most part, they are ordinary people who decided to pick up weapons and start robbing their countrymen. You have had as much, if not more training than most of them. The group that attacked us were no exceptional warriors, and I believe you would be able to handle most of them in a one-on-one fight. You are taking steps to become self-sufficient, which is not something most men your age give any thought about until they are forced to do so," Ola reassured him.

"That's nice of you to say, Ola. But don't forget, I was forced to do so myself. If the Hoyt hadn't attacked my barge, I would still be living the same naïve existence I was before. I was ignorant of how the world actually works, and it seems like I learn something new every day that shocks me."

"This is true, but you could have sailed out of Thornata with your captain and never looked back. Instead of burying your head in the sand, you elected to make this journey and learn something, not only about the world but also about yourself. You could have been content to let me protect you on this journey, but you insisted on learning how to fight. You are an impressively proactive young man."

This statement brought to mind a question Adel had been thinking about for days. He had been cautious about asking too many questions, not wanting to anger the big ogre or send him back to his previous silent and withdrawn state. Still, Ola had been more talkative of late, so why not ask now and see if he would provide an answer? The worst that could happen would be for Ola to fall back into his previous silence. While Adel did not want this, he felt the question was worth the risk.

"Ola, where did you learn how to fight? I've never seen anybody who fights like you. Who taught you? How old were you?" Adel asked, hopeful that he might get a real response this time.

There was a long moment of silence, long enough that Adel was concerned he had angered his companion with the personal question. The ogre made no sound, and only the singing of the crickets broke the silence of the evening for close to a full minute. Just as he had accepted that Ola was ignoring him completely, the ogre responded.

"Nobody taught me. I had little choice but to teach myself. It is the same for most of my race. Tell me, Adel, how much do you know about the ogres and our culture?" Ola asked.

"Not much, but I have heard that for the most part your people prefer to remain secluded in the Ogra Mountains far in the southern reaches of the Empire. It's one of the reasons I was so surprised to see you so far north," Adel said, choosing his words carefully as not to offend Ola. He had heard many unpleasant rumors about the nature of ogres that he had concluded were false during his time with Ola. There was no sense in bringing up such vicious stories.

"Everything you say is true, and you are polite to pretend you have heard nothing else. I am not ignorant to the things that are said about ogres. Still, your discretion is appreciated. But do you know why we prefer to remain secluded from the rest of the Empire?" Ola pressed.

"Not really. I heard it is mainly that ogres resent interference from the outside world," Adel replied, having no better answer to offer.

"Again, true enough, if not a complete answer. Tell me, have you ever heard of a place called the Ogre Pits?" Ola asked, a hint of sadness and pain creeping into his usually rough voice.

"No, I don't believe I have ever heard of such a place," Adel said, wondering what could evoke such emotion in the ordinarily stoic ogre.

"I thought not. The Empire does everything it can to keep them quiet. You see, Adel, in the far southern provinces of the Empire, hunting ogres is like a sport to some men. It is treated as being similar to a man hunting a deer so he can eat it or use its fur. The difference is they are not hunting us to kill us, not directly at least. The ogres who are hunted and captured by men in these provinces are taken to the Ogre Pits and sold as slaves," Ola said.

"Slaves? But slavery was outlawed in the Empire hundreds of years ago!" Adel exclaimed in shock, unable to believe such a thing could be true.

"Indeed, it was. Slavery of men is forbidden in the Empire. However, in the eyes of the governments of the southern provinces, ogres are not considered human at all. So, when we are captured, we are taken to the Ogre Pits, and once we are there, we never leave." The sadness was still in Ola's voice but was steadily giving way to anger. "You see, the ogres who are taken as slaves are forced to fight one another for the entertainment of their captors. Well, for entertainment and gambling purposes, of course. Gold has a way of making men do despicable things, especially when there is no oversight. Any ogre who refuses to fight is killed on the spot. It is a good method of intimidating any others who might have delusions of resistance. We are forced to fight and kill our own kind over and over until we face an ogre who is skilled enough to release us from our suffering."

"How is this possible? How can the Empire allow such a practice to continue?" Adel was appalled.

"You must have heard other stories about ogres, Adel. I have heard them myself, though always in hushed tones. Men do not realize that we ogres have far better hearing than they do. I assume you never heard that particular rumor in a tavern? I have heard that we are mindless, bloodthirsty savages. They believe we kill for amusement and live like wild beasts. The Empire hears these same stories and writes us off. We do not matter, because we are nothing but savages."

"You aren't, though! Anybody who has ever spoken to you could not possibly believe it."

"Your face when I opened my door in that inn was the same as most when they see me. You were scared when you saw what had opened the door. Please understand, I am not trying to shame you, Adel. You have no control over the lies you have been led to believe; it is not your fault. Most people have no interest in talking to me long enough to learn the truth about me. It is hard to explain to people why they are mistaken when they refuse to listen. To be honest, not many people have much interest in learning about my past, yet another regard in which you are a remarkable person, Adel."

Adel was speechless, scarcely able to believe what he was being told. He did not want to believe what Ola was telling him could be true. He knew that men in distant provinces lived by codes of honor that were different from his own. Still, he would never have imagined anything like this, and the knowledge filled him with a deep sense of shame in what his people had done to Ola's. Slavery was wrong; this was why the Empire had outlawed it so many centuries ago. To think the law turned its back on an entire race of people that were considered to be lesser creatures was unthinkable to him. The longer he sat there thinking about the injustice of it all, he found himself sharing Ola's grief and rage.

"I'm sorry, Ola, I never would have imagined. You were a slave at the Ogre Pits?" he asked delicately, wanting to know more of his story, but not wanting to cause Ola pain.

"Aye, I was. I was captured when I was a few years younger than you, snuck up on while fetching water for my village. I had to learn how to fight on my own; the other option was death, which I refused to accept. I lived as a slave in their games for almost six years, fighting and killing my own people so those wealthy men could make a profit off of their deaths. There were times when I thought about simply laying down my sword and letting myself be killed, desperate for release. It was no life that I wanted to live. But the instinct for survival won out every time." Adel had never heard such pain in anybody's voice. He would never have expected it from this fierce warrior.

"So, what happened? You told me ogres are kept as slaves until they die. Did you find a way to escape from them?" Adel asked, in spite of his reluctance to ask him anything more that would bring back the pain he had experienced in the Ogre Pits.

"No, I did not escape, at least not on my own. I was rescued late one night. When we were not fighting, we were kept in steel cages. I wasn't sleeping; I rarely did in those days. There were perhaps a dozen of us in this particular block of cages. I saw a man approaching with a torch; I assumed it was one of the slavers until he drew near and it became apparent he was not. He began to speak to us, speak to us as though we were human, which was something we had not experienced in many years." Ola paused for a moment, seeming to fight down a surge of emotion before continuing. "He said he was sorry for the suffering we had endured and that he was there to set us free. We did not know what to think. I suspected it was a trick, an excuse for the slavers to slaughter some of us. He came to each cage and held his torch to the lock.

The Path of the Rawl Wielder

As he did so, the flame seemed to grow hotter, hotter than any flame I had ever seen before, hot enough to melt the metal locks and open the cages."

Adel felt a sudden understanding of what had happened. Along with this came an understanding of the reason Ola was here with him now. This must be the reason Ola had dedicated his life to serving the Children of the Rawl.

"The man who set you free, he was one of the Children of the Rawl, wasn't he?" he asked, already feeling confident he already knew the answer.

"Yes, he was. He told us we were free to go where we wished, and most of my fellow slaves chose to return to our people in the Ogra Mountains. However, I could not do this; I could not continue to live my life in fear of becoming a slave again. I had no doubt the slavers would pursue us. I also did not want to see my own people, and I had no desire to return to my home. To do so would be a daily reminder of fellow ogres I had faced in the Pits. So, I went to the man and offered him my service. He agreed to bring me here, to Thornata, to the Temple of the Rawl. I entered the service of the Children, not because I had to, but because that is what I wanted to do. I am no longer a slave. I am a willing helper to the men to whom I owe my life."

Upon finishing his tale, Ola seemed exhausted, the first time on their voyage that Adel had seen him display any sign of fatigue. Adel could not fault him, for the ogre had endured horrors beyond anything he could imagine, and retelling them must've been an exceptionally challenging thing to do. This thought brought one last question to his mind, and he resolved to leave his companion be after he had his answer.

"Ola, why did you tell me all of this? I can't imagine that it is an easy thing for you to discuss," he asked.

"These days of traveling with you have revealed that you and I are not so different. We were both thrown into dangerous situations that we had no control over. We are both determined never to allow that to happen again. It is easier to speak to a person who understands some of what I have been through in my life. Our circumstances were different, but our positions were much the same. You should get some rest, Adel; I want to get an early start tomorrow. We are still a few days from the Temple of the Rawl. The sooner we get there, the better."

Adel lay down but found that sleep would be elusive for him this night, much as it had since the Hoyt had first attacked the barge. It seemed like he learned more about the true nature of the world every day, and he did not like much of what he was discovering. He felt an immense amount of pity for his traveling companion, but also a great deal of respect for what Ola had endured. Such trials would have broken him, would have broken almost any man, and yet Ola had survived. He had moved past his horrors to live a meaningful life. Adel doubted he would be able to claim the same if he had been in the same predicament. It gave him a sense of faith that he was traveling with the best companion he could have asked for and a sense of pride that the ogre had seen enough from him to tell him this most personal of stories.

Chapter Seven

Many miles to the west of the spot where Adel and Ola had made their camp, another much larger encampment was filled with a tingling sense of foreboding. A large number of Hoyt forces had gathered in the foothills of the Bonner Mountains north of the city of Kolig, and dozens more were arriving by the day. The Thornatan government had no idea they had this many men at their disposal, and the Hoyt intended to keep it that way until it was too late. They had spent many years expanding their influence in Thornata, and soon they would be ready to execute their leader's plan. Yet their leader was none too pleased at this particular moment, a fact of which the entire encampment was well aware. When their leader was unhappy, it meant bad things for the people who'd put him in such a mood. The men went about their tasks in silence, the idle chatter that would typically accompany their work conspicuously absent. An uncomfortable feeling hovered in the air that had nothing to do with the spring humidity.

Idanox had led this group since they were no more than a handful of hardened men raiding the occasional trading caravan. Their organization had grown significantly in recent years, their numbers gradually swelling from dozens to hundreds and eventually into the thousands. Now the Hoyt were spread across every corner of the province, ready to carry out his plans. He had worked hard for many years at establishing the network of people that would be required to achieve his lofty goals. Despite all this hard work, however, his followers seemed incapable of completing even the most menial tasks that he asked of them. Even those as simple as capturing a teenage boy had proven to be beyond them. That's what he was being told at the moment. A handful of his commanders gathered in his tent, each of them looking as though they would rather be anyplace else in the world.

Idanox was a sharp-featured man, and those features intensified when he became angry. He had never been a man whose emotions were difficult to ascertain, nor had he ever cared enough to hide them. His desires took precedence, and if he was angry, that was the concern of others. He was lean, and not exceptionally tall either, but he commanded an intimidating presence nonetheless, in nothing more than the way he carried himself. Idanox was always the most intelligent man in any room, and his bearing showed that he knew it. His jet-black hair and eyebrows were uncommon in this province, where most of the native people bore blond or brown hair. Idanox did not mind looking different; in fact, he enjoyed standing out. It was what he had strived toward the entirety of his adult life.

"You see, sir, seven men under my command spotted the boy and an ogre traveling along the western shore of the Moyie Sea. One of them hurried to send word via messenger pigeon that they had found the boy, while the others moved to take him into our custody. When his companions did not return with the boy, the remaining man went to check and found all six of them cut down. We cannot be certain exactly what went wrong," one of the commanders was explaining.

The man looked as though he knew this would not be a satisfactory explanation as soon as the words left his mouth. His face was slightly green, as though he were in danger of falling ill. Any illness was about to be the least of his concerns.

What went wrong, Idanox thought, *was allowing a simpleminded fool like you to find yourself in a position of power.* It was a mistake Idanox planned on correcting shortly.

"The message we received three days ago said the

boy had been captured and was on his way to this camp. Would you care to explain why that is?" Idanox asked coldly, allowing the man to redeem himself, though it was an opportunity he knew would be squandered. The fool had already shown he lacked the intelligence and common sense that Idanox required of his commanders.

"Sir, you must understand, it was six men against two. Our man assumed there would be no complication with the capture of the boy. He expressed as much in his message to me. Due to the high level of confidence, I was comfortable in informing you that the boy was in our custody," the blithering idiot said, trying desperately to explain away his incompetence.

To his credit, the fool appeared to understand that his excuses were woefully inadequate; he was sweating more copiously by the minute. Perhaps he was smarter than Idanox had suspected, though it wouldn't save him now. The opportunity for this man to display evidence of his unsuspected brilliance had already passed.

"Oh, I see. That makes perfect sense, Commander. What reason could you possibly have to expect that there might be complications? What had the boy done besides smash over a dozen of our boats into wet firewood? Besides that, there was absolutely no indication whatsoever that capturing this boy may not be a simple task, was there?" Idanox asked rhetorically, to which the commander was at least intelligent enough not to attempt to offer justification. No response was provided, which was probably for the best. Idanox could safely assume more words coming out of this man's mouth would enrage him further.

Blithering fool, Idanox thought. He had obviously not prepared his men for the type of resistance they might face, despite the mess this boy had made of things on the Moyie River. Now the Hoyt were six men fewer, soon to be seven. At this crucial juncture, every warm body mattered, and they could not afford these types of losses. There was nothing to be done for it now. All he could do was adapt to the circumstances he had been dealt, the same as he always had. But first, this commander needed to be disciplined. If he could not be trusted to oversee the capture of a mere teenage boy, he was unfit to command Hoyt men in the days ahead. This was especially true when those days were sure to present far more significant challenges than a boy.

"Walk with me, commanders," he instructed the men surrounding him as he walked from his tent and out into the camp.

There were hundreds of men in the camp. They had come from across Thornata, gathering in the foothills of the Bonners at his request. They had come to prepare for an assault that had been years in the making. This was good; he would require a broad audience for this display, and he had one. Putting his fingers to his mouth, he let out a loud whistle to catch the attention of as many men as possible. Hundreds of men stopped what they were doing, turning their attention immediately on their leader. Idanox never spoke unless he had something important to say, and everybody present knew it.

"My dear brothers, may I please have your attention for a moment? I merely want to tell you that I appreciate all of the hard work you are putting in to ensure everything goes according to plan. The sweat and blood that you have put into our efforts have not gone unnoticed. The Hoyt are the future of Thornata, thanks to all of you. However, when our plans go awry, the people responsible need to be held accountable for their failure," Idanox cried out, projecting his voice as widely as possible.

Without further explanation, the knife was out of his belt. The bumbling commander, Idanox had already forgotten his name, did not suspect what was about to happen.

Of course not, Idanox thought, for the man had already displayed a profound lack of intelligence and foresight; it was to be expected. Still, Idanox could not help but feel mildly annoyed by the look of shock upon the fool's face as the knife plunged into his gut, and then his chest, and then finally his throat. The man fell to the ground, but Idanox did not have the patience to wait for him to finish dying, so he began to speak again, ignoring the man at his feet.

"This man's incompetence placed our goals in jeopardy. It placed the lives of every man in this camp and across the province in danger. Let it be known that anybody who stands in the way of our objective will meet the same fate. I know that none of you will fail me in the same way. Thank you again for your service, my brothers. You may return to your tasks," Idanox said. He turned away from the crowd as his former commander finished bleeding out on the ground. He did not look back as he stalked away. Somebody would have the mess cleaned up before he left his tent again, he was sure of that much.

Beckoning for his remaining commanders to follow him, Idanox returned to his tent. The dead commander was already out of his mind, relegated to the past. The mistakes had been made, and there was no point in dwelling on them. It was time to work on correcting them. It was time to move forward, and the future presented challenges of its own to be faced. That was how he had always dealt with such situations. Idanox possessed an exceptional ability to move on from failure and into a new plan. The boy had to be dealt with immediately, and they needed to finalize the Kolig strategy. He had sacrificed everything in pursuit of his goals, and the foolishness of lesser men would not thwart him, now or ever.

"The boy was last spotted along the western shore of the Moyie Sea. Based on his travel path from Kalstag, I have no more doubts. He is heading for the Temple of the Rawl. After what happened on the river and the direction he is traveling, he must possess the power of the

Rawl; there is no other explanation. The place has long been rumored to be in a valley of the Bonners north of us. If we move quickly, we can intercept him before he reaches the temple. Do I have a volunteer to oversee this?" Idanox asked of the men assembled.

After a moment's hesitation, several of his commanders stood to volunteer their services. The cowards obviously did not want to meet the same fate as their former comrade, and none of them looked enthusiastic about volunteering for the assignment. His preference would have been to handle this matter himself, but the attack on Kolig was drawing close, and it would require his full attention. Choosing the commander who he thought the most capable of not bumbling the operation, he laid out his instructions.

"Take no fewer than three dozen men; I want this done right this time. Kill the ogre if he still travels with it; it is of no use to us. I want the boy alive, if possible. He could prove to be a powerful ally, but if he proves to be too much of a struggle, kill him too. I would rather see him dead then wandering the countryside as a potential threat to our cause. Understood?" Idanox said, careful to lay out his instructions in the simplest terms possible. The men he had gathered were loyal, but none of them were remotely close to intelligent.

Of course, that's why they came to fight for me in the first place, he thought pleasantly to himself.

The commander nodded his understanding and

hurried out of the tent to make his preparations. Idanox was silent for a few moments, remembering how much simpler things had been when the Hoyt was a small gang of bandits causing small amounts of chaos. Now he had everything he had worked toward within his grasp, thousands of men following his lead, and it was exhausting. Idanox told himself that all of the stress and hard work would be worth it once he had forced the Empire to name him the Duke of Thornata. Then he would have time to rest, for a while, at least. Realizing the rest of his commanders were awaiting their orders, he shook himself from his daydream.

"Do we have any update on the elf?" The nervous glances the remaining men exchanged told him all he needed to know.

"Sir, we dispatched a dozen men to the tavern called The Purple Dinosaur in Kalskag. They were instructed to make an example of the elf, to ensure that the people know the Hoyt will not tolerate such insolence."

"Very good, I can assume the message has been delivered and received?" Idanox asked, pretending he could not spot the apprehension etched across their faces. He had learned long ago that it was better to never tip your hand about all of the knowledge you possessed.

"I'm sorry, sir. The elf has proven to be quite formidable. His name is Keeler, and it seems he had a lengthy career as a pirate in the southern provinces."

"So, you are saying that twelve men could not handle one elderly pirate? What was their excuse?" Idanox was already imagining the example he would make of this new set of fools.

"Well, sir, I'm afraid I don't know what their excuse is. An associate of Keeler's approached two of our men in Kalskag. He handed them a large sack and told them that any Hoyt who came to The Purple Dinosaur would meet the same fate. There were twelve severed hands in the sack. We have not recovered the rest of them. Shall we send more men?"

"Forget it. The elf is no threat to us. Let him run his dump of a tavern in peace. I will not waste further Hoyt lives attacking him needlessly. We need our men more than we need to send a message to some has-been pirate."

It was not an approach Idanox would typically take. He would love nothing more than to see this elf killed for his insolence. But this was a sensitive time for the Hoyt, and they could not afford to throw away the lives of their men on such a vanity mission. He was irritated that this Keeler had helped the Rawl wielder elude him, but it was a grudge that did not profit him to pursue. He needed to refocus on the task at hand.

"We need to ensure that we are ready within the next two months for the attack on Kolig. Where do we stand?" Idanox asked.

"We have successfully infiltrated the Kolig city

watch, sir. We have over a dozen men within their ranks and expect to have at least a dozen more before the time for the assault has come," one of the commanders advised.

This is a good start, Idanox thought. Men planted inside the city watch would be able to open the gates to the city at the right moment. This would allow the Hoyt forces to sack the city without having to breach the gates by force. The Thornatan Army had a relatively small number of men stationed in Kolig; the city watch would be their greatest adversary. With their best line of defense breached from within, they would not be able to put up much of a fight.

"How much resistance can we expect once we are inside the walls?" he asked.

"The city watch has around four hundred men, though only a third of them are on duty at any given time. If we strike at night, many will be sleeping in the barracks, and our men on the inside can deal with them before they have a chance to interfere. The army will not want to engage with us in the streets. They will fear civilian casualties. Our attacking force may have to overcome two or three hundred men at most," the commander said with confidence.

Everything was falling into place, and Idanox was confident that the defenses of Kolig would collapse in short order. Once the Hoyt were in control of the city, they would also have control of the waterways of the

Kival River, giving them leverage over the city of Kobuk to the south as well. He stopped before he got ahead of himself. First they needed to gain control of Kolig successfully, and then they had to hold it long enough for the next part of his plan to fall into place.

Idanox had chosen the city of Kolig as the starting point of their war for several reasons. The person in control of Kolig could easily cut off shipments to the city of Kobuk by the river, thus crippling two cities in one stroke. Its location right on the shore of the Kival River made it a relatively simple city to hold against an outside force, as there were limited ways to move a sizeable force against it. Once the Hoyt were in control, Idanox would order the demolition of the bridge that spanned from the city gates over the river. Once this was done, the lone way to approach the city in force would be by boat, precisely as Idanox wanted.

The duke would send the Thornatan Army as soon as he heard the Hoyt had taken Kolig. Idanox was counting on this. With the bridge destroyed, the military would have no choice but to cross the river in boats. Once thousands of soldiers were in the water, Idanox's master trap would be sprung. The waters from the Bonners to the north flowed so swiftly in the spring and summer that a massive dam had been constructed north of Kolig. It was designed to prevent flooding and manage the irrigation of crops, but it would serve a much more lethal purpose for the Hoyt. Once the army was in the river, Idanox would order this dam opened, drowning a sizeable chunk of the Thornatan Army before they could react.

Idanox was confident the army generals would not see this coming. The opening of the dam would no doubt destroy a large portion of the city as well, and a great number of civilians would likely perish. The Thornatan Army would assume they had taken the city to have control over it, not to destroy it. The military would be decimated by the thousands, leaving the rest of the province more vulnerable to attack.

By this time next year, the Hoyt would be in control of the duke's palace in Oreanna, and Idanox would in control of the province. The emperor would face a choice of marching the Imperial Army thousands of miles to retake control of the province or allowing Idanox to have power and reign as duke. If he did elect to march against them, it would serve Idanox's purposes well enough. While he did not seek a war with the Empire, he had allies who would be all too happy to see such conflict arise, and they would reward him richly for his valiant efforts on their behalf. If the emperor elected not to attack, the Hoyt would be able to rule unchallenged.

Realizing that he had looked too far into the future despite his determination not to, Idanox scolded himself. There was still work to be done, and he could enjoy his victory once it had been won. Once again, he began addressing his commanders.

"Once we are in control of Kolig, I want you to arrange regular patrols through the streets. Any civilians who cause issues are to be killed at once, preferably publicly, and make it as messy as possible. This should help keep the rest of the populace in line. Intimidation is an effective sedative for a restless population. It will take several weeks for the Thornatan Army to arrive; we cannot lose control of the city before they do. Understood?" Idanox reiterated.

His commanders nodded their understanding and began to file out. Again, Idanox felt the excitement welling up within him. Everything he had been promised was within his reach. He had performed his duties to perfection, and his reward would soon be his to enjoy. The most challenging weeks of his life lay ahead, but he harbored no doubts in his ability to execute his plan to perfection.

Idanox was perhaps the wealthiest man in the entire province, and he had been for many years. He had been born into a wealthy family, but upon inheriting their wealth, he had grown his fortune considerably. He had made most of his fortune by running a timber business, the most prosperous in the entire Empire. But despite all his wealth and power, he had never felt he had received the respect that his genius demanded. In many ways, he realized, he felt the same as many of the peasants across the province, struggling for recognition. This, of course, had been instrumental in persuading such men to join his cause. The vast sums of gold he had at his disposal to offer in payment for their loyalty did not hurt either.

Idanox had built the Hoyt from the ground up, an organization that welcomed anyone, no matter how poor or seemingly useless. He may be obscenely wealthy, but he did not give off the aura of superiority that many of his peers did. The people felt like he could understand their plights and had flocked to him in droves. Now they were gathering here, his fiercely loyal army, ready to win him the position he had always deserved. The duke and his fellow nobles had looked down at Idanox for years, thinking him no more than a simple wood merchant, a man who had fallen backward into his father's fortune.

It would all change soon enough, he told himself. Soon, he would finally receive the respect and admiration that he had always known he deserved. Those that had looked down on him would soon be bloody corpses looking up at him. Smirking in self-satisfaction, Idanox moved to his bed to enjoy the few short hours of rest that were allowed to him. There was still much work to be done, and none as capable of doing it as he.

Chapter Eight

The sun was at its highest point in the sky on the warmest day of the year so far. Under its harsh glare, Adel was ready to be done with this journey. For the better part of the past five days, he and Ola had marched westward through the foothills of the Bonner Mountains, the trek becoming more complicated all the while. Up and down rolling green hills they had trudged, each one higher and steeper than the one before. They had worked their way along dirt trails thick with bushes that eventually gave way to evergreen trees as they climbed ever higher. Adel was a physically fit young man, but having spent most of his past few years on a ship, he had never undertaken such an arduous journey on foot.

They had eventually reached a narrow pass that wound its way between two massive peaks, the rocky trail still slick from the swiftly thawing snows high above. They had needed to take great care not to slip, for the hard rocks they marched over would be unforgiving to anybody unfortunate enough to take a fall. Their walk had been relatively easy since that point, through a lush green valley full of blooming spring wildflowers, though the heat was beginning to test both Adel's endurance and patience. Early in the day, he had admired the beauty of the mountain valley, though hours in a harsh sun had him ready to see the end of it. If there was an inch of his body not coated in sweat, he could not find it.

"You told me we would reach the Temple of the Rawl today. How much longer?" he asked the seemingly tireless ogre, amazed as always by his endless stamina. If Ola ever got tired, he had never revealed as much to Adel.

"Once we reach the far end of this valley, there is only a short climb. We will reach the temple by nightfall," said Ola, his voice not reflecting even a hint of weariness.

Resigning himself to the fact this entire day would be spent walking under the burning hot sun, Adel let out a sigh of exasperation and kept moving forward. There was no point in complaining; Ola would not be convinced to stop and complete the journey the next day. The ogre was confident it was merely a matter of time before the Hoyt found them again. Ola was equally convinced that they would be completely safe once they were within the Temple of the Rawl. As little as he was enjoying the walk this day, Adel had no desire to encounter the Hoyt again, so onward he plodded. Despite his weariness, he was looking forward to reaching the Temple of the Rawl, and he was hopeful they would have luxuries such as a bed and maybe even a place to bathe. A more complete meal would also be a welcome sight.

Determined to take his mind away from the blazing heat, Adel turned his thoughts toward the journey that he would soon complete. He found it best to allow himself to focus on his surroundings enough to keep placing one foot in front of the other. Otherwise, it was better to keep his thoughts inward. He had set out to start a new life and, in many ways, that life would begin today when they reached the Temple of the Rawl.

Ola had still not told him much about the Children of the Rawl, claiming he did not want to fill his head with preconceived notions. Frustrating though this was, Adel understood the ogre's logic. Perhaps it was, in fact, better to see things for himself before forming opinions. Ola himself had been a lesson in this, for Adel's previous notions about ogres being warlike savages were long since forgotten. After days of the ogre's company, he was ashamed to have ever held such ideas in his head.

They had continued to train with the practice swords in the evenings, and Adel had continued to improve. His endurance was growing daily, as was his power and technique. In spite of this, he had still not managed to land a single strike on the exceptionally skilled ogre. They had not discussed Ola's past any further, though the ogre did continue to seem more talkative since their battle with the Hoyt. He would frequently comment on their surroundings, pointing out rare plants or animals, and would often inquire about Adel's comfort and well-being. Adel suspected that the ogre might have never told anybody the entire story that he had been entrusted with, a trust he did not take lightly. He was also delighted to have a more talkative traveling companion.

The closer they drew to the Temple of the Rawl, the more Adel wondered if he had made the right choice to leave his life on the barge behind. He could have stayed and sailed out of Thornata with Boyd and the others, but he had chosen to remain in Thornata, despite the continuing threat posed to him by the Hoyt. After the encounters in Kalskag and on the shores of the Moyie Sea, there could be no doubt they were actively hunting him. Was he a fool for staying behind?

It was a question he had asked himself often, but he knew he'd never have been able to live his life acting as though nothing had happened. How could he possibly pretend that he'd never discovered this power sleeping within him without seeking answers? He had to learn more about this ability, had to learn what he was truly capable of doing. He would never be able to put an end to the questions racing through his mind until he did so.

Realizing they were drawing near to the far side of the valley and the sun was beginning to fall lower, Adel smiled. Once again, his thoughts had helped to pass the time. They came in handy, even if they drove him mad at times. The daydreaming that had often gotten him scolded on the barge had helped pass the day's walk away. It was then that he took note of Ola's slowing pace. Adel was immediately on alert; it was unlike the ogre to slow his pace for any reason while they were traveling. He glanced hurriedly in every direction, searching for any sign of approaching enemies. His hand inched close to the pommel of the sword that Captain Boyd had given him.

"Ola? Is there something wrong?" Adel asked.

"No, Adel, there's nothing wrong. There is no need to be alarmed. I just wanted to warn you that the guardians of the temple will be greeting us soon, and I did not want them to surprise you," Ola replied.

"Guardians of the temple? Who are they?" Adel's curiosity was piqued now. Ola had mentioned no such guardians until now.

"I can promise that you have never met men like these before. They have an intimidating appearance, and I say that as somebody who has been told the same thing about himself. Rest assured, they will not harm us. The Children are expecting your arrival, so there will be no delay. The guardians will merely greet us and send us on our way as welcome guests," Ola assured him.

"They are expecting me? How do they know that we are coming? Did you send them a message?" Adel queried, quite puzzled.

"No, no message was needed. Understand that the Children are extremely powerful in the way of the Rawl in their own right. I do not doubt that they are aware you are drawing near. In time, I'm sure they will teach you how to use your power to sense other Rawl wielders nearby. The Children will have alerted the guardians that you are welcome to enter the temple," Ola said, an explanation that utterly failed to satisfy Adel's curiosity.

They were aware of him drawing near? That was a strange thing to say. One day, would he also be able to sense the presence of fellow Rawl wielders? Once again, he was filled with apprehension. How much were these people able to learn about him before he had even met them? What if they had already decided he was not fit to learn from them? Would they greet him at the door and politely ask him to leave? He would not have the opportunity to pose these questions to Ola because, at this moment, one of the guardians revealed himself in front of them.

He appeared at the far end of the valley, which was now no more than a few hundred yards away. Ola had warned Adel to be prepared for an intimidating person, but he could never have imagined what was waiting for them. He was sure his eyes must be mistaken until the man took his first step toward them, and he felt the earth quiver ever so slightly beneath his feet. He had heard tall tales in his childhood about the legendary giants, but it was said they had all died out centuries ago, if they had ever existed at all. Some men believed they had never been anything other than stories told to frighten gullible children. His own eyes were telling him quite a different story.

The giant was still a hundred yards away. Its size was difficult to fathom, the tremors produced by its footsteps striking the earth intensifying with each step. If this was one of the temple's guardians, it was easy to understand why Ola felt so assured of their safety. The giant was now finally close enough for Adel to begin to make out its features. Until this point, Ola had been the largest man Adel had ever met by far, his six-and-a-half-foot frame towering over everyone else. Yet next to this giant, Ola might as well be a newborn kitten.

Though he had no way to measure for sure, Adel guessed the giant's height to be between thirty and forty feet. His clothing was fairly simple, fur pants and tunic and leather shoes covering rock-hard skin. In one hand the giant carried a massive wooden club, the club on its own perhaps as large as Ola. The ogre had reassured Adel he had nothing to fear, but now that the giant was mere steps from them, he could not help but feel a shred of apprehension. If it were to attack them, there was little they would be able to do to stop it, Ola's exceptional fighting skills notwithstanding. At last, the giant spoke, his voice deep and booming yet strangely gentle and reassuring at the same time, like a grown man attempting to soothe an infant.

"So, you return at last, Ola. We have not seen you in quite some time, my old friend. I am glad to see you are returning safely. Who is this young one you are bringing with you?" the giant addressed Ola. Unlike the ogre, its facial structure was familiar enough for Adel to make out a smile, which allowed him to breathe slightly more comfortably.

"It is good to see you again, Klaweck. I have indeed been away for a long time, but my travels have not been fruitless. This young man is Adel. I believe him to be the one the Children have been seeking for so many years," Ola replied. His voice was friendly, though Adel thought he sensed a slight undertone of apprehension that he would never have suspected the mighty ogre capable of showing. Apparently, even the mighty Ola was not completely free of fear.

"You think so, do you? Elim called me up to the temple last night and told me to expect you today, along with a special guest. He also told me that you have been pursued and that we should be ready for a fight. Who has been bothering you?" Klaweck said, his tone hard to gauge, even harder than those of the taciturn ogre.

"The Hoyt have pursued Adel for weeks; he

possesses the power of the Rawl. No doubt they hope to turn him to their cause or kill him if that fails. He made a mess of some of their boats on the Moyie River, and they were not particularly happy about it. They went after him in Kalskag as well. We were attacked on the shores of the Moyie Sea, and they wanted to capture him alive. That group was far from impressive, but we should assume they will send better next time," Ola explained.

"A wielder of the Rawl, you say? Then you are truly a special guest indeed. It has been years since we have welcomed such an important guest. Rest easy, young Adel. My fellows and I will ensure that you come to no harm during your stay. I am Klaweck, and this is my promise to you." Adel was stunned by the eloquence with which the giant spoke. Much like ogres, the tales he had heard had pegged them as mindless, bloodthirsty monsters. It appeared as though the giants had been painted with a similar brush in error. Again, Adel felt a twinge of shame at his preconceived notions.

"Thank you, Klaweck. It is a pleasure to meet you as well. Rest has been a hard luxury to come by for many weeks now. I shall sleep easy knowing that you and your fellows are keeping watch," Adel said, growing more comfortable in the giant's presence by the minute. He did not know if he would ever grow used to the giant's logic-defying size, though he sensed Klaweck was sincere in his welcoming statements.

Before Klaweck could reply, the blast of a horn

sounded throughout the valley, echoing off the nearby peaks and deafening the trio. Adel spun around, searching for the source of the horn, and was stunned to find dozens of Hoyt men positioning themselves on the rocks around them. The valley was narrow at this point, though the Hoyt archers were still positioned far enough away that Adel and Ola would prove to be difficult targets. A dozen more were approaching from behind, scheming to cut off any attempt at escape. It was one of these men who called out to them, his voice echoing off the walls of the valley.

"Well, here is a sight to behold! I never thought I would see a giant or an ogre, yet here they are in front of me. They look every bit the stupid brutes the stories say they are." This comment elicited an angry growl from Ola. The Hoyt smirked in satisfaction before continuing. "You have led us on a merry chase, boy, but it is over now. Come with us now, and we will leave your pets to wallow in the mud or whatever it is they do for amusement. Idanox is very much interested in speaking to you. If you try to resist, they will both die, and you will be coming with us anyway. What will it be?"

"I'm not going anywhere with you, Hoyt scum! If you try to take me, you will meet the same fate as every one of your bastard friends who have tried so far!" Adel shot back, trying his best to sound confident and intimidating, hoping his fear of the seemingly impossible odds was not evident. The smirk that curled across the

Hoyt's smug face showed that Adel's bravado did not fool him. Apparently, an obnoxious level of arrogance was a requirement to join the Hoyt.

"Have it your way, you stupid boy. I'm not playing your games. Take him and kill the others!" the Hoyt shouted.

The Hoyt men began to advance, and out of the corners of his eyes, Adel could see their fellows in the rocks nocking their longbows. He drew his sword, but at that moment, Ola seized him and began to drag him away from the Hoyt, shoving him against a tree and shielding him with his own body. It was at that moment Klaweck let out a bellow unlike anything Adel had heard before. Adel's ears rang, and the ground beneath his feet trembled from the sheer force of the giant's voice.

The advancing Hoyt hesitated for a brief moment. It was obvious they had not anticipated such a robust response from the giant, who had remained silent up until that moment. That brief moment of hesitation proved to be a deadly mistake.

Klaweck charged with a speed that defied his incredible size, a minor earthquake rattling the valley with each step he took. Six Hoyt were dead before they could even think of reacting. One mighty swing of Klaweck's club sent them spinning through the air as though they were feathers caught in the wind, their bodies shattered by the impact of the blow. A few of them flew so far that Adel could not even see where they had landed.

The remaining six men were in a panic. Their commander was desperately trying to cry out orders as the club came down on his head with splintering force. When the club came back up, the commander was no longer recognizable as human. The Hoyt on the ground desperately began to flee, though a few more of them were doomed to be caught in the back by another devastating swing of Klaweck's club.

Their comrades positioned in the rocks had begun to fire on Klaweck, and Adel saw two arrows strike the giant in his shoulder and arm. If these caused the giant any pain, he did not show it. If anything, Adel thought these might as well have been flea bites to Klaweck, a minor annoyance that did no harm but to anger him further. The giant now turned his attention to the archers who were continuing to fire on him. He broke into a sprint toward the north end of the valley where over a dozen archers were attempting to pepper him with arrows. He cleared the distance with incredible speed, his club going to work once more on the Hoyt.

From where he was positioned closer to the south side of the valley and behind Ola, Adel could not make out what was happening to the north where Klaweck was battling. Thus, he was quite surprised to hear a sharp crack in the tree above him. He looked up, expecting to find an arrow lodged above them, and was shocked to find instead that a Hoyt, a man around six feet tall, had struck the trunk of the tree with enough force to split the trunk nearly in half. Klaweck had thrown the man from several hundred yards away, and yet he had struck with enough velocity to kill him instantly.

Adel became aware of more noise behind him. Turning to peek around the trunk of the tree, he was stunned to find two more giants racing down the rocks toward the remaining Hoyt archers. The Hoyt never had a chance; they were wiped out within seconds. Ola eased his grip at last, allowing Adel to step away from the tree and sheath his sword. Klaweck was returning from the north end of the valley, pulling arrows from his body as he went and tossing them aside like minor annoyances.

"I see you haven't lost your edge, my friend," Ola commented as Klaweck drew near. Adel's eyes were drawn to the giant's club, the end of which was covered in blood.

"Did the fools honestly think they could take Adel by force? Rest easy, my young friend. No Hoyt bastard will ever get close to you while you are at the temple. My fellows and I will see to that," Klaweck said, a reassurance Adel had no qualms about taking to heart after the unbelievable display of power and ferocity he had just witnessed.

"A few of the rats who attacked us on the valley floor ran off. Please take care of them. Better if there are no survivors to run back and tell the rest of the Hoyt where to find us, as much as I wouldn't mind disposing of more of the scum," Klaweck said to the two giants who had arrived in the midst of the battle. They set out eastward at a jog without question, the shaking of the earth easing as they moved farther away. Adel had no doubt the fleeing Hoyt fighters would not get far.

Adel was still in shock at the sheer ferocity that this mild-mannered giant had demonstrated moments before, but he managed to tremble out a quick word of thanks nonetheless. Ola thanked Klaweck as well before turning to Adel and indicating they should proceed to the Temple of the Rawl without further delay.

"Yes, you had best get up there before the Children start to worry. Have no fear; I will have patrols arranged to sweep the area regularly, just in case any more try to get in. The Hoyt will not interfere with your business with the Children. We know these mountains better than anyone; they will never get close to you. It's been a pleasure to meet you, Adel. I look forward to having an opportunity to speak with you again. Good luck with your training," Klaweck said as they made their departure.

Leading the way out of the valley, Ola showed Adel to a stone pathway that began to wind its way up into the mountains. The path became steeper until it finally became a stone staircase cutting its way up the hill. The ogre's pace was quicker than before; it was clear he was every bit as eager to see this journey completed as Adel was.

Adel's mind was flooded with curiosity about

Klaweck and the giants who guarded the Temple of the Rawl.

"How many giants guard the Temple of the Rawl?" he asked, scrambling to keep up with the ogre's long strides.

"There are eight of them. There are always at least three of them close to the temple, and the others patrol the nearby mountains to monitor potential threats. You would not suspect it due to their size, but they are exceptional at avoiding detection. They are the best hunters I have ever seen. Of course, they would have to be. Just imagine how much they need to eat to survive," Ola responded. "It's possible Klaweck already knew about the Hoyt and did not want to alarm you. They prefer to deal with threats quietly when possible. The Children prefer a quiet lifestyle, and Klaweck and his giants allow them to live that without fear."

"I thought the giants had all died out years ago," Adel said, relieved that his assumptions had been proven false.

"For the most part, they did. Klaweck and his group are one of a few tribes left in the world. For as few of them as there are, there are even fewer females among them. Klaweck's tribe has none at all. One day there will be no more giants; a race cannot continue without offspring. They are aided somewhat by their long lifespan; Klaweck is over ninety years old and will likely live for another ninety. But still, one day they will be gone from this world, and when that day comes, the world will be a poorer place for it," the ogre explained.

Ninety years old? Klaweck had moved with the speed and agility of a young man, despite his massive stature. Adel would have loved to learn more about the giants, but he knew those were questions best reserved for another time. He focused on the path ahead, which was becoming steeper by the minute. He thought sarcastically to himself that Ola's definition of a short climb was different from his. Just when he felt the climb would never end, they reached the top of the steep hill, and there was the Temple of the Rawl.

Adel had traveled to most of the major cities in Thornata, but he had never seen such a structure before in his life. It appeared before them without warning, obstructed from view until they reached the top of the stairs. In some ways, it resembled the temples of worship found in cities across the province, but it was also clear that this temple was built not for prayer, but rather to withstand an assault of incredible magnitude. A massive outer wall surrounded the temple proper. Made up of the most enormous blocks of stone Adel had ever seen, it rose at least sixty feet into the air. Who could have possibly built such a structure? Its scale was beyond anything Adel could have imagined.

At the center of the wall was a massive door that appeared to be made of the same heavy stone. How was it possible for such an enormous door to open? Almost before the thought had crossed his mind, the door swung open, much more rapidly than should have been possible. Standing in the entryway was a solitary figure dressed from head to toe in long robes of dark green.

As they drew closer to the figure, Adel could see it was an old man, his wrinkled face and bright white beard becoming more apparent by the step. The irony of the fact that this man referred to himself as a child was not lost on Adel. Once they were within speaking range, the old man's face split into a wide smile. He gazed upon Adel like a grandfather welcoming his favorite grandson.

"Welcome, Adel. My name is Elim. On behalf of the Children of the Rawl, welcome to the Temple of the Rawl; we have been expecting you. You must be tired from your journey, though I am afraid your true journey has only just begun. Please, come inside. We have a great deal we need to discuss."

Chapter Nine

Adel stared upward in awe as he passed through the great stone doorway of the Temple of the Rawl. Not only were the walls as high as any he had ever seen, but as he walked through, he could now see they were also thicker than any he had ever seen, perhaps twenty feet thick. The entryway resembled a short tunnel more than a standard doorway, their footsteps echoing off the walls as the trio made their way through the entry. Such a structure defied all preconceptions he had once held of what was possible. They had barely cleared the tunnel that passed through this wall when the door closed behind them. It apparently closed of its own accord, for looking back, Adel could see nobody pushing it shut, nor any gears that would indicate a mechanical system. The temple itself was before them now. It was not as massive as the wall surrounding it, but still a dramatic structure nonetheless.

The walls of the Temple of the Rawl had been constructed with the purest white marble he had ever seen. Adel could not begin to imagine the years of labor that would have been required to bring so much of it up to the top of the steep mountain path. It was a simple structure—no ornate sculptures adorned the outside—yet the marble alone was enough to leave him awestruck. There was a large courtyard between the temple and the outer wall. Elim led them down a cobblestone path toward the entrance to the temple without delay. He led them past the lush green courtyard abloom with flowers of every color Adel could imagine. It immediately struck Adal as a peaceful area, one in which he could envision himself enjoying hours of relaxation. They were inside the temple within moments, and Adel was not expecting what met his eyes.

Upon seeing the spectacular exterior of the Temple of the Rawl, Adel had expected more of the same magnificence inside. To his surprise, he found the interior rather drab. They had entered a massive central room, but there was virtually nothing inside of this room, the lone source of light coming from windows high on the walls. There were hallways to either side that appeared to lead to other sections of the temple, but this first room was not as awe-inspiring as Adel had expected after seeing the spectacle that was the outer wall. He looked toward Elim, trying to conceal his disappointment, but Elim seemed to sense his trepidation.

"This room is quite simple; we are aware. But it serves our purposes well enough. Sometimes, I have found that less is more. Don't be concerned, young Adel. All will be quite clear in good time, I assure you," the old man said with a warm smile.

Elim led the pair to the center of the massive room before coming to a halt. They stood in silence for a moment before Adel noticed more figures slipping from the shadows of the surrounding hallways. All of the Children bore a similar appearance to Elim. All wore the same dark green robes, and all appeared to be ancient beyond measure. Once again, the irony of the fact that these men called themselves children was not lost on Adel. Adel had not expected the Children of the Rawl to be actual children, but their ancient appearance came as a mild surprise. There were six of them in total. Once all were gathered, Elim began to speak.

"Welcome, Adel. Welcome to the Temple of the Rawl. As I am sure you have surmised by now, we are the Children of the Rawl. We have been awaiting your arrival for a long time. Allow me to begin by assuring you that as long as you are within the grounds of this temple, you will be safe from any and all who might attempt to pursue you. We are aware of your troubles with the Hoyt, and they will not extend within these walls. Rest easy knowing that nobody can harm you here," he said in the gentle manner in which a grandfather may reassure his grandson. Adel scanned the faces of the men, all smiling warmly at him. After a long silence, he realized they were waiting for him to reply.

"Thank you for accepting me into your home, Children of the Rawl. Ola believes you can help me understand and control the power that I possess, the power of the Rawl. Is this true?" Adel asked.

"Ola speaks truly. We can help you understand your power, and in time, perhaps we can help you understand how to wield it. With enough training and perseverance, you may be able to use it in ways that you cannot even begin to imagine. Please understand, Adel, that we will do everything in our power to teach and guide you. In the end, your path is your own to walk. We can guide you along the route we feel is best, but ultimately, you must choose your own way," Elim replied.

Adel did not care much for the way Elim seemed to hedge every statement he made. He supposed the old man was merely trying to temper his expectations, but he wished Elim would speak with more confidence. He assumed the Children did not want to get his hopes too high. Still, Elim was speaking in general and sweeping statements and had yet to state anything specific that the Children could do to help him. He had left his life behind and traveled a long way to seek their assistance.

Determined to receive at least one solid answer before this meeting adjourned, he pressed on.

"How shall we begin with my training then?" Adel asked, trying to keep impatience from seeping into his voice.

He did not want to be rude, but he was eager to learn more about the power that had revealed itself on the river. He had journeyed for weeks, searching for answers, and now that they were within his grasp, he was anxious to have them at last. He scrutinized the faces of the Children of the Rawl as he asked, trying to determine their intent based on their expressions. His efforts were in vain, their peaceful smiles as difficult to measure as the emotions of the ogre with whom he had traveled across Thornata.

"First, we will discuss exactly what your power is and the known history of the Rawl. Once you have a broader understanding of the power you possess, we will begin the process of helping you learn to master its use. These lessons will start small, and over time we will progress to more challenging uses of the Rawl," replied Elim, the gentle smile never leaving his face. The rest of the Children made no sound at all, merely continuing to smile serenely at him.

Again, Adel was slightly disappointed. He had hoped to begin learning to use his power immediately, but he would not question the Children's plan. He was confident they knew the best method for teaching him what he needed to know. It seemed obvious now that they would not start with lessons on using rivers to annihilate boats. Most people probably did not learn they had this power in such a manner. He did not like being kept in the dark, but he resolved to accept it, at least for a time.

"Are all of you like me? Do you possess the Rawl as well?" he asked, his curiosity about the Children growing by the moment.

"Yes, we do possess the power of the Rawl; however, you must understand that our use of its power is quite limited. We are able to harness its power here in this temple, but outside of the temple walls, our ability to use it is limited and comes at great personal cost. One of the costs of old age, I'm afraid. I will explain this further once we begin our training, I assure you," Elim replied patiently.

Adel's confusion continued to grow by leaps and bounds; perhaps he should get used to that feeling. Would his power also be restricted to the Temple of the Rawl? If so, how had he been able to use it on the river? Deciding there was no use in pestering Elim with further questions at this point, he nodded his understanding. For the first time since arriving, he felt his weariness begin to catch up with him once more. The adrenaline that had flooded through his body during the Hoyt attack in the valley below had started to wear off. Elim seemed to sense this; it was as though he could read Adel's mind.

"You have traveled far, and your recent encounter with the Hoyt has no doubt left you exhausted. I will show you to the kitchen where you may eat your fill, and then I will show you to the room we have set aside for you so you may rest. We will begin our training in the morning when you are sufficiently rested," Elim said.

Thankful for the opportunity to eat and rest, Adel and Ola followed Elim into one of the small hallways that ran outward from the central chamber. Similar to the central hall, the passage and the kitchen it led to were unadorned and straightforward, though there were at least a table and chairs for them to sit. There were no windows in the kitchen; the light emanated from candles that gave off an intoxicating scent Adel could not identify. The warm glow of the candles gave Adel a sense of home that he had not felt since his mother had died.

Elim motioned for Adel and Ola to sit at one of several wooden tables while he gathered a variety of bread, meat, and fruits to set before them. Realizing for the first time how hungry he was, Adel devoured the food ravenously. He had not starved on their journey to the temple, for Ola had carried a sufficient supply of food, but the rations had merely been enough to sustain them. Having access to a more complete meal was a treat Adel was grateful to have. Once they had finished their supper, Elim again motioned for them to follow him.

He led them through a series of unremarkable passageways until they arrived at a pair of wooden doors directly across from each other. Elim motioned to Adel that the room on the right was to be his.

"You may rest here during your stay with us, Adel. I thought perhaps you would feel more secure with Ola sleeping directly across from you, so we have prepared that chamber for him. You should find everything you need within your chambers. Sleep for as long as needed. When you awaken in the morning, you will find food waiting for you in the kitchen. Once you have eaten, please come back to the central chamber. I will be waiting to begin our first lesson. Sleep well, Adel." He departed without waiting for a reply.

"You may have already figured this out for yourself, but they don't get many visitors," Ola remarked to Adel, the first time the ogre had spoken up since their arrival.

"Yes, that is the impression I had. They are still quite welcoming, though. Will we continue with our sword training now that we are here? I would like to, and I feel as though I am making progress," Adel said, not wanting his newly forged bond with the ogre to fade.

"That you are, there is no doubt about it. Very well, if you wish to continue our lessons, I will speak to Elim in the morning and ask him to leave you enough time for a sword lesson daily. Do not hesitate to knock on my door if you need anything, Adel, but rest assured you are quite safe here. Klaweck and his giants keep watch, and there are additional protections around this temple that you will learn about in due time. Sleep well, my friend," Ola said before disappearing into his own chamber.

Adel remained in the corridor a moment longer, realizing this was the first time the ogre had referred to him as a friend. Even though Ola had warmed to him as their journey had progressed, it still came as a pleasant surprise. He had become resigned to the fact that he would be nothing more than a charge to be protected by Ola. The Children of the Rawl may indeed wish to help him, but he sensed from their brief encounter that it would be difficult to view them as friends. It brought him a small measure of comfort to know he had a true friend to lean on in the days ahead.

Entering his chamber, Adel was taken a bit by surprise. He had expected more of the same unremarkable appearance that most of the temple seemed to feature and was shocked to find a bed with plush cotton blankets and a roaring fireplace. There was a basin he could use to bathe with hot water already waiting for him. The Children of the Rawl had even left a set of cotton bedclothes for him to slip into for sleep. He climbed onto the bed and lay back in bliss. He could not remember ever being so comfortable. Within minutes he drifted off to a night of sleep more restful than any he had found since before the Hoyt had attacked the barge.

Morning came seemingly in the blink of an eye. Feeling well-rested for the first time in a long time, he dressed without delay. He was anxious to get started with his training. He knocked on Ola's door, hoping the ogre would join him for breakfast, but there was no answer. Surmising that Ola must either be sleeping or long gone by now, Adel decided to try to find his way back on his own. Finding his way back to the kitchen proved to be simple enough, despite the labyrinthian corridors that seemed to twist and turn in every direction. As Elim had promised, there was food waiting for him—a generous helping of smoked ham and sweet cakes—which Adel devoured ravenously. He could get used to having all this food available.

Once he had eaten his fill and made his way to the central chamber, Adel found Elim waiting for him. The room was still mostly empty, but now there was a small wooden table positioned at the center of the room. Elim sat in one of the two chairs and motioned for Adel to have the other. Settling in, he wondered what the first day of his training had in store for him. His heart raced in anticipation.

"I trust you were able to get some rest?" Elim inquired. "The past few weeks must have been quite strenuous for you."

"Yes, thank you. I slept more peacefully than I have in many days. Thank you for breakfast as well, it was quite delicious," Adel commented, which drew a quick smile from the old man.

"Many years ago, before I found my calling as a

Child of the Rawl, I worked as a cook in the home of a wealthy dignitary. It is comforting to know that my skills have not been completely lost to the relentless march of time. I usually have nobody to cook for but my fellow Children, and I fear they would not comment if the food were not up to their expectations. You may have noticed, they are not the most vocal group of men you will ever meet."

"You have nothing to fear," Adel reassured him.

"Ola tells me you wish to continue the combat training the two of you begun during your journey. I think this would be a good idea and I shall see to it that you have time for this each day. The two of you may train in the courtyard; you will have plenty of room there. Please do take care not to tread on the flowerbeds though. My fellow Children are quite attached to them," Elim said.

Adel thanked the old man again, wanting to be courteous but also hoping their idle chat was coming to an end. He had come here to learn about the Rawl and was ready to begin. Apparently sensing this, Elim smiled briefly before starting to speak.

"Tell me, Adel, when you used the Rawl against the Hoyt on the river, how did it make you feel? Can you remember what you felt at the moment you used it? Please describe it for me as vividly as you can; no detail is insignificant." He leaned in toward the boy, his wizened face curious.

The Path of the Rawl Wielder

This was a difficult question for Adel to answer, recalling that at the time he'd been unaware he was using any sort of power. He hadn't even been confident that he was not dreaming or hallucinating. He recalled that when he had woken, he had been certain the whole incident had been nothing but a dream. It also did not help that he had collapsed immediately afterward, but he took a deep breath and tried to put it into words as best he could.

"I remember being very angry. The Hoyt had attacked us twice at that point, they were killing my friends, and they were going to kill the rest of us. I was taking shelter in the captain's box, as he had ordered me to do. I can't explain what compelled me to step out of the box, but my instincts told me that I should. I don't remember everything I felt during the time I was using the Rawl. I remember feeling incredibly powerful, as though nothing could stand against me. At the same time, I didn't understand what was happening, and I even thought I was dreaming at one point. It was as though the river was feeling the same emotions I was. Arrows were flying everywhere, and it is a miracle I wasn't hit. It was over so fast, and I was so exhausted that I lost consciousness immediately," Adel elaborated, feeling as though he had utterly failed to explain adequately.

Elim nodded his understanding but did not reply for a long moment. Adel waited, expecting a reply, but none was forthcoming. Once it became clear that the old man was not going to interject, Adel decided to continue.

"When I woke, it still felt as though it had been a dream. I was convinced that it was until my captain told me it had really happened. It was so confusing. I had no idea what had happened or how it had happened. I don't know what I would have done without my captain helping me find Ola and Ola bringing me here." Again, Adel paused, not sure how else he could further elaborate. Elim waved his hand, indicating no further explanation was required.

"Your first experience was similar to those of many before you over the centuries. Within the library of this temple, the Children of the Rawl have documented these discoveries for many years. In most cases, a person has no idea they possess such abilities until pressed into a moment of extreme need. Frequently, situations of life and death lead the power to reveal itself to the wielder. It leads us to wonder how many people have possessed this gift over the centuries and have never discovered it," Elim said.

Adel tried not to let his confusion show. He had spent weeks attempting to comprehend how he could have possessed this ability without realizing it. Now he was being told that he was not the sole case, which was somewhat reassuring. Though if there were others, why was this temple so scarcely populated? Shouldn't there be more Children? Dozens, or hundreds even? This line of thinking led him to a question.

"Can you tell me more about the Children of the

Rawl? Who are you? You say that you have been documenting people with my abilities for a long time. Why is that?" Adel asked. The old man hesitated for a moment before answering.

"These are fair questions, Adel. After all, you are placing a great deal of trust in us. So, I will attempt to answer them to the best of my ability. The Children are those of us who possess the gift of the Rawl but have bound ourselves to this temple. We have committed ourselves to the continuing study of the Rawl and its users. For nine hundred years there have been Children in this temple. The name is a bit of a misnomer, I grant you. You are very kind not to point it out, but I am sure our age has not gone unnoticed. Like you, most of us discovered our abilities at a young age when we found ourselves in danger or overcome with emotion. As old age drew near, we came here, forsaking the remaining years of our lives in the outside world so we could carry on the work of the Children. In our advanced age, our ability to use our power is limited, but we can still pass on what we know to youthful wielders such as yourself," Elim explained before falling silent.

"You have not answered all of my questions. You mentioned work beyond training new Rawl wielders. What is that work, and why is it so important?" Adel pressed, determined to not allow the old man to evade him.

Again, Elim seemed puzzled by Adel's continued

persistence. Perhaps having all of the time in the world while locked away in this temple had caused him to forget the urgency of younger men. There was yet another long moment of silence; the old man appeared to be having an internal debate as to what his reply should be. As Adel was opening his mouth to press the issue further, he began to respond.

"Tell me, Adel, what do you know of the lands that lay to the west of the Empire?" Elim asked.

"All that I know of is the Thrawll Desert. I do not know anything about it, other than it is a barren wasteland. The stories I have heard say it is completely devoid of life," Adel replied, puzzled by the question.

"This is all true. However, another sad truth is that a woefully small number of people are aware of why this is so. The Thrawll Desert was once every bit as lush, diverse, and full of life as the Empire. Home to people, plants, and animals, much like Thornata and the other provinces. However, seven hundred years ago there was a great war, and once that war ended, those lush, green, fertile lands were no more, replaced by the emptiness of the Thrawll Desert."

"This is an interesting story, but I fail to see how it is an answer to my question," Adel snipped, his patience with the old man's evasiveness gone.

"Silence! I am answering your question; however, there are things you need to understand before you will be able to comprehend my reply. If you are unable to focus on what I am telling you, perhaps we should postpone the start of your training!" Elim rebuked, his kindhearted voice gone cold and steely, the benevolent smile nowhere to be found. Elim's patience with Adel's constant line of questioning was wearing thin.

Adel leaned back, surprised at the force of the rebuke from the kindly old man. He did not see how the history lesson Elim was waxing on at length about would help him understand anything. Did Elim not understand the reasoning behind his impatience? Still, he did not want to anger the old man further and jeopardize his opportunity to learn about the power of the Rawl. Seeing no reason not to hear the man out, he nodded his agreement to listen, and Elim continued.

"The people of these lands to the west led lives similar to those of the people living here in the Empire. They were completely unprepared for the enemy that came for them, a people called the Thrawll. They fought back against these invaders as fiercely as they could, but in the end, they were no match for the Thrawll. The Thrawll were not merciful to their victims; any living creature found within the lands they'd invaded was slaughtered on sight. Every man, woman, child, even the animals and the plants. If you were to wander in the region now called the Thrawll Desert, you would find not a single trace of life. Not an insect, not a blade of grass, nothing. Calling it a desert is a bit of a misnomer, for even in a desert there is life. But the men of the time had no better word for the desolate wasteland that the Thrawll left behind," Elim said.

Elim paused for a moment, and Adel reflected on what he had been told. These Thrawll had wiped out every living creature in an entire region? Even the plants and animals? How was this even possible? This sounded like another tall tale a mother would use to frighten her children. It was similar to what he had been told about ogres and giants, all of which had been false. No sooner had he thought this question to himself then was Elim answering it.

"No doubt you are wondering how this was possible. Even if the Thrawll could kill every living creature within a land, how could they possibly transform that land into such a barren wasteland? To put it quite simply, Adel, the Thrawll have the same power as you and me; they command the power of the Rawl. From every account we have from that time, they command it with skill and mastery far beyond what any human wielder has ever displayed. This is why the Children keep records of Rawl wielders. This is why we feel it is so important to do so. We believe that one day, a week, a year, or ten centuries from now, the Thrawll will come to the Empire and seek to do the same as they have done to every other land they have visited. When that day comes, powerful Rawl wielders will be needed to stand against them. Without such people, we will stand no chance," Elim explained.

The Path of the Rawl Wielder

Adel sat back in his chair, trying to absorb everything Elim had told him. If there were indeed a race of Rawl-wielding creatures in the world who might one day seek to conquer the Empire, he would need to be prepared to fight them. He had come here hoping to understand his power and learn to control it, perhaps even to use it to defeat the Hoyt who had attacked and murdered his friends. Now he understood his training at this temple was much more important than he could have realized.

"Where do these Thrawll come from? Why do they invade other lands and turn them barren?" he asked, not sure if he wanted to know the answer, sickened by what he had been told already.

"The records lead us to believe they came from the far south, but we are uncertain if that is their original home or another land they had already conquered. The reasoning behind their actions is unknown; there is no record of them speaking to or attempting to negotiate with their victims. Of course, the people they conquer leave behind no records of any kind, so much of what we know is guesswork and speculation. It was speculated at the time they perhaps stole the life from the land around them as a means of preserving their own, though this is a theory we have never been able to confirm. Every record we have tells us that they are not natural creatures like you and me but rather some other type of life-form using the Rawl to further their causes, for reasons only the

Thrawll know," Elim explained.

Adel felt fatigued even though he had slept through the night and been sitting in a chair all morning. The weight of the knowledge Elim had dropped on him was more significant than any physical burden he had ever had to carry. At that moment, he felt like it would have taken less out of him to turn around and walk all the way back to Kalstag. He was ready to sleep again already. Perhaps this was why Elim had been so reluctant to elaborate. Adel had not thought anything the old man could tell him would overwhelm him, but here he was, utterly exhausted. Elim seemed to sense this and smiled reassuringly.

"Rest easy knowing this, my friend. The Children have found no evidence the Thrawll are moving against the Empire in the near future, at least not directly. However, we do see worrying signs, including the rapid rise of the Hoyt. In the texts from the last Thrawll war, there are tales of internal conflicts in the lands that were doomed to be conquered, conflicts that split the people apart from each other. Men living in those times believed the Thrawll were responsible for this, wanting to sow division in the lands they planned to invade, dividing and then conquering their victims. Again, records are scarce, but the little we do know comes from people who fled those lands before the conclusion of the war. Still, the similarities are troubling, and it is a possibility we need to be prepared to face."

The Path of the Rawl Wielder

Adel wondered if this could be true, if the Hoyt could indeed be pawns in a grander game. If this was the case, the Hoyt would need to be stamped out, a task in which Adel would be happy to take part. Eager to ensure Elim understood this, he spoke up.

"I am happy to take part in the fight against the Hoyt, especially if it means I could help prevent the Thrawll from invading the Empire. I hope in the training ahead that I prove to you I am capable. If you have confidence in me, I will do whatever you command if it can help defeat the Hoyt or the Thrawll."

Elim did not reply right away, leading Adel to wonder if he had misspoken, but Elim eventually let a wry smile escape from behind his thick white beard.

"My young man, I would never presume to command you. The Children of the Rawl do not command those who possess the power or the Rawl. We hope only to educate them on the nuances of the gift they possess. As for you, Adel, we hoped that in time you would agree to become our leader. We believe the time has come for wielders of the Rawl to play a larger role in the events that unfold in this world. However, we have bound ourselves to this temple, and outside its walls our power is severely weakened. We need a young man like you, one who can lead us and serve as our champion across the Empire. Whether you agree to take on that responsibility will be your choice to make when the time comes."

This statement floored Adel. He had come here thinking the Children of the Rawl would request his service in exchange for their knowledge, a price he had been willing to pay. The thought of becoming their leader bordered on ridiculous. He had just recently discovered his power. How could he expect to lead a group of old men who had wielded it for decades? Still, he knew his training had to begin before he could truly consider such things.

"I am sure you are tired of sitting here and talking. I have given you much information to process. You will find Ola in the courtyard. Go and practice with your sword; such skills are important. It is a beautiful day, so take it in and enjoy it. Such times are a useful reminder of the beauty in the world that we need to defend. I will prepare a lunch. After you have eaten and rested, we will begin more practical training," Elim said.

Adel nodded somewhat reluctantly; he was eager to begin his training but knew he needed to take time and process everything he had been told this morning. Thanking Elim for his time, he rose and made his way toward the courtyard, more determined to improve his skills than ever before.

Chapter Ten

The night was black as they come, precisely as the Hoyt had hoped it would be. The only light came from the sliver of a quarter moon partially concealed by cloud cover and the torches at the gates of the city of Kolig far off in the distance. Idanox paced impatiently, unable to remain still, eager to see things get underway. His master plan was finally about to spring into motion, and these final moments of waiting were bordering on intolerable for him. He stalked back and forth on the hilltop with the anxiousness of a large cat stalking its prey. Idanox glanced back at the city for the signal every few seconds, determined not to miss the moment when it came.

The city of Kolig would fall this night; he harbored no doubts about that. He had prepared too thoroughly for any other result. The Thornatan Army had disregarded the threat of the Hoyt at their own peril. They thought them no more than a ragtag gang of bandits and thieves, content to continue scraping out an existence by robbing shipping barges and trading caravans. This was the night the army would learn the consequences of their willful ignorance. This was the night they would regret it. The moment Idanox's rise to power would truly begin was fast approaching. When future generations told tales of Duke Idanox, they would start with the fall of Kolig.

In many ways, it was ironic. The government of Thornata had made little effort to put a stop to the Hoyt, perfectly content to allow the gang to prey on the weakest of their citizens. Rich men cared little for the plights of the poor, after all. Idanox had been no different until he had recognized the incredible potential of angry peasants in large numbers. This was a point Idanox had used to significant effect when recruiting men to the Hoyt. The duke and his army did not care for them or their suffering in the way Idanox did. The Hoyt could offer them a more fulfilling existence, one in which they could pull themselves out of poverty and despair. It was an argument that usually worked. Commoners did not think like nobles and rich men. They saw only what they perceived as disregard toward them by those in power. It was a trait Idanox was able to prey on quite effectively.

Now here he was, commanding a force made up of former farmers, blacksmiths, merchants, and all manner of peasants. Not so long ago, he would never have permitted such commoners to even be in his presence. What a fool he had been, completely overlooking the potential of such people. They may lack intelligence and sophistication, but such traits were unnecessary. They would stand in the way of them blindly following his orders, an obstacle he could not accept. He had figured it out first, and now the government of Thornata would be forced to see him for what he truly was, though the realization would come too late. He was a man who was a threat to them, a man more worthy of ruling than they were. They would soon regret disregarding the needs of their commoners for so long.

Turning away from the city, Idanox surveyed the men he had brought with him. Row after row of heavily armed fighters, they were far from the mob of disorganized thieves the Thornatan Army would expect. Idanox had brought over two thousand men with him to Kolig. It was more than he was likely to need, but failure was not an option. It would set his plans back by months, if not years. He was focused not solely on taking the city, but also killing as many Thornatan soldiers as possible once they came to reclaim it. If he was not able to deplete the army of thousands of soldiers, the Hoyt could not hope to seize the capital city of Oreanna.

The army had no idea such a force was at the doorstep of one of their province's largest cities. Their arrogance had long been blinding them to the threat that had been building. In their arrogance, they had ceased regularly patrolling the countryside years ago, yet more disregard for the poor peasants living in smaller communities. When the attack came, they would have no warning. The city would fall before they could bring the bulk of their defenses to bear, and the Hoyt casualties should be minimal. He was relishing the thought so intently that he almost missed the signal when it arrived, two torches atop the gates, waving at him. His men inside the city were ready to open the gates. He hurried down the hill and ordered his commanders to sound the attack.

Row after row of Hoyt fighters began to jog up the hill and then down the other side toward the bridge spanning the Kival River and ran right to the gates of the city. The battle would not last long. His men planted on the inside of the city would have already significantly weakened the garrison of men defending Kolig and ensured there would be no warning of the impending attack. The large number of men had been brought to Kolig more to control the civilian population once the city was under Hoyt control. They also needed a sufficient number of men inside the city to draw the appropriate response from the Thornatan army. The more soldiers that came to liberate the city, the more they could wipe out in one fell swoop.

The Path of the Rawl Wielder

The gates of Kolig began to open as the first rows of Hoyt fighters reached the far side of the bridge, and Idanox gazed down from the hill and smirked with satisfaction. It was done; now that his forces were inside the walls, the city was as good as his. Kolig had physical defenses as formidable as any city in the province, but they made no difference. His men were already past them. The army had not even bothered to place a sizeable watch on top of the walls at night; there would be no warning. The Thornatans did not have enough men inside to stand against such a force. All he had to do was sit back and wait for his men to complete the formalities.

The signal came even sooner than he had expected, and he crossed the bridge and entered the city triumphantly the hour before dawn. He felt like a conquering hero, strolling down the streets of the city, the savior come to free them from the oppression of the corrupt Thornatan government. He was pleased to see his men had not needed to burn or destroy many buildings to get their point across. It was better to keep the people under the impression that the Hoyt had no intention of destroying their city. There were bodies of slain Thornatan soldiers and Kolig city watchmen still lying in the street with the occasional civilian lying along with them.

Good, he thought, *let the people of Kolig see what fate will await any who dare to resist me.* The more tokens of his victory were strewn across the city, the better.

Pete Biehl

He made his way confidently to the governor's mansion, which now belonged to him. A small contingent of bodyguards surrounded him every step of the way. It was a necessary precaution in case any of the citizens of Kolig had the idea to make an attempt on his life. He could not count on every citizen of Kolig seeing him as the savior he was. There would always be ideologues who refused to see matters as they truly were, and eventually, such people would need to be stamped out. There was no room for disorder in the Hoyt regime.

A small group of Hoyt fighters had rounded up the governor and his staff. They sat gathered in front of the mansion. Idanox approached the governor with a smile. His smile was met with a glare and a spit aimed at his face. The spit missed, but Idanox still could not allow such an insult to pass in front of his new subjects. They needed to understand the repercussions of such an act.

Drawing his knife, he slit the man's throat without ever saying a word to him. The people of Kolig needed to see precisely what type of man would now be governing them. Idanox could be a kind and just ruler, but he would never allow anyone to perceive him as weak. The days of a spineless Thornatan government were coming to a close. As the governor collapsed to the grass, choking out his last few breaths, Idanox turned to his men.

"String the governor up by his feet from the city gates. He will make a fine decoration. Take his staff as well; place them in cages in the main city square. Any time anyone in this city decides it is a good idea to speak out against us, pull one of them out of their cage and kill them. Make sure it is public and painful. That should show the people of Kolig exactly who is in charge of their city now. There is no need for hostility between us, but they need to understand how things have changed," Idanox instructed.

The victory in Kolig was only the beginning. Idanox knew the type of brutality that would be required to hold this city. He had always known, and he felt no urge to shy away from it. If anything, he reveled in the prospect of violence. He much preferred handling things in this manner to the diplomatic approach he had been forced to employ in his past life. Things ran so much more efficiently when you were unconcerned with the bothers of diplomacy.

The governor's staff were dragged away, some of them begging for mercy as they went. Their cries meant nothing to him. The only relevance the rest of their lives would have would be to help him maintain control of the city until the army arrived. Once that happened, their purpose would be fulfilled, and their use to him ended. They could survive the coming conflict or perish, it mattered not to him. He ordered one of his bodyguards to gather his commanders here at the mansion; there were preparations to be made and no time to waste. The governor's mansion of Kolig was not as luxurious as his former manor home, but it would serve him well enough for the time being.

He made his way to the dining room of the enormous mansion, taking a seat at the head of the large table. He noted the governor had not lived in the same poverty many of the residents of his city were forced to endure. He would need to make sure to point this out to his men. It was always good to remind them of the lives their oppressors led while they scraped out a living in poverty and despair.

The attack had proceeded exactly as he had planned, if not better. He had never dared to hope Kolig would fall so easily. It was indeed gratifying to see his carefully laid plans executed to perfection. His men had not even needed to damage this beautiful mansion in any way, and he appreciated that. Artwork and fine cutlery adorned the room, all paid for by the hardworking taxpayers of Thornata, of course. It gave him a sense of pride to have liberated such belongings from the corrupt governor. He would have to remember to take some of them with him as trophies of his victory, spoils of a battle well fought. His commanders were beginning to arrive, so he snapped his attention back to the matter at hand. There would be time to revel in the glory of his achievement later.

"Well done, my good men, my dear brothers. Kolig is ours. Without a doubt, the word is already beginning to make its way to the other cities in the province. The duke will have no option but to send the

The Path of the Rawl Wielder

Thornatan Army to retake the city. He cannot afford to leave one of his cities under our control. To do so would make him appear weak to his subjects, and he cannot tolerate that, even if it is the truth. It will take weeks for them to muster a large enough force and weeks more for them to march here. We have plenty of time to make our preparations for their arrival. Have we secured the dam?" Idanox asked, allowing his happiness to show.

He did not show hints of his emotions often, but he felt his men deserved to know they had done well this night. True, they had only done so because they had his genius guiding them, but they need not know that. Best if they felt their own contributions were more invaluable than they actually were.

The massive dam to the north of the city was the keystone of his plan, the weapon they would use to destroy the Thornatan Army. However, it was crucial they not suspect this. If they moved against the dam first, his plan would fall to pieces. He did not think they would do so; they were still ignorant of his true intentions. Opening the floodgates of the dam would destroy much of the city, but the duke would believe his goal was to hold and rule the city as his own private kingdom. They would recognize the error of their thinking too late, not understanding he had far more lofty goals to pursue. By the time they realized this, they would have already assisted him in doing so.

"We have sent a hundred men to secure it; it

should be ours within the hour. The governor had a token force assigned to defend it, so we expect no complications. We are already making arrangements to ensure it will be under heavy guard day and night. We will see to it that all men guarding it are familiar with how to open the floodgates." The reply brought a smile to Idanox's face.

"I want no fewer than five dozen men guarding it at all times. Ensure that all men who are stationed there understand the importance of their task. They are not to open the floodgates until the bulk of the Thornatan Army is on the river; we want to ensure maximum casualties," Idanox elaborated, fighting to contain the excitement in his voice. He had to put on the aura of a pragmatic leader. It was difficult when all he wanted to do at that moment was gloat.

He was confident the plan would work to perfection. He had invested too much time and too many resources to accept failure. He went over the remainder of his instructions, reinforcing the fact that he wanted their stay in the city to be as calm as possible. Rebellions were to be put down brutally and rapidly. They could not allow the populace to possess even a shred of belief that they could overcome their occupiers. The bridge that spanned from the gates and across the river was to be destroyed before dawn. This would ensure the army had one method with which to enter the city, and the same method would prove to be their demise. Dismissing his commanders, he retired to the governor's private quarters for some well-deserved rest.

Alone at last, Idanox was once again able to relish his victory. There was nothing that could stand in his way now, or at least almost nothing. There was still the matter of the young Rawl wielder. He had dispatched dozens of men to see him eliminated. Weeks had passed, and nothing had been heard from those men since their departure. He had deployed a few scouts; those had also failed to return. This led him to believe the mission had failed yet again. The boy must be more formidable than he had feared. He would have preferred to oversee the attack on the boy personally, but his preparations for this battle had prevented it.

He had hoped to capture the young man and hopefully sway him to join the Hoyt. A Rawl user would be a powerful and useful ally in the days to come; however, it appeared such an alliance was not meant to be. He would have been satisfied knowing the boy was dead, but even that reassurance was eluding him. He assumed the boy had reached the Temple of the Rawl, and even Idanox was not bold enough to attempt an assault on that ancient fortress. If half the rumors he had heard about the temple and its residents were true, such an attempt could easily spell the end of the Hoyt. He doubted even the entire Imperial Army could sack the Temple of the Rawl.

It was a shame, he conceded to himself. The boy

would have been a useful weapon indeed if the Thrawll decided to go back on their promise to him. There was nothing he could do about it now; perhaps there would be another chance to capture or kill the boy later. It did not do to dwell on worst-case scenarios. For the moment, he was victorious, and everything he wanted was finally within his grasp. He retired to the chambers reserved for the governor of the city of Kolig. It was a fitting reward, one that had been wrought by nothing more than his own ingenuity. Yes, it was a sweet reward indeed, one that would have to satisfy him for the time being.

Chapter Eleven

Focus, concentrate, but do not allow any strong emotions to fight their way into your mind." Elim's voice was calm, reassuring. "No anger, no fear, no doubt. One must never rely on the motivation of emotion to wield the power of the Rawl. You must learn to summon it as easily as putting on your shirt or taking a drink of water. Our emotions will always fight to force their way in, but you must learn to master them."

Adel clenched his teeth and focused as Elim instructed, but still found himself unable to do what he was being asked to do. The frustration kept fighting to creep its way in, no matter how hard he struggled to keep it at bay. With every failed attempt, it became more difficult to keep his emotions out of his mind as Elim was urging him to do. For three days now he had come and sat at this table and tried to perform this task, and for three days he had failed miserably. What was he doing wrong?

The pitcher of water and the empty goblet sat there, two feet from his face, taunting him. His task should be a simple one: move the water from the pitcher into the goblet. It would be simple enough if he were allowed to use his hands, of course. Instead, Elim had requested he complete this task using nothing but the power of the Rawl. The problem was that Elim had given him no instruction on how to do this, merely a command that it should be done. Each day he had sat in this chair and failed, and each day Elim had reassured him he would succeed when he was ready to do so. The old man's blind optimism had been a comfort at one point, but now it merely infuriated Adel further. Three days, and he had not managed to move a single drop.

Realizing he was no longer able to keep his frustration at bay, Adel sat back in his chair, momentarily setting his task aside. His struggles didn't make any sense to him. When faced with the danger of the Hoyt attack, the Rawl had come to him easily, even though he had been entirely unaware of his abilities. Now he was well aware of their existence and unable to call on them no matter hard he tried. The struggle filled him with doubt. It had occurred to him multiple times that perhaps he did not possess any power after all. Perhaps somebody else on the barge had been the one to command the river and hadn't even known it. What if the Children were mistaken about him? How many more times could he fail before they would ask him to leave?

"It's hard to keep the frustration from my mind when I fail time and time again!" he snapped, not at directly at Elim but rather to the entire world around him, his impatience finally boiling over.

"Rest assured, Adel, these struggles are not only normal, but they are a crucial part of the learning process. Those who never struggle never have the opportunity to build true strength. It's a fact that the Hoyt leader Idanox has never learned, to his detriment. By the time your training is complete, such a feat will come to you as easily as breathing." Elim's reassuring smile frustrated Adel further.

"But there hasn't been any training! All you have done is sit there and tell me to move the water. You have not told me how to do this! How can it be done without any instruction?" Adel quipped, this time very much directed at Elim, his face hot with anger. He knew he should not snap at the old man. Elim was trying to help, but his temper was finally getting the better of him.

"Think about your struggles like this, Adel. When you were a child, did your mother tell you how to breathe? How to chew your food? Even how to walk? No, she did not. These things come naturally as part of the growing process. So it is with using the power of the Rawl. We are here to help you on your journey, to show you possibilities. It is just as your mother showed you the possibilities of life. In a manner of speaking, you are only a child when it comes to using this power, and you must learn on your own how best to wield it. The process is different for every Rawl wielder, and it is not my place to set you on the path I think is best. Ultimately, everything you learn will be for you to decide." Elim was as calm as ever. If he took any offense to the way Adel had lashed out at him, he did not show it.

Adel was silent for a moment, trying once more to master his emotions as Elim had told him, and failing all the while. How could Elim not understand his struggles? He was not learning to walk; he was trying to learn how to wield an incredible power. How could he do this without further instruction? At this rate, he would be staring at the jug of water until he was as old as the Children. It was evident he would be unable to focus correctly anymore. He exasperatedly ceased his attempts to move the water.

"I think it would be best if I stopped for today. I do not think I will be able to succeed in my current state of mind. I do not wish to frustrate myself further. With your leave, I will seek out Ola for my sword training," he said, making every effort to be as cordial as possible.

"Of course, my friend. You require no leave from me. You are your own master, never forget that," Elim replied, the optimism in his voice as annoying as ever. Adel forced a smile and thanks as he rose from his chair and made his way out into the courtyard. He blinked against the brilliant sunshine. Each day had been more beautiful than the previous, and the quaint silence of the high mountain meadow had been a source of great comfort to him since his arrival. Summer would arrive in earnest before long; the days had already begun to last longer.

If his training with Elim had been the source of his frustration the past few days, his sessions with Ola had been his relief. He wondered if this was why Elim had thought it a wise idea to continue them. The ogre was still besting him with relative ease, of course, but the ability to engage an opponent he could see and feel was somewhat relaxing. He found Ola outside, already training on his own, his massive sword fending off imaginary foes in the air around him. Noticing Adel's approach, Ola sheathed his massive blade and retrieved the two practice swords.

"How go your lessons with Elim?" Ola asked, though Adel was sure the ogre already suspected the answer.

"Each day he sets the water in front of me, and each day I fail to move it. I am beginning to think I am wasting my time here. The Children may be mistaken about me. Maybe I have no power, after all. Perhaps I should leave and find myself a job on a barge. Perhaps it's all I am good at," Adel replied, unable to mask the disappointment in his voice.

"Perhaps you are making progress, even if you are unable to see that progress," Ola suggested, handing Adel his practice sword.

"How is that possible? I either move the water, or I don't, and to this point, I have been unable to move a single drop!" Adel exclaimed, his anger beginning to boil over once more.

"Think back to when we first started training with the sword, Adel. You were unable to fend off my attacks for more than a few seconds. Each day you improved, and it was clear for me to see it, yet still, you thought you made no progress. You even told me as much, do you remember? But every bruise you sustained in those early days was a lesson, and every one of those lessons made you a better swordsman. Perhaps you are sustaining a different type of bruise every time you fail in your Rawl training. Maybe Elim can see progress, even though you cannot, simply because you do not yet understand how to look for it," Ola said.

Adel reflected on this for a moment. It was true, in his early days of sword training it had seemed as though he would never improve. But improve he had, nevertheless. During their last session, he had held off a particularly ferocious assault by the ogre, one that would have broken his defenses in moments only weeks earlier. Could the same thing be happening now with the Rawl?

The Path of the Rawl Wielder

He was not sure, yet this talk with Ola had undoubtedly given him a renewed sense of hope. Ola had become a good friend to him these last few weeks, a friend Adel was genuinely grateful for here at the temple.

***

When Adel walked into the great room the following morning to find the familiar table and pitcher of water waiting for him, he faced them not with trepidation. This time, it was with an eagerness to try again. Ola's words of encouragement the day prior were still ringing in his head. He was making progress, even if he could not see it, and for the first time he was confident of that fact. Today he would prove it. Elim's smile of greeting did not bother him this day; he knew this would be the day he succeeded. The old man would be smiling much wider before too long, he would see to that. The two did not exchange words; no words needed to be said. Adel knew what he was being asked to do, and no words would help.

Adel took his seat, as calm and relaxed as he had been since he had arrived at the temple. Elim's words from the day before were racing through his mind. Summoning the power of the Rawl had to be as natural and effortless to him as breathing, walking, or eating an apple. He glanced at the goblet, then at the pitcher. Having decided that an approach similar to his sword training would work best, he cleared his mind, focusing on nothing except the water.

First he stared hard at the pitcher of water, then he glanced at the empty goblet, his intended target. What if the water moved from the pitcher to the goblet, without him directing it specifically on what it should do? What if the water moved because he wanted it to do so? Yet the water did not move, sitting still as ever in its pitcher. Adel had thought this simplistic approach would work, and yet it had not. Allowing his focus to break, he looked to Elim.

"What am I doing wrong, Elim?" Adel asked.

"That is for you to discover on your own, Adel," Elim replied, apparently unaware of how much this oft-repeated answer angered him.

Adel was angry now, the anger causing his blood to rush to his head, which began to throb. Remembering that he must not lash out in anger in an attempt to use his power, he rose from his chair, needing to step away for a moment.

"I need a drink of water. Excuse me," he said, beginning toward the kitchen.

"Certainly, my friend. But why leave the room? There is water right here," Elim suggested, pointing to the untouched jug and goblet.

Adel reached for the pitcher to find Elim had already lifted it from the table. The old man motioned for him to pick up the goblet, indicating he would pour the water for him. Adel lifted the goblet with a quick word of thanks, extending it toward Elim, who remained motionless. His head was paining him more than ever, and he needed the water badly. It was at that moment the liquid began to move.

It began moving gently, inching its way up the side of the glass pitcher, gradually picking up speed as it breached the rim and began to fall into the goblet. Once the goblet was nearly full, it stopped. The remainder of the liquid settled back at the bottom of the pitcher. Adel looked at the old man closely, assuring himself Elim had not moved at all, yet the water had moved from the pitcher to the goblet. Adel stared down at the goblet in disbelief. His headache and thirst were forgotten. He looked up at Elim, who was smiling in satisfaction at him.

"Well done, Adel. You have moved the water from the pitcher to the goblet. Do you understand why you were able to do so?" the old man asked, his kind eyes glowing with delight.

"I don't understand. I wasn't even thinking about moving the water; I just wanted something to drink," Adel stammered, struggling to believe his own eyes as he gazed at the full goblet in wonder.

"Exactly, Adel. You were thinking about a result, not a task. Think back to when you destroyed the Hoyt blockade. Were you thinking about moving the river, or using the water against the Hoyt?" Elim asked.

"No, I was angrier than I had ever been, thinking and wishing I could kill them all," Adel replied, beginning to understand what Elim was trying to tell him.

"Understand this, Adel. The Rawl is summoned by focusing not on what you want it to do, but rather what you want your result to be. Over time you will learn to focus its power in more specific and unique ways, but do not allow yourself to believe that you are completely controlling it. The Rawl and its wielder must work together. It can serve you well, but you must never allow yourself to believe you are fully its master. The consequences of such arrogance could prove dire. The first Children of the Rawl believed that the Rawl possessed a will of its own, that is was a living entity. Maybe not in the same way you and I are, but alive nonetheless. They believed the Rawl and its wielder were symbiotes, each needing the other to survive. We have studied this for centuries and have been unable to confirm this belief beyond doubt. But there is one thing we do know. It is a power so vast that it is beyond the full comprehension of mere humans," Elim warned.

Adel leaned back, reflecting on this for a moment. Not wanting to lose his momentum, he thought to himself that perhaps he was not so thirsty after all; maybe the water should remain in the pitcher. No sooner had the thought crossed his mind then the water began to move once more, climbing up the side of the goblet and floating through the air, coming to rest back inside the pitcher. The rush of excitement was hard to contain, and he proceeded to move the water back and forth from pitcher to goblet. The movement became faster with each repetition, the grin splitting Elim's ancient face growing along with Adel's confidence. With each repetition, the power responded more easily to his request.

Once he had moved the water perhaps a dozen times, Elim set the pitcher back on the table and motioned for him to pause. Adel did so, but not until he'd raised the water from the pitcher and then dropped it back inside with a mighty splash and a triumphant smile.

"I am proud of what you have accomplished here, Adel," Elim said. "But I must ask you a question. Do you understand why you must not rely on emotion to summon the power of the Rawl?"

Adel thought about this for a moment. If he was angry, why could he not channel his emotion to use his power more effectively? If he was scared, why could he not use that fear to call upon his power to protect him? Stumped, he looked up at Elim and shook his head.

"If you grow reliant on emotions to use the power of the Rawl, what will you do when they are not there? If you only summon it when you are angry, how will you summon it when your rage is spent? Even more of a danger, what if your emotions are too powerful for you to control? What if you are so angry that you fuel your power into doing far more damage than you intended? If you can master the art of using your power without such aids, it will always be at your disposal and within your control."

That makes sense, Adel thought. If he used emotions as a crutch for summoning the power of the Rawl, it might fail him at a crucial moment. It had worked on the river, though he had been unaware of his actions at the time. He needed to learn to wield the power in a safer, more proficient manner.

"That makes sense, Elim. Thank you so much for your help and for allowing me to learn this lesson on my own. I can't wait to learn more."

"You have done well today, my young friend. Now you understand that you truly do have access to an incredible power, and you are able to summon this power when you require it. From this point forward, your lessons will expand to other areas, other ways you can manipulate the world around you to your advantage. For now, enjoy this triumph. Our lessons shall resume in the morning," Elim said.

***

In the weeks that followed, Adel found his confidence growing along with his proficiency at wielding his newly discovered abilities. In one lesson, they went to the courtyard, and Ola fired arrows into the sky. Under Elim's guidance, Adel was able to channel short bursts of wind into redirecting their flight, bringing memories to Adel's mind of the arrow that had changed direction for no apparent reason while racing toward him during the attack on the barge. Ola and Elim flat-out refused his request to truly test his ability by firing an arrow directly at him. They assured him the skill would be there for him in the unfortunate event he should require it in an actual battle, and that practice was too hazardous. No amount of protest could sway them on this, even the suggestion that Ola merely fire at his legs.

In another lesson, several of the Children struck flint against stone, and Adel was able to channel the Rawl to create a large flame from the minuscule sparks the strikes produced. Once he formed the flame, he was able to move and bend it to his will, controlling the direction of its movements and the pace of its growth. Once he had completed the exercise, he was able to withdraw the air from the flame and put it out in an instant. Elim seemed particularly pleased that he had managed this challenge without lighting any of his teachers on fire.

Adel's favorite lesson was one that occurred by the good fortune of an early summer thunderstorm. He woke one morning to the sound of the massive thunder blasts echoing off the surrounding peaks, and Elim eagerly led him out to the courtyard. After many failed attempts, Adel was able to stop and redirect a lightning bolt before it could strike the ground. That feat left him utterly exhausted yet incredibly proud of himself. Elim explained that in time, he might even be able to create lightning of his own; however, this was a far more advanced skill than he was ready to attempt at this time. Apparently, the Children were in no hurry to have a novice Rawl wielder calling down lightning strikes in the area of their temple.

Elim also taught him ways of using the Rawl to defend himself from enemies without harming them. In one such lesson, Adel was taught to draw moisture from deep within the earth, turning the solid ground into thick mud that was impossible for all but the strongest of men to walk through. During a rainstorm, he practiced turning puddles of rainwater into ice, a handy method of slowing down pursuit.

All the while, his lessons with Ola continued as well, each more intense than the one before. The ogre seemed determined to test the limits of his abilities further each day, and each time Adel's limits seemed to expand in response to the hard lessons. He was still nowhere close to being the ogre's equal, but Adel was confident he could hold his own against most opponents if forced to defend himself with a blade.

It was during one of these lessons that the doors from the temple swung open and Elim came walking briskly toward them, a young woman by his side. Adel had not seen this woman before. Her somewhat tattered garb gave the impression she had been traveling for some time, leading him to surmise that she had arrived at the temple recently. Her dark brown hair perfectly matched the hue of her eyes and dark leather clothing. Adel could not help but notice the longbow, sword, and many knives that hung from various areas of her frame, which was far from unappealing to a man of his age. Seeing them approach, Ola halted the lesson, a smile splitting his rough face at the sight of the young woman.

"Alsea, it has been quite some time since I have seen you. You are well?" Ola asked the young woman in greeting, seeming quite pleased to see her.

"Not so well, unfortunately. The Hoyt have attacked Kolig and seized control of the city. It took me nearly a week to sneak out so I could bring you this news. The Hoyt have patrols everywhere; they don't want anyone leaving the city. The governor is dead, and now Idanox plans to lure the Thornatan Army into a trap," the young woman replied, obviously not one to waste time on pleasantries during such dire times.

Adel could not believe what he was hearing. The boldness of the Hoyt did not catch him off guard, but rather the ability to organize well enough to seize control of one of the province's largest cities. It was quite an accomplishment for a ragtag band of thieves that the Hoyt had the reputation of being. Having seen firsthand the cruelty the Hoyt were capable of during their encounters on the river, he grew immediately concerned for the well-being of the people of Kolig.

"Ola, Alsea was able to get close enough to overhear some Hoyt men discussing their plans. They have seized control of the dam upriver. Once the army arrives and begins to cross, they will open the dam and drown them. The Hoyt have destroyed the bridge leading to the city gates, leaving the army with the sole option of crossing the river in boats. We cannot allow this to happen; this could leave the entire province vulnerable to a takeover by the Hoyt. An unstable province is a dangerous one, even for us. The Hoyt have shown a great interest in our young friend here, and they cannot be allowed to assume a position of power. I want you to go with Alsea back to Kolig and attempt to warn the army of the danger." Elim elaborated.

"Oh, I will go, but I can't guarantee they'll be too eager to take the word of an ogre. I doubt the Thornatan Army will think of me as being much better than the Hoyt," Ola replied.

"If they do not listen, you will have to seize control of the dam yourselves to ensure a safe crossing for the army. I agree, the army will be reluctant to heed your warnings, but we cannot sit back and allow the Hoyt to succeed," Elim said.

"I want to go with them."

All eyes shifted to Adel.

"I'm sorry, but who are you exactly?" Alsea asked, one eyebrow arching until it had almost disappeared into her hairline.

"I will fill you in on that later," Elim interjected before Adel could respond. "Yes, Adel, I was going to suggest you accompany them as well."

Now it was Adel's turn to be surprised, and he was not alone. Alsea looked skeptical, and Ola seemed downright shocked, assuming, of course, that Adel had grown as skilled at reading the ogre's various facial expressions as well as he believed he had. His assumption was soon confirmed.

"Are you certain this is a good idea, Elim?" Ola asked. His tone was respectful, as it always was when addressing the old man, but his skepticism was apparent.

"It will be a good opportunity for Adel to test his newfound abilities in a setting with higher stakes. With you two by his side, I do not doubt he will be quite safe. Besides, his skills may be of use if things go badly. This is a dire situation, and I think we would be foolish not to deploy every resource we have available to face it. Many innocent lives are at stake," Elim explained.

Ola didn't appear to be entirely convinced by the argument, and the expression on Alsea's face still betrayed her skepticism. Still, it was clear neither of them were comfortable with challenging Elim further on the matter. With the issue settled, Elim urged them all to get some rest; they would need to leave at the first light of dawn. Adel headed for the kitchen, finding himself suddenly famished. He was excited to finally have the opportunity to test himself in the real world, and determined to prove he was up to the challenge.

Chapter Twelve

It was a damp and dreary morning that greeted Adel as he stepped out into the courtyard of the Temple of the Rawl. Mist filled the courtyard, giving the high mountain clearing the appearance of a swamp. It was quite a switch from the bright sunny days of the past few weeks, eliciting a small groan from Adel, who had been hoping for sunny skies to accompany them on their journey. Seeing that Elim, Ola, and Alsea were already waiting near the massive front gates, he hurried his pace, eager not to slow the group down. Ola offered a quick word of greeting, but a curt nod was the sole acknowledgment he would receive from Alsea. Adel had surmised from her response the day before that she believed he was a potential liability on this journey, and he was quite eager to prove her wrong.

His confidence notwithstanding, he could not help but feel ill-equipped when compared to his two traveling companions. He carried the sword he had been gifted by Captain Boyd, along with the small dagger. Ola once again carried his massive sword strapped to his back, as well as a shorter sword and several long knives on his belt. Alsea had a bow and quiver of arrows on her back. She also carried a belt of throwing knives and daggers at her waist along with a short sword. She had donned clean clothing as well, again made of dark brown leather. This plethora of weapons, along with the determined expression etched across her face, was enough to convince him that he would not want to test his newfound combat skills against her.

"Good morning, Adel." Elim greeted him with his usual benign smile. "Would you be kind enough to open the gates for us this morning?"

Adel looked up at the massive stone doors. He knew they must be heavier than he could possibly imagine. Not to be deterred, he focused his thoughts, homing in on the fact that he needed the gates to open for him. The power responded immediately. An enormous gust of wind seemed to come from nowhere, passing over their heads and striking the massive gates with enough force to ease them forward. He glanced at the others to find Elim smiling in pride, and even Alsea with a slightly impressed expression that vanished the moment she noticed him looking at her.

"You have come so far in a very short time, my young friend, and your abilities will serve you well in the journey ahead. However, do not believe for a moment that you have learned all you must know. I urge you to return to this temple as soon as you have helped Alsea and Ola retake Kolig from the Hoyt. Heed their advice; it will serve you well in the days ahead. Both are exceptionally skilled, and I have no concerns about your safety as long as they are with you. Remember your training, and your power will be there for you if you need it," Elim said.

"I will," Adel promised. "Thank you, Elim, thank you for all that you have taught me and for seeing my potential even when I could not see it myself."

With that, the three companions were off, though not before Adel brought them to a brief halt so he could close the gates behind them. Alsea took the lead, and Adel quickly learned that much like Ola, she was not going to move at a leisurely pace. They descended the long stone steps into the valley below at a speed that seemed to border on reckless to Adel, given the damp state of the rocks and the dense fog surrounding them. Determined not to hold the group back, he merely pushed on, taking each step as gently as could, trying his utmost not to stumble. Within an hour, they had reached the valley floor. Adel looked up, hoping for a last glance at the Temple of the Rawl, but it was invisible through the dense fog above them.

Klaweck was waiting for them not far from the path. Despite having already met the giant, Adel could not help but be awestruck by the sheer size of the man. In the back of his mind were images of the speed and ferocity with which Klaweck had dispatched the Hoyt men who had attempted to capture Adel. To now see Klaweck waving in greeting and smiling from ear to ear was almost off-putting.

"Leaving so soon, Alsea? But you have only just arrived," Klaweck greeted the young woman.

"Unfortunately, there is no time for rest, Klaweck. Elim wants Ola and me to get back to Kolig and hopefully stop the Hoyt ambush before it happens," Alsea replied. Adel could not help but notice the omission of his name and tried his best not to let it bother him.

"Well, you have a Rawl wielder on your side. Should be an easy enough feat, especially if they're as competent as the Hoyt I have encountered. Have you finished your training so soon, Adel?" Klaweck asked, turning his attention to Adel.

"Not finished, but Elim thought some practical experience would be good for me. I hope he is right," Adel replied.

"Well, if Elim thinks you are ready, I am sure you are. You must be a fast learner indeed. I will keep you no longer; safe travels, my friends. I look forward to your safe return!" Klaweck bade, and they were off once more.

If Adel thought Alsea had moved quickly on the steps, he had been sorely mistaken, as her pace hastened even more now that they were on relatively flat terrain. She did not make any attempts at conversation, nor did Ola. Adel thought once or twice of trying, but was worried he would run out of breath trying to talk and keep up with the blistering pace of their march at the same time. They had cleared the valley in no time at all and were soon making their way down the foothills.

It had taken Ola and Adel five days to traverse these rolling foothills, though with Alsea leading the way, Adel surmised they would reach the plains by the end of the next day. It gave him an appreciation for the consideration Ola had shown him, not forcing him to march so fast on their first trek. They had been walking for five hours before she came to a stop and suggested a short break. Adel's legs were burning with exhaustion, but determined not to show it, he smiled and nodded his agreement as though they were out for a pleasant afternoon stroll. Apparently not one to need things as trivial as rest, Alsea announced she was going to scout the surrounding area during the break.

"She's not happy I'm here, is she?" Adel asked once she was out of earshot.

"Don't take offense, Adel. It's nothing personal. Alsea likes to keep people at a distance. You are right, though. She argued with Elim furiously last night about including you on this journey," Ola replied.

"I'm not deadweight. I think I will be of value on this mission!" Adel shot back, exasperated.

"I agree, and let me be clear, she does not think you are deadweight. You are the first Rawl wielder other than the Children who we have seen in the time the two of us have served them. You have to understand your importance. Alsea believes it is reckless of Elim to send you on this type of journey with incomplete training. She understands how important you are, and thinks it is reckless to put you in harm's way. That is all there is to it. She has no personal issue with you, that I can assure you."

It was not the response Adel had expected, but it did make sense. Perhaps Alsea was even concerned that he would be injured or killed in her company and she would be seen as responsible for that. Everybody he had encountered these past weeks was of the impression that he was an important person, a viewpoint he was still struggling to wrap his mind around. Still, Ola's explanation did give him a small amount of sympathy and understanding for Alsea. It was short-lived compassion that died a few minutes later when she returned and barked impatiently at them that it was time to proceed.

Onward they marched, making their way steadily east through the foothills. After several more hours, the sun was beginning to fall behind them, and Adel was hopeful that with only a few hours of daylight left, they would soon make camp for the night. Of course, Alsea showed little interest in stopping. Adel assumed Ola was also not about to make the suggestion, which is why the next words to come out of the ogre's mouth came as a great shock to him.

"Stop now!"

Alsea stopped and turned to face Ola, who had served as the rear guard for their entire journey. The ogre held up one finger, freezing her before she could speak. Adel had become better at reading Ola's facial expressions these last few weeks and believed the ogre looked quite alarmed. Within seconds, the ogre was beckoning them to lean in closer to him.

"We are surrounded," he whispered. "There are Hoyt fighters in the hills around us. I can hear them moving closer. They are making a great effort to conceal their presence. I think our best move is to pretend we are unaware they are there. If they do not expect any resistance, we may have a chance. If we tip our hand, I think they will open fire on us from long range." Adel had heard and seen nothing to indicate this but had learned on their journey to the Temple of the Rawl not to doubt the ogre's keen senses.

"How many of them do you think there are?" Alsea asked.

"It's hard to be certain, but I would guess over two dozen, spread out all around us in a circle. Let's keep on walking as we have been. Try to act natural, but be ready for a fight, because we're going to get one."

Alsea nodded her agreement and continued. Adel's heart was racing. Knowing the attack was coming was every bit as bad as being caught unawares. A few times, he found his fingers inching toward the pommel of his sword, but he knew if he drew it now that he would give them away. There was no Klaweck here to save them this time. If they were going to survive, they would have to fight off an enemy that outnumbered them immensely.

The first crack of a bowstring rang out, splitting the silence like the cry of a morning rooster. Evidently, the Hoyt were not interested in talking to them this time; they were going to kill them all and be done with it. Instinct took over, and Adel summoned the power of the Rawl, throwing up a protective curtain of wind around them, sending the first arrow, and then the dozens more that followed, careening harmlessly away. The trio stood in the center, perfectly safe as Adel's powers sent nonstop wind gusts blasting outward. Without breaking his focus, he reached down and drew his sword, knowing the Hoyt would move in and engage them up close once they realized the futility of their arrows.

Alsea drew her bow faster than Adel's eyes could follow, sending arrow after arrow out through Adel's wind curtain, the outward gusts he was generating speeding them toward their targets even faster. He could see the Hoyt now, drawing closer on each side, still trying to breach his wind curtain with arrows. His training had built up his endurance, and he was confident that he could maintain until they ran out of arrows, or Alsea killed them all with her own. She was striking them quicker the closer they came.

At last, the Hoyt seemed to tire of firing at the wind curtain and rushed forward, drawing swords and axes. Adel released the wind curtain, although he pushed it outward as he did so, catching their attackers in stride and throwing them off-balance. Then he raised his sword in the defensive position Ola had taught him and braced himself for the first real sword battle of his life.

An axe-wielding attacker raced toward him, screaming incoherently. Adel braced himself, believing if he could avoid the man's first wild swing, that there would be an opening for him to strike. He never got the chance to find out as one of Alsea's arrows caught the man through his temple when he was still ten feet away and dropped him where he stood. Adel turned in all directions, remembering Ola's instruction never to leave his back facing in one direction for more than a second.

Another attacker was rushing in now, though not as boldly as the first, his sword slashing out at Adel. Adel parried the first swing, then the second. The man was slightly stronger than he was, but Adel was faster and accustomed to defending against a much stronger opponent. Seeming to realize his sole hope of defeating Adel was with brute force, the Hoyt charged like a wild bull, striking out with uncontrolled, ferocious swings. Adel was able to parry these, but the sheer power of their impacts rocked him off-balance and he swayed backward, praying he was not being driven back into another Hoyt's blade. Just as Adel was sure the next swing would rip the sword from his hand, Alsea was there again, darting up to the Hoyt with catlike quickness, shoving one of her daggers into his chest and then his neck before he even knew she was there.

Knowing Alsea had him covered on one side, Adel spun around in time to see Ola cleave a Hoyt almost in half with one swing of his massive sword. He saw another Hoyt standing a dozen feet away, setting up to hurl his axe at the massive ogre, not willing to engage up close. Once again, Adel called on his power, and another wind gust sent the axe spinning harmlessly away. Ola was in his face before the man could draw another weapon, one large hand closing around the Hoyt's head, driving it down into the blade of his sword.

Adel spun again, looking in every direction, but all the attackers seemed to have fallen. Alsea was walking from body to body, shoving a dagger into each for good measure, obviously fearing some may be faking their own deaths. Ola was wiping the blood-soaked blade of his sword in the grass. The battle finished, Adel, at last, began to feel the effects of his extended use of the Rawl. His endurance had increased during his training at the temple, but he had never held a wind barrier in place for so long.

He was not on the verge of collapsing, but he was fatigued.

"You handled yourself well, Adel," Alsea called out to him, much to his surprise. He turned to smile at her, in time to see her drive her dagger into yet another prone Hoyt opponent.

His surprise gave way to a feeling of pride at having at least partially won over the skeptical young woman. While his companions had done most of the physical fighting, there was no doubt they would have all been killed by the flurry of arrows if it had not been for his fast and effective use of his power. Elim had been right; when he had needed his powers, they had not failed him. His training had allowed him to call on the power of the Rawl at will and utilize it in the precise manner he needed. He allowed himself a small smile as Ola slapped him on the back.

"I know we are all tired after that, but I think it best if we push on a bit farther. The Hoyt likely threw everyone they had at us just now, but I don't want to risk stragglers sneaking up on us in our sleep. Ola, please keep those wonderful ears of yours open, just in case," Alsea said.

Even though he did not want to walk any farther, Adel could not help but acknowledge her reasoning was logical. There was always the possibility of more Hoyt fighters nearby, and they did not want to be caught off guard. He also did not care to sleep surrounded by the bloodied corpses of the fallen Hoyt fighters. So, for two more hours, they continued their trek east through the foothills until, at last, the sun had dropped so low behind them that they had little choice but to set up camp for the night.

Alsea and Ola agreed it was best they do without fire this night, so their supper was a cold mixture of bread and vegetables. It was a rude awakening after the excellent suppers Elim had prepared for them in the Temple of the Rawl. Once the less than satisfying meal was complete, Ola set out for a nearby stream to refill their water skins, and Adel allowed himself to lean back against a tree and relax. It felt good; it was the first opportunity he had to rest since the attack. It was not the comfort of the plush bed he had enjoyed in the Temple of the Rawl, but after their long day, it felt perfect to Adel. To his surprise, Alsea began to speak to him unprompted.

"I'm sorry if I've been a bit abrupt with you today, Adel. Thank you for what you did back there. If it weren't for you and your power, it would have been the end of us," she said.

"There's no need to apologize. I understand you don't want some inexperienced boy to get under your feet. I do try to pull my own weight, though. Besides, the Hoyt would probably not have been here if they weren't looking for me," Adel responded.

"You did far more than that. You are not getting

underfoot; you are a crucial part of this task we must find a way to complete. Please understand, I have served the Children for six years now and you are the first Rawl wielder we have discovered in those years. At first, I thought they were foolish to put you in harm's way so soon. But that is not the case at all. You are a capable man, and quite able to defend yourself. I was wrong to doubt you, and I am sorry for that. You are far from a boy, and besides, I doubt you are more than a year younger than me," Alsea said, flashing him another rare smile.

Now Adel's curiosity was piqued. How had someone a year older than himself come into the service of the Children at such a young age? How was it she was so skilled and capable of defending herself? She was an enigma he hoped he would be able to unravel. He was on the verge of asking these questions when Ola returned with their water and snapped him back to the task at hand.

"So, have either of you given thought to how we are going to persuade the army they are walking into a trap? Most men see an ogre and their first instinct is to kill me and mount my head in their hunting lodge. I'm guessing they will not want to listen to my advice on war strategy. The two of you are young enough that they will likely disregard you as children. Generals don't want children telling them how to do their job. I don't want to be negative, but I can't imagine them taking us all that seriously," Ola said, bringing up once again the entirely plausible possibility that the army may not view them as a credible source of intelligence.

"I have given that quite a bit of thought, and I suspect you may be right," Alsea replied. "I doubt there will be much the three of us will be able to do to convince Thornatan generals that crossing the river by boat is a bad idea. Men in power tend to believe their ideas are always right. They will think Idanox means to rule the city as some sort of king and, therefore, won't believe he would open the floodgates and destroy a good portion of it. Military commanders tend to be stubborn men who always feel they know best. They haven't gotten to their rank by listening to advice from riffraff like us."

"But we can't sit back and allow the Hoyt to drown half the Thornatan Army, no matter how foolish their commanders may be," Adel pointed out. "Not to mention the innocent people of Kolig who would be washed away in the flood as well."

"You are right, and we are not going to allow that to happen," Ola replied. "However, I think we need to face the fact that an ogre and a boy and girl hardly old enough to be considered grown will not be taken seriously."

"I assume you have an idea, Ola?' Alsea asked.

"We secure the dam ourselves, the three of us. The army is then able to cross the river and retake Kolig from the Hoyt, hopefully killing Idanox and most of his men in the process. They won't know what we do to help them. We won't be thanked for our service, but they will survive," Ola suggested.

"Everything I overheard while inside the city indicated the dam would be heavily guarded. Dozens of men will be protecting it, if not more. Do you really think we can do it, just the three of us?" Alsea asked.

"I don't think we are going to have a choice in the matter, but yes, I do. Adel just showed us how much of a difference he can make in such a battle. What do you say, Adel? Do you think you can use your power well enough to help us overcome the odds? Be honest with us, because frankly, this plan depends heavily on you," Ola said, turning to face him.

Adel considered this question for a long moment, not wanting to rush into a promise he would not be able to keep. It was true that his skills had grown immensely over the last weeks, but had they become powerful enough to face such a test? His confidence had grown by leaps and bounds, but this was different, there were hundreds, perhaps thousands of lives that would be depending on him, including the two sitting with him now. It was a humbling moment indeed, recognizing what the price of his failure could potentially be.

However, at the same time, he knew what was at stake. In the end, he did not have a choice in the matter. The army would never hear them out, and there was no other way. He could act, or he could stand by and allow thousands of people to perish at the hands of the Hoyt, like his friends on the barge. Adel had made a promise to himself upon discovering his power that he would not allow such a thing to happen again. He would not allow it to happen here. His mind made up, he responded to Ola's question with one straightforward statement.

"Let's do it."

Chapter Thirteen

For the better part of the next five days, the trio made their way east and then south through the foothills of the Bonner Mountains. Once they had finally traveled far south enough to avoid the more jagged peaks of the range, they turned their course westward once more toward the city of Kolig. The journey was long and arduous, made all the more strenuous by the pace at which Alsea forced them to march. Though the trip was exhausting, none of them could resent this; all of them were desperate to reach the Hoyt-controlled city before it was too late.

Adel, in particular, was determined to prevent disaster from striking the people of Kolig more than it already had. He had traveled to the city many times aboard Captain Boyd's barge and had found the people to be among the kindest and most generous in the province. The thought of such innocent people living under the brutal rule of Idanox and his Hoyt scum infuriated Adel and drove him to push through his exhaustion. Even one innocent life lost because they delayed would be one innocent life too many for him to bear. The images of what the Hoyt had done to his fellow crewmen on the barge passed through his mind regularly. Each time they did, his pace quickened. He had been unable to save those men, but he could do something for the people of Kolig.

Fortunately, the rain had cleared after their first day away from the Temple of the Rawl. Less happily, the rain had been replaced by oppressive heat and humidity. The brutal conditions made their already tiring journey all the more exhausting. By midday each day they were covered in sweat, and they were struggling to fill their waterskins often enough to keep themselves moving. Adel often found himself wondering if the Rawl could be used to alter the weather, though he supposed that would not be an intelligent use of his limited energy. Onward they pressed, refusing to let anything slow them down.

When they stopped to take their few hours of rest in the night, they would discuss their plans for taking control of the dam north of the city. Sometimes Alsea would tell the others about the things she had seen inside the city under the Hoyt occupation. One instance in particular made Adel's blood boil. A fruit merchant in the city center had defiantly thrown a piece of rotting fruit at a Hoyt patrol. In retaliation, the Hoyt brought out one of the prisoners they kept in cages in the city center and forced the merchant to watch as they disemboweled the unfortunate man. They then released the fruit merchant after a vicious beating, though not before ransacking his stall of all food and coin.

The stories of Hoyt brutality made Adel's urgency to reach Kolig all the more intense. Part of him was even looking forward to facing the scum, now that he had the tools with which to fight them. When they came up against his power, they would hopefully feel a bit of the same helplessness the people of Kolig must be feeling now. He would be all too happy to give them a taste of their own medicine. He scolded himself every time these thoughts entered his mind. He forced himself to remember Elim's warning about using his emotions while wielding the power of the Rawl. He would need to keep a level head when the time came.

An hour after breaking camp on their fifth day, Alsea brought them to a halt and motioned for Ola to join her. She called for Adel to keep a lookout as the two knelt together to examine the ground. It seemed she had spotted some type of tracks. Adel scanned their surroundings, wondering if Alsea had found signs of nearby Hoyt. After a few minutes of hurried conversation, the pair rose and called for Adel to join them. As he approached, Alsea pointed out spots where the ground appeared to have been disrupted recently.

"A large group of men passed this way within the last day, men wearing very cumbersome clothing," Ola explained. Very cumbersome clothing meant one thing to Adel: armor. Could the army have made it this far already?

"Do you think it was the army?" Adel asked, alarmed.

If the army reached Kolig too far ahead of them, they might be unable to prevent the Hoyt trap from being sprung. If the army were caught and decimated in a flood on the river, there would be little to stop the Hoyt from continuing their bloody conquest of Thornata. Alsea felt sure the Hoyt planned to march on the capital of Oreanna once they had wiped out the force that was sent to retake Kolig.

"Not the entire army, but most likely a sizeable scouting force. If the army plans to enter the city by barge, they are likely sailing down the river. But yes, I would bet they are at least several hours ahead of us. If their ground scouts are this far, their boats cannot be far behind. They are certain to reach Kolig by nightfall, and that is if they are moving slowly. We need to hurry," Ola urged.

So onward they pushed, their pace increasing to a light run, desperate to reach the dam before it was too late. Adel had visited Kolig enough times to know the dam was situated around a half mile north of the city and at a slightly higher elevation. He had sailed past it many times, usually admiring the ingenuity that had gone into building such a structure as he did. If the floodgates were to open completely, the water would flow far too quickly for the army to avoid the rush in their slow-moving barges. He forced the images of the worst possible outcome out of his head. It would not happen; they would not allow it to happen. By the dawn of the next day, Idanox would be dead or captured, and the Hoyt who survived would be scattered in a hundred directions or waiting to meet a hangman's noose. It was the sole outcome he would allow himself to entertain.

It felt as though the hours of daylight were slipping away far more swiftly than usual as they raced south in their desperate attempt to reach Kolig. Adel even felt as though the sun was falling faster than usual, mocking their efforts. Ola assured him they were gaining ground, but the ogre still seemed concerned by the lead the army scouting force had on them.

At last, as the sun was slipping out of view to the west, they crested a rise, and there was the city of Kolig below them. Adel's heart dropped like a stone in the river as his eyes took in the horrific sight below him.

The army had set up a base encampment not far from where the bridge had once crossed to the city gates. Several hundred soldiers were milling around this camp.

The Path of the Rawl Wielder

The far more alarming concern was the sight of close to a hundred Thornatan army barges, already in the water, making their way steadily downriver. They were already in a vulnerable position; the Hoyt could open those floodgates at any time and wreak havoc. It appeared they were merely waiting for the army to draw closer to the city walls. Adel assumed this was so it would be easier for their archers to pick off any men who survived the initial rush of water.

Adel could scarcely believe it; they had arrived too late to intervene. To have come so far to fail at the end of the journey was agonizing to him. The thought that he would soon be watching all these helpless people die, the same as he had when the Hoyt had attacked the barge, was too much for him to bear. The feeling of despair was too much for him; he wanted to collapse right there. Turning to his companions, he was shocked to find a look of pure determination planted on Ola's face. Obviously, the ogre was not ready to give up on their plan yet, but what could they possibly do?

"We need to change the plan, and we don't have much time! Alsea, you and Adel get as close to the river as you can. They are bound to open the floodgates within minutes. When they do, it is going to be up to Adel to slow the flow of the river long enough to give the soldiers a chance to make it to shore. I'm going to get to the dam. If I hurry, I may be able to close the gates before too much water flows downriver," Ola commanded, taking immediate charge of the situation.

"Are you insane? You can't take the dam by yourself! Have you forgotten they have dozens of men guarding it? They will kill you before you get anywhere close! There is no chance of getting close to the controls without Adel's powers to help even the odds," Alsea cried out in protest.

"We don't have a choice. Adel will need to focus completely on stopping the river, and he needs you to protect him from anybody who tries to attack him. Me going alone is the only chance we have. Now stop arguing and move!" Ola barked.

With that, the ogre was off, not waiting to entertain further protests, sprinting toward the dam as fast as his massive legs could carry him. Alsea looked for a moment as though she was considering giving chase, then turned to Adel. The two exchanged a brief look; no words were necessary. They did not like the sudden change to the plan, but they both knew Ola was right. Like it or not, this was their only chance, and however slim it may be, they had to try. They raced down the hill at a dead sprint, desperate to reach the shore as soon as possible. Each of them feared the floodwaters would be upon the soldiers before they could make it to the riverbank.

To Adel's amazement, they made the edge of the river before the Hoyt opened the dam. Gazing out across the water, he saw most of the barges were within the range of any longbows the Hoyt had stationed on the city walls. The Hoyt had not opened fire, evidently content to let the river do their dirty work for them. How could the soldiers not suspect anything was wrong with the Hoyt allowing them to approach the walls with no resistance?

"We shouldn't get any closer to the walls. If the Hoyt notice what you are doing, they will shoot at us. It's a long shot across the river, but a skilled archer could pull it off," Alsea said, bringing them to a stop a short distance north of the river and the city walls. "We have to try to warn the army what's about to happen!"

The two cried out as loud as they could to the men on the barges, trying to warn them of the impending trap. A few men did turn to look their way, confusion upon their faces. To their dismay, the soldiers did not seem to be heeding their warnings. Whether they could hear them or not was uncertain. Maybe the soldiers thought the young man and woman were playing a child's game with them. Those expressions of confusion turned to sheer horror at the sounds of grinding gears and moving metal to the north. It was too late.

There was no mistaking the sound; the floodgates were opening. Within moments of the sound of the gears, there was another far more ominous noise, the sound of thousands of tons of water being released from the reservoir toward the helpless soldiers. Over the sound of the river, Adel could not hear them, but he could see them, frantically gesturing toward the shore, urging their barges away from the onslaught that was approaching, but it was no use. They could not escape; the water was racing toward them at a pace that no oarsman could match. The tidal wave would be upon them in seconds, and to make matters worse, the Hoyt archers on the city walls were now beginning to let their arrows fly at last. Adel knew there was only one way to save the soldiers now, and it fell entirely on his shoulders.

"I'm counting on you, Alsea. If the Hoyt realize what's happening, they will try to send men after me. You have to hold them off until Ola can close the dam," he said to Alsea, surprising himself a bit at the calm of his own voice, not allowing himself to consider the possibility that the ogre might fail. Ola had not failed yet, and he would not do so today. Adel somehow knew he would find a way to break through the Hoyt defenses no matter what.

The young woman nodded in agreement, drawing her bow and setting an arrow to the string. The rushing water was in sight now, crushing down on the soldiers like a hammer falling toward a nail. Adel observed its approach, still shocked by his lack of panic at the sight of the unimaginable tidal wave bearing down on them. Reaching out for the power that he had only recently learned was his to command, he began to go to work. All the while, he desperately hoped he was equal to the enormity of the challenge before him.

Chapter Fourteen

Ola raced toward the dam as fast as his long legs could carry him. He did not know how intense the resistance would be along the way, but he knew it did not matter. He knew even if Adel were able to slow the flow of the river, the young man would not be able to keep it up for long. The boy was still too new to his power, and though he would try valiantly, eventually his strength would give out. Even a far more experienced Rawl wielder would not be able to hold back the river indefinitely. It was up to him to make sure the floodgates did not open, or if they did, that they were closed before too much damage could be done. He was moving so fast that even his sharp ogre ears almost did not hear the voice crying out to him over the sound of the wind racing past his head as he sprinted.

"Halt! Stop right there, ogre! I said stop!"

Thinking he was soon to face his first Hoyt fighters, he spun immediately, his hand reaching for the hilt of his sword. He was shocked to find not a Hoyt fighter, but perhaps a dozen Thornatan soldiers closing in on him from the left. The chain mail and emblems on their shields left no doubt about their identity. What was in doubt were their intentions toward him. The apprehension etched across their faces and the manner in which they gripped their weapons were not promising signs. It appeared these men bore the same predisposition toward ogres as most of their countrymen. He did not have time for any delay!

"Captain, it's an ogre! They didn't tell us the Hoyt had ogres fighting with them!" one man cried out, lowering his spear toward Ola as if to charge. Ola tensed up, but threw his arms out wide, trying to appear nonthreatening. He would prefer to settle this matter without violence if possible; there would be plenty of bloodshed soon enough.

"Wait! I am not here fighting for the Hoyt. I am trying to get to the dam as quickly as possible. The Hoyt are planning to open the floodgates and drown the men down on the river before they can escape. I am trying to stop them, but I cannot delay any further. Please come with me and help me take control of the dam," Ola cried out, his empty hands spread wide.

He hoped they would listen to him, though his past experiences in life did not afford him much optimism. He was on the same side as these men, but if they refused to listen to him, he might have no choice but to kill them, a prospect he did not relish. Whatever his cause, he doubted their commanders would look upon such an act favorably.

"You're not going anywhere, ogre. You're coming back to base camp with us for questioning. We need to be sure you aren't fighting with the Hoyt. Now, I'm going to need you to lay the sword and knives on the ground slowly. Don't make any sudden movements now, ogre. My men will put your hands in shackles as a precaution," the captain of the patrol declared.

No sooner had the words left the captain's mouth than the unmistakable humming of bowstrings rang out from the right. A small group of Hoyt fighters had closed in, apparently thinking the soldiers were trying to reach the dam, and had opened fire. The captain was struck several times, falling to his knees, his blood immediately staining the grass beneath him. His men scattered in confusion, though not fast enough to save several more of them from being struck as well. The archers did not seem to be targeting Ola, their focus solely on the men in army uniforms. This would prove to be a fatal mistake on their part.

Ola reacted instantly, charging the Hoyt archers

with reckless abandon, his massive sword in hand. His long legs once again proved to be a saving factor. They allowed him to close the gap with lightning speed, limiting the effectiveness of their bows by shortening the distance between them. They did not understand his intent toward them until it was too late. Two of the archers were dead before they could drop their bows and draw their swords. Their three companions followed them into death within seconds, unable to match close combat skills with their massive foe, meeting violent ends at the edge of Ola's sword.

Ola spun back toward the soldiers; their captain was dead along with two others. The men who remained standing were staring at him, obviously awestruck by the way he had so easily overpowered five opponents. Their amazement meant nothing to Ola, and the silent stare down was interrupted by the horrifying sound of gears grinding. The Hoyt had begun to open the floodgates. The delay of dealing with the soldiers had been a costly one. He had to move, regardless of whether his attack had convinced the soldiers of his allegiances or not. If they were smart, they would join him. If they were not, they would stay out of his way. If they were incomparably foolish, they would try to stop him. If that were the option they chose, he would do whatever was necessary to reach the dam and close the floodgates.

"We have to close the floodgates! Follow me if you are willing to fight by my side, get back to your camp and warn your commanders if you are not, but do not try to stop me. This is the only warning I will give you. I promise I will kill any man who tries to interfere, regardless of his allegiances," Ola declared, and off he was again, sprinting toward the dam. He did not bother to turn and see if any of the soldiers followed him; it did not matter anymore. They were not fast enough to overtake him if they intended to attack, and he saw no arrows flying after him. He had no choice but to take control of the dam with or without their help.

It took longer than he expected for the arrows to start flying at him from the dam. Perhaps the Hoyt men stationed at the dam had figured that once the floodgates were opened, there would be no more threat of an attack against them. Once the Hoyt fighters atop the dam spotted him at last, they opened fire at once. Most of their shots were well off the mark; they were obviously not used to firing at a target that could move as swiftly as Ola could. He was near to the dam when the first group of men intercepted him, spears and swords swinging wildly.

The Hoyt were ferocious fighters, attacking with sheer recklessness and ferocity. These types of tactics typically allowed them to defeat their foes through fear and intimidation. Ola felt neither emotion as he met them head-on, his massive greatsword in hand. Idanox had likely selected some of his best, most reckless fighters to guard the dam. He had chosen well; these men possessed skills far beyond the Hoyt fighters Ola had faced before. But these men had never met an adversary like Ola, a veteran of hundreds of battles, and he would not be so easily intimidated by their wild tactics. He had faced off with and defeated foes far more fearsome than these, and they would have no fear from him.

The first spear thrust missed its mark but was close enough for Ola to seize the weapon and rip it effortlessly from the hand of its owner. He wasted no time getting rid of the weapon, shoving it into the gut of his nearest opponent. A split second later, his sword cut down the previous owner of the spear, who was still struggling through his amazement to draw another weapon. He took hold of the spear once more, tugging it from the gut of his first victim and thrusting it cleanly into the chest of another. Letting go of the spear, Ola grasped his sword with both hands, his feet moving agilely, twisting his body in every direction, a dance designed never to leave his back exposed for more than a second. In combat against multiple foes, an exposed back meant death, a message he had fought to pound into Adel's mind during their training.

The Hoyt were dumbfounded that a man so large could move so gracefully. They attacked with wild abandon, but their strikes were unable to find the elusive ogre. Seemingly every second, another of the Hoyt met his end at the end of Ola's sword. The ogre was completely covered in blood and sweat, though he paid it no mind, his focus solely on dispatching one attacker after another. Within a minute, all of the first rush of attackers were dead. He spun at the sound of footsteps approaching from behind, prepared to fight once more, but was surprised to see the surviving members of the Thornatan patrol approaching. He tensed momentarily, unsure of their intentions toward him.

"Let's go, we have to get the dam closed before the water kills them all!" the man in front called to him. Apparently, seeing the waters of the river racing toward their brothers in arms had brought them to their senses.

Better late than never, Ola thought irately to himself.

Ola joined their rush toward the dam. It appeared the gears that controlled the floodgates could be accessed through a small box situated at the far end of the dam. Ola could make out several dozen Hoyt fighters lining the top of the dam; they would have to fight their way through all of these men to close the floodgates. They were nearing the causeway over the top of the dam when Ola took his first injury from an arrow that finally found its mark and struck him in the left thigh. The wound hurt, sending waves of pain radiating through his leg and into his torso. But it did something else, something the Hoyt hadn't anticipated. It made him angry, and an angry ogre was an ogre you did not want barreling down upon you with a greatsword in its hands.

The Thornatan soldiers who followed him would likely spend the rest of their lives telling stories about what they saw next. The infuriated ogre did not slow from the arrow, but instead charged onto the causeway with renewed fury. His recklessness was growing by the second, but he had no time to take a more measured approach. He did not doubt Adel would do his best to hold the water at bay. But the young man was still inexperienced at using his power, and he needed Ola to put an end to this at once. He ran out onto causeway and straight at the Hoyt fighters who lined it.

Now the Hoyt were at a disadvantage. In spite of outnumbering their opponents vastly, the narrowness of the causeway prevented them from attacking in force. No more than three Hoyt could stand against the ogre at a time. They soon learned that three men were not enough to hold their ground against the ferocious Ola and his sweeping greatsword, no matter how determined or reckless they may be. His combination of unmatched skill and brute strength were too overwhelming for any Hoyt fighter to match.

Ola rushed on, hacking and hammering his way past opponent after opponent, many of whom tumbled from the dam into the raging water below as he cut the life from them. He was not keeping count of how many fell to his blade, nor of how many cuts and thrusts he was receiving in return, though they were numerous. The occasional sharp pain was dismissed before taking the time to identify the source. He had to fight until he reached the controls or until he could fight no more. All that mattered was closing the floodgates before it was too late, if it wasn't already. Everything else was irrelevant.

The dam had been open for several minutes now, and Ola was not sure how long Adel could hold back the flood. He did not look downriver; he did not have time to look at what was happening below. He understood that averting his eyes from his attackers even for a moment would likely be the end of him. Considering the circumstances, the end of him would probably mean the end of the city of Kolig and the Thornatan Army. He could only hope Adel was managing to hold back the river. If he did not, nothing Ola did here would matter.

At last, he had neared the far side of the dam, the box housing the gate control ten paces ahead of him. One last group of Hoyt fighters blocked his way. One charged him wildly, and Ola's ferocious counterattack left the man's body lying in three bloody pieces on the causeway. The three remaining men tried charging as one. Two of them landed minor cuts on the ogre, cuts that were mere scratches compared to the mortal wounds they received in return, all of them falling dead upon the causeway within moments.

Ola staggered on toward the control box, slipping on the blood of his fallen foes as he lurched over their bodies. As he arrived, he found the door was too small for his massive frame to squeeze inside. He turned toward the soldiers who had followed him across the dam, urgently motioning for one of them to go inside and close the gates. As one man rushed past him, he was aware of the others staring at him again. Were they not used to the sight of an ogre by now? Or did they still think he was a Hoyt operative, even after watching him hack his way through countless Hoyt fighters? It was at this moment Ola became mindful of the extent of the injuries he had sustained while fighting his way across the dam.

In addition to the first arrow that had struck him, two more now protruded from his body, one from his side and one from his left arm. He counted perhaps a dozen additional wounds taken from swords, axes, and spears to his torso, arms, and legs, all of them bleeding profusely. The injuries were far more severe than he would have suspected during his attack. His rage was beginning to fade, and so was the adrenaline that had accompanied it, allowing him to keep fighting. The pain he had so effectively compartmentalized was now beginning to spread throughout his body in sharp waves. He fell to one knee, his eyesight starting to spin. Just as he heard the gears moving once more, indicating the dam was finally closing, he slipped out of consciousness, the blackness he had fought against in such desperation overtaking him at last.

Chapter Fifteen

Adel did not know how much time had passed since the floodgates had opened, nor was he aware of much of anything else that was going on around him. He could feel Alsea near his right side, and occasionally a word of encouragement made it through the deafening sound of rushing water. Apart from those brief moments that her voice broke through, there was nothing else. As far as he could tell, nobody had tried to attack them yet, though if they did, he was relying totally on Alsea to protect him.

All that existed in his world at that moment was the water crashing down on Kolig, and he was the only thing standing in its path. He knew that at that moment, he alone was preventing the death and destruction that accompanied it. All he could allow into his mind was the singular focus that he had to try to stop it. Even a momentary break in his concentration could spell disaster for thousands of people.

As the water had initially come bearing down on them, Adel had feared panic might set in and he might freeze up. To his surprise, his training with Elim took over, and he was able to react instinctually, halting the rush of the river in its tracks. He kept his breathing slow, as Elim had taught him, trying to think of stopping the water being a task as menial as any other. Elim had once warned him that breathing too heavily, as one might when exerting oneself, could cause his energy to run out sooner. Adel did not know how long it would take Ola to close the floodgates, but he knew he needed to be prepared to hold the water for a long time if necessary.

He had discovered within moments that he would not merely be able to stop the flow of the water in its tracks; there was too much of it to hold in place. The mounting pressure would exhaust his strength within moments. Instead, he began redirecting its flow, diverting it from its standard path and into the only place he could think of to put it. So it was that a massive ball of water was floating in midair, about twenty feet from the banks of the river. It was a tactic similar to the one he had used instinctively to crush the Hoyt boats on the Moyie River all those weeks ago. However, this ball of water had exceeded the size of that one within seconds. With every passing minute, it continued to grow exponentially. It was a sight that must appear quite absurd to anyone who happened to be observing, but Adel did not have time to dwell on the humor of the situation. Diverting the flow of water eased the strain of holding back the river just enough to allow him to keep doing so.

The problem with this strategy was becoming more apparent to Adel by the second. The ball of water was growing exponentially, its girth expanding so rapidly that he was not sure how much longer he would be able to hold it in place. His energy was holding up so far, but the power required to maintain it was increasing every second. Not only this, but there was also the fact that he had no idea of what he would be able to do with all of this water once Ola had managed to close the floodgates. This was assuming, of course, the ogre succeeded in doing so. If he merely released it where it was floating, the city would still sustain massive damage and casualties. Deciding this issue could be dealt with after the floodgates were closed, he attempted to force it to the back of his mind. He could not allow himself to become distracted if he hoped to keep holding the river at bay.

Adel was mildly surprised that his energy had not seemed to diminish. Holding this water was a feat far more strenuous than any he had attempted during his training at the Temple of the Rawl. He had to assume the pressure of the life and death nature of the task at hand would not allow his body to feel the fatigue that should be setting in by now. His heart was racing and his head was pounding, but the adrenaline would not allow his body to feel the effects of his prolonged use of the Rawl. There would no doubt be a price to pay later for his reckless and prolonged use of his power, but that did not matter now. All that mattered was he could not fail to contain the river. He would gladly pay the consequences later if it meant saving the lives that were at stake now.

He could not hear or see anything happening at the dam upriver, and for long minutes he sought to block out the world around him. Was Ola close to securing the floodgates? Was the ogre even still alive? He had no way of knowing the answers. If Ola failed, the water would keep coming until his strength gave out. That would be the end of the army, and him and Alsea as well. At last, after he had lost all sense of time, he could feel the pressure of the flowing water beginning to ease. The strain of holding it back was lessening with each passing second.

Ola must have been successful in closing the floodgates of the dam! Adel felt a rush of elation as he realized they had succeeded at stopping the Hoyt from massacring the Thornatan Army. It was a task that a short while earlier had felt impossible. As he felt the river's flow return to normal, he halted his efforts to redirect the water. However, there was still a massive orb of water merely floating in the air in front of him. The time had come to consider his options for what to do with it. No longer straining to redirect the current, he could still hold the orb for a while, though not indefinitely.

The floating orb must be as large as the Temple of the Rawl, if not bigger. The strain of holding it in place was not yet too severe. But Adel knew it was only a matter of time before the cost of using his power in such an intense manner caught up with him. He needed to find a place for the water before that happened. If he collapsed from exhaustion before finding a solution, the consequences could be as severe as if they had failed completely, and he and Alsea would likely be washed away. He glanced about in every direction, searching for an answer to his dilemma.

Adel momentarily considered moving the water south of the city and then releasing it back into the river to resume its typical path. This option did not seem especially wise; the sheer amount of water could still lead to damage downriver, including flooding to the city of Kobuk to the south. He had not saved Kolig to see Kobuk pay the price for his inability to find a solution to this dilemma. He could not merely dump the water back into the river and hope for the best.

He could attempt to move the water to the east and release it, but this also presented certain complications. The land to the east contained vast stretches of farmland. Releasing the water there could potentially destroy their crops, crops that fed a large portion of the province. Saving people from floods and subjecting them to famine was also not an appealing prospect. For the first time, he began to feel the fatigue starting to creep in. He needed an answer, and he needed one now. Adel was trying to think of a third possibility when Alsea's voice managed to cut through to him.

"Adel, there is a group of Hoyt fighters approaching from the north. There are too many of them for us to try to fight. They will be here within two minutes. You have to do something with that water, and we have to get out of here now," she urged him. Of course the Hoyt would have left some forces outside of the city. It would be necessary to deal with the army base camp and any survivors of the massacre on the river.

Her warning gave him the idea for which he had been searching. If he dropped the water to the northeast, it would eventually flow back down to its regular course, but much of it would be soaked up in the relatively empty plains along the way. The earth would be saturated, and there may still be minor flooding downriver, but not likely enough to cause any severe damage or kill anyone. Almost anyone, he corrected himself. The Hoyt who were advancing on them would be right in the path of the water. But as he saw it, the Hoyt had made conscious decisions that had led them to such a fate, unlike the innocent people who would be harmed if he released the water elsewhere. It would be nigh impossible to drop the water without killing somebody. If somebody must die, it may as well be those responsible for this predicament.

Turning his focus to the northeast, he moved the ball of water through the air, trying to hurry. He could feel the strain of his excessive use of the Rawl beginning to take its toll on him now, but he had no choice but to be quick. He knew he did not have much time before the Hoyt reached them, and if the Hoyt reached them, they would kill both of them without hesitation. If the Hoyt murdered him before he safely diverted this water, the consequences for innocent people could be catastrophic. Once he had moved the water what he felt to be a safe distance, he called out to Alsea.

"Grab onto me, hold on tight. I don't want to risk you getting swept away if the water comes this way," Adel said. He was confident if the water did come toward them, the Rawl would instinctively protect him, but that same protection may not extend to Alsea.

As soon as he felt her hands lock tightly around his waist, he released his hold on the water.

The sound was unlike anything he had ever heard, drowning out everything else around him. It struck the ground with such force that he could feel the tremors through his boots as if a thousand giants had begun to stampede around them.

The water cascaded around them like a raging ocean tsunami. Every bit of Adel's focus was fixated on using his power to keep the water moving around them, preventing it from sweeping them away. How many gallons of water was it? He guessed that it must be hundreds of thousands, if not millions. To his surprise, the process took only a few seconds. When the water had cleared, all that remained of the attacking Hoyt were a few scattered bodies. They were barely recognizable as human, shattered from the sheer force of the impact. How many Hoyt had the water swept away?

Once it was over, the thing that seemed the most unusual to Adel was the silence. Apart from a slight ringing in his ears, there were several long moments of absolute silence. Turning toward Kolig, afraid of what he would see, he was relieved to find the city seemed completely intact. There was also no sign of damaged boats or dead soldiers in the river, and the army was continuing toward the city unimpeded by the devastating floodwaters the Hoyt had tried to unleash on them. Hoyt archers still fired on them, but the army should still be able to reach the city and liberate it now. They would capture Idanox, and that would be the end of the Hoyt. Adel could hardly dare to believe it.

"You did it!" Alsea exclaimed, breaking away from him and smiling more radiantly than he had ever seen her before.

Adel was glad she had spoken. It had seemed for several long moments that he must be dreaming, that it was not possible he had succeeded. He allowed himself to shoot her a quick smile, surprised to find her still beaming radiantly back at him. The beauty of her smile seemed to be making him weak in the knees. It took a moment for it to dawn on him that this was not the effect of Alsea's smile. His prolonged use of the Rawl had caught up to him at last.

His legs were the first to feel it. They were no longer able to support the rest of his body, and he sunk to his knees, his resistance futile. Alsea placed a steadying hand on his shoulder, ignoring his feeble attempts to wave her off. The fatigue was setting in fast now, his eyes growing heavy as though he had not slept in days. He felt much as he had on the barge after using his power for the first time. He could hear Alsea saying something into his ear, but he could not make out the words. Adel tried to lift his head to look at her, but his head felt heavy, along with his eyelids. Within seconds, his exhaustion had triumphed in their brief battle. Before he could attempt to fight it off, the need to sleep overwhelmed him, and he collapsed right there on the plains overlooking the city he had just helped to save.

Chapter Sixteen

It required quite a bit of effort for Adel to fight his way out of his exhausted slumber. His mind was seemingly reluctant to face the splitting headache and aching muscles that awaited him. His eyes strained and struggled to stay closed until he forced them open. The light that greeted his opening eyes emanated from several nearby candles. They burned dimly, but to his sensitive eyes, the sun itself may as well have been burning by his side. As his eyes began to adjust, he was able to make out the form of Alsea sitting in a chair by his bedside. It took him a few seconds more for his mind to truly register the fact that he was in a bed, inside of what appeared to be a large tent. His last memory was of collapsing in the mud by the riverbank. A bed inside a tent was a welcome change of scenery.

"It's good to see you awake again, Adel. You have been out for a long time," Alsea greeted him, bending over his face to examine him more closely, her dark brown eyes scrutinizing him.

"How long, exactly?" Adel asked, trying to sit up, only to feel her hand gently but firmly on his shoulder, holding him securely in place.

"You have been sleeping all night; the sun will be up soon. You are inside a Thornatan Army tent, and there is no need to be concerned. They brought you here to keep you safe; there are still a small handful of Hoyt fighters who need to be rounded up. Needless to say, they were quite grateful for your actions last night. There would not be much of an army left if it weren't for you. I promise there is nothing for you to concern yourself with at the moment. The best thing you can do is lie down and regain your strength," Alsea assured him.

It was all coming back to him now. Their desperate race to reach the city before it was too late, the sound of the floodgates opening, and the incredible strain of holding the water at bay until Ola could close the floodgates. Ola! He was reminded now of the ogre and his desperate solo mission to close the floodgates. He looked frantically around the tent, searching for any hint of his friend. Realizing Ola was not there, he asked a question he dreaded the answer to, but knew he must ask nonetheless.

"Is Ola here as well? He obviously managed to close the floodgates, and it's a good thing he did it when he did. I don't know how much longer I could have held on. A few more minutes, and that would have ended very badly for everyone," he said, hoping more than anything that Ola had survived his courageous assault on the dam.

"He is here, though he is wounded badly. He was brought in by a scouting party he encountered on his way up to the dam. He didn't look great, but he's as tough as they come, so don't worry too much. The army was not too keen on allowing an ogre into their camp, but this scouting party vouched for him. In fact, they were quite in awe of him, a rather unusual attitude for men to have toward an ogre. They said they saw him cut down dozens of Hoyt men single-handedly so they could close the floodgates. They said they had never seen anything like it. The army has healers working on him now. The men who saw what happened are calling him a hero. I'm not sure how many of their comrades believe their story, but it pretty much sounds like the Ola we know and love," Alsea replied.

Adel was immediately concerned for his friend's well-being and once again tried to rise from his bed, to find Alsea's hand holding him down once more. She bent in closer, smiling gently at him but never removing her hand from his shoulder. Despite how gently she smiled, it was quite apparent she was not going to let him out of bed, no matter how hard he might protest.

"There is nothing you can do for Ola now, Adel. We must let the healers do their work. He is resilient; I can assure you he will survive. You need to rest and worry about yourself for the time being. You may not be wounded, but what you did took its toll on you; I can see it. You can't see yourself, but I have never seen you looking so gaunt and exhausted. You pushed yourself to the utmost edge of your abilities last night, and you need time to recover your strength. I hope we won't need it anytime soon, but you never know. I'd rather have you at full strength, just in case we need your talents again," she said. Her voice was as kind as it had ever been, but she left no illusion that he had any choice in the matter.

Accepting she was not going to let him out of bed and that he was still far too weak to be able to do anything about it, Adel conceded defeat and allowed his muscles to relax once more. He even allowed himself to enjoy the gentler treatment he was receiving from Alsea. It was a nice change of pace from being marched through the foothills of the Bonners at breakneck speed. It occurred to him this might be an excellent opportunity to ask the questions he had about the mysterious young woman.

"Alsea, while we are stuck here, can I ask you something? Why do you serve the Children of the Rawl? Ola told me his story, but I do not know much about you. Why would you willingly risk your life on a journey like this? I'm sorry if this is too personal, but I thought since you won't let me leave this tent that we may as well get better acquainted," Adel said, unsure if she would be willing to answer, and hoping he would not anger her by asking.

Alsea appeared quite taken aback by the question; perhaps she had thought him uninterested in her past. She looked away from him, her eyes scanning the tent but resting on nothing. She did not reply to his question for a long moment, so long that Adel wondered if he had overstepped his bounds in asking it. Much like Ola, it seemed Alsea was uncomfortable talking about herself. He imagined that, as with Ola, there were unpleasant memories in her past that she did not care to recount. Just as he resigned himself to the fact that she would not answer, she began to speak.

"The Children took me in when I had no place else to go. They did not demand my service in return for this, but I insisted on it. I wanted to earn the kindness they had shown me, wanted to prove that I deserved it. Truth be told, I did not know what else to do with my life. So, I offered them my services, and I have worked on their behalf ever since," Alsea said.

"Why did you have no place else to go?" Adel asked, regretting this question the moment he spotted the expression of pain that darted across her face. It was there for a second before she had hidden it once more, the girl obviously well-practiced at concealing her emotions. There was another long pause, but this time his question was not to be answered, for no sooner had she opened her mouth then the tent flap opened and three Thornatan soldiers entered.

The man in the middle appeared to be in charge, judging by his bearing. In addition, Adel spotted a series of stripes on the sleeve of his uniform that he was fairly certain indicated the man was a general. The two men flanking him were massive, each well over six feet tall, and their expressions were not the least bit friendly, leading Adel to believe these must be the general's bodyguards. This time Adel was firmer in his desire to sit up, and Alsea complied, at last. She removed her hand from his shoulder and allowed him to rise to face the general on somewhat more even terms. To his relief, she allowed him to rise on his own without her help. He did not want to show any signs of weakness in front of the soldiers. It was bad enough that they had walked in to find him lying in bed.

"I'm glad to finally find you awake, young man. I am General Bern, and I am the commander of this army. I understand that I owe you my thanks. My men tell me that were it not for you, I would not have many men left to command." Bern's words were friendly enough, but also had a hard undertone, and no smile found its way to his face. It was as though he wanted to leave no room for misunderstanding who was in command of this situation.

"Thank you for your hospitality, General Bern.

My name is Adel." The pair shook hands, the general's grip conveying the same message as his tone of voice.

"General, do you have any update on our friend's condition?" Alsea cut in, apparently reading Adel's mind.

"The ogre?" Bern replied with a slight twinge of disgust in his voice. "The healers have finished with his wounds, and they assure me he will make a speedy recovery. From what the healers tell me, he was apparently quite eager to come and see you. I am told they had to give him a sleeping draft to make him sleep. He is resting comfortably now."

"His name is Ola, and he is every bit as responsible for saving the lives of your men as I am," Adel blurted out.

The outburst lacked the decorum he would have typically tried to maintain in the presence of such an important person, but he was none too pleased with the tone the general had taken at the mention of their ogre friend. Bern would not have an army if not for Ola, and Adel found his lack of acknowledgment of that to be disrespectful. He had known the man for the span of a few minutes, but he already felt this was not a man he liked much.

Adel's bluntness seemed to catch General Bern off guard. This was obviously a man who was not used to being spoken to in such a manner. His face reddened slightly and he locked his steely eyes on Adel, who met his gaze. Bern's men may have no choice but to allow him to speak to them in any manner he chose, but Adel would not stand for it.

"I'm sure Ola will be quite pleased to find his friends unharmed," Bern replied diplomatically, doing a rather poor job of concealing his displeasure. Adel suspected the general was more used to dealing with people who were required to defer to his authority without question. "Now, Adel, pardon my forwardness, but I would like for you to explain exactly how you were able to contain the flow of the river. My first thought was that you must be a mage, but my advisors seem to believe that such a feat is beyond the powers of even the strongest mage. Were it not for so many eyewitness accounts from my men on the river, I must admit I would doubt the story, meaning no offense to you personally. So please, Adel, I would like to hear your story in your own words."

"Begging your pardon, General Bern, but Adel has only just woken up, and he is exhausted. As I'm sure you can imagine, such a feat is incredibly demanding. Can your questions wait until he has had more time to recover?" Alsea interjected politely.

"Begging your pardon, girl, but I have more pressing matters of concern then the boy's weariness. He will answer my questions now, and unless you have something of substance to add, you will hold your tongue. The boy can enjoy his nap when I have finished my questions. He is inside a tent that is the property of the

Thornatan Army, and he is on my schedule, not his. In this camp, my word is the law. Interrupt me again, and my men will remove you from the tent," Bern snapped, the forced calmness of his voice beginning to break at last.

He was now utterly failing to hide the condescension that he seemed to feel they deserved. Once again, Adel felt that General Bern was obviously a man who was accustomed to getting whatever he asked whenever he asked for it. The challenge of such a young woman must not sit well with him.

Alsea looked furious at this point, appearing as though she would love nothing more than for the general's men to attempt to remove her from the tent. Adel was no more pleased than Alsea with the general's attitude toward them, but decided trying to diffuse the situation would be a wiser course of action. While the sight of Alsea roughing up the bodyguards would no doubt be amusing, he felt they should strive to maintain a good relationship with the general, despite his boorish behavior. Nevertheless, he also felt it was essential to make it clear to General Bern that they would not be intimidated by his tough talk.

"It's quite all right, Alsea. I am happy to answer General Bern's questions. However, General Bern, I would also ask that you speak to me and my companions with more respect. Gentlemen, I can assure you that trying to remove my companion from this tent forcefully would be a serious mistake on your part. I've seen her angry, and trust me, you don't want to be on the receiving end of that," Adel said, directing this last comment to the bodyguards.

The bodyguards exchanged quick, confused glances; evidently, they were not used to being addressed directly in such a manner. Their function was to stand silently and appear intimidating, and it was obviously a distinct shock to them that they were failing in this instance. Unsure of what to do, they seemingly settled on standing silently, trying to look more intimidating. Their confusion paled in comparison to the look of fury now residing on their general's face.

"Oh, do forgive me, sir. How can I possibly atone for showing such disrespect to two children and their pet ogre? I have had enough of your games, boy. Answer my question at once. How did you stop the flow of the river? I can assure you that refusing to answer me at once would be a serious mistake on your part. This is a temporary encampment, but I can have a stockade built in no time at all if that is the path you wish to travel. It's up to you, boy," Bern shot back, mimicking Adel's prior statement, any attempt at false decorum thrown to the wind.

Adel would never know how General Bern would have replied to the insult he was about to utter, his patience with the buffoon of a man at its end. At that moment, the sound of men crying out broke the silence outside the tent, accompanied by an overpowering stench of smoke. Cursing, General Bern turned tail and charged out of the tent, his guards close behind.

Alsea and Adel looked to each other, not saying a word, their facial expressions showing each that the other shared their confusion. The stench alone told them there was a fire nearby, but how had it happened so suddenly? This confusion would not last long, however, as a loud voice rose above the cacophony of noise, a soldier addressing General Bern outside the tent.

"General, several tents along the northern edge of the camp have been hit with flaming arrows. An attack by the Hoyt, no doubt. They must not have enough numbers left to engage us directly, but the flames are spreading quickly, and we have no way to contain them."

"No way to contain them, you fool? Gather every bucket you can find and get men down to the river filling them. Begin a chain of men, passing the buckets from the river to the encampment. Deploy a search party to find the Hoyt scum who launched this attack; they are not to return to camp without their severed heads in hand! Once the fire is out, I want every single man on perimeter patrol replaced at once. They are to report to me immediately for discipline," General Bern said.

The stench of smoke was growing more overwhelming by the second, and Adel soon found himself struggling to draw breath. There was no way soldiers with buckets would be able to gather enough water to drown a blaze this intense. These soldiers would all die trying to save their camp. His distaste for the oafish General Bern notwithstanding, he could not allow that to happen. He rose from the bed at last, his legs wobbling from lack of use. Spotting him moving, Alsea moved to try to stop him.

"No, Adel. You have not rested enough. There is nothing you can do. Leave this to the army; they can handle it," she tried to tell him, coughing out the last few words, beginning to struggle from the stench of the smoke herself.

"No, Alsea, they cannot, and even if they can, who can say how many of them will die in the process? Most of these men aren't like that oaf who was just in here. They are brave men fighting for their people, and they came here to save the people of Kolig. I won't let them die like this. I have enough strength for this, I promise you. We are wasting time," he insisted. He knew she wanted to keep him safe, but the need of the army would have to take precedence now.

She moved out of his way begrudgingly and took her place at his side, drawing one of her long knives in the process. She was not about to allow him to leave the tent on his own. If he collapsed again, he would require her protection. Silently, he thought to himself that he was relieved to have her by his side.

It did not take long to see they would have been forced to flee the tent within a few minutes anyway. The flames were racing in their direction, kindled by the dry cloth of the tents. The army would have been wiser to concede the tents as lost and withdraw rather than try to fight the blaze. But Adel had seen enough of their commanding officer that he knew such a wise action would not be forthcoming. Adel would have preferred to move closer to the river before beginning his work, but there was no time for that. Every second that went by, the blaze became more challenging to contain; he would have to start at once.

His first instinct had been to pull water from the river to drown the flames, but now he doubted such an attempt would work. The river was so far away that he was concerned his exhaustion would not permit him the strength needed to move such a vast quantity of water over such a great distance. Instead, he focused on a tactic Elim had taught him during his training, stealing the air from candles as a means to put out their flames instantly. Elim had compared fire to a living creature that required air to breathe. He would have to apply that lesson here, though on a much larger scale than he had ever attempted before. Taking a deep breath and immediately hacking it back up from the smoke, he reassured himself that he could do this. *If you can stop the flow of a river, this is no major feat*, he told himself.

He raised one arm, pointing at the approaching inferno, finding the act of pointing toward his target helped his focus. He started with the tent closest to where he stood, choking the air from the flames. Confident now that he could do what was needed, he spread his power wider, extinguishing the fire in several tents at a time. Typically, he would attempt to pace himself through such a task. But every second wasted was another second that men may be dying in this blazing inferno, so on he pressed, building speed to his work as he went.

The task did not take as long as he had feared it might. Within minutes, the entire fire had been suffocated. Thick black smoke and a few slightly burning embers were the entirety of the evidence that seconds earlier a blazing inferno had threatened to engulf an entire army encampment. Adel fell to one knee, the exhaustion he had so successfully set aside now rearing its head once more. The smoke-filled air impeding his breathing did not help matters. He had not rested enough from the ordeal at the river, but he knew there had been no other choice.

Alsea's arm was around his shoulders in seconds, trying to help him to his feet. He rose with her help, though he was unsure where they should go. Soldiers were milling about, confused by the sudden end of the fire, but none of them were paying any attention to Adel or Alsea. The smoke was so thick that returning to their fortunately undamaged tent was not an appealing prospect. He had little time to think on the matter as a gruff voice interrupted his train of thoughts.

"I must admit, I thought my men were seeing illusions when they told me some boy had stopped the river from drowning them. I will give credit where it is due, lad. I have never seen anything like that before in all my years. You have my thanks for the lives you have saved here today."

Adel turned at the sound of the voice with Alsea's help to find General Bern and his bodyguards approaching. Immediately apprehensive, Adel tried to shrug off Alsea's arm, not wanting to show the arrogant general any sign of weakness. He was exhausted and in no mood for another confrontation with the unpleasant man. To his surprise, he found Bern seemed in no hurry to resume his interrogation right then.

"My men will show you to the tent where your friend is recovering; you can stay there until you have had ample time to rest. The smoke should not be so thick in that area, and hopefully you will be able to rest. I will check in on you later; I must assess the damage this attack has done to us and discipline my sentries for allowing this to happen. We can only hope our scouting party finds and eliminates the attackers. I did not mean to be abrupt with you earlier. You have my apologies, and once more, my thanks for what you have done twice now. Please feel free to ask my men for anything you require. I will have an officer assigned to see to anything you need. I will order that food be brought to you shortly," General Bern said, again to Adel's surprise.

Without waiting for a reply, Bern was gone, heading into the damaged wreck that used to be the northern end of his encampment. Adel relaxed a bit. He had fully been expecting another tense confrontation with the man and was grateful that such was not the case. He was certain that Bern would not allow the matter to rest for long, but he would accept the reprieve. Relieved they were soon to be reunited with Ola, he turned to the bodyguards and nodded his readiness to be led to their new accommodations.

Chapter Seventeen

Adel spent most of the following day and night in bed, sleeping off his fatigue from his two exhausting uses of the Rawl. He had not been so weary since the first time he had unwittingly summoned the power on the Moyie River. To his credit, the abrasive General Bern had not disturbed them again that day, for which all three of them were grateful. The trio surmised he must have his hands full with the cleanup and recovery effort after the Hoyt attempt to burn down the camp. It was fine by them; the more time that passed before they had to speak to the insufferable man again, the better.

It had been a tremendous relief to find Ola sitting

up in his bed upon their arrival in his tent. He was arguing with an unfortunate healer, demanding to join the battle outside. Adel and Alsea were able to calm him, assuring him the danger had passed for the time being and no new battle had taken place. Upon examination, Alsea determined the healers had done an excellent job treating his wounds, which had been significant. Adel believed nearly any other man would have succumbed to such severe injuries, but the ogre seemed well on his way to recovery merely a day later.

Adel had managed to stay awake long enough for Ola to recount his attack on the Hoyt forces guarding the dam. Once again, he was left in awe of Ola's incredible skill and courage. With significant help from Alsea, he also managed to brief Ola on their efforts to hold back the floodwaters. They talked as well of their brief and unpleasant encounter with General Bern. Ola scowled openly at the mere mention of the general's name, and Adel surmised the ogre had experienced the man's less than charming personality firsthand as well.

His weariness had overwhelmed him within minutes of arriving at the tent, his companions scolding him for his attempts to ward it off. Assuring him they would wake him if his powers were needed again, they persuaded him to lie back in the bed that the soldiers had brought in for him. He had fallen asleep within seconds of his head hitting the pillow. He woke twice that day, managing to keep his eyes open long enough to eat and relieve himself before sleep's inviting arms drew him back in.

When he came awake at last, Adel was surprised to find dawn was already approaching again. There was a great commotion outside the tent. He sat up at once, fearing the camp may once again be under attack. He flung his legs out of bed, hoping his feet would not fail him as he tried to rise. His eyes darted around the tent, searching desperately for his sword. Alsea caught him before his feet could hit the floor, whispering to him reassuringly with her hands firmly on his shoulders.

"There is nothing to fear, Adel. The army is beginning to break their camp. A messenger just left, and we were about to wake you. The general will be here to speak with us within the hour," she said.

The mention of the intolerable General Bern's impending visit did not put him in a particularly good mood. Still, Adel could not deny that his body was feeling the effects of his long rest in an enjoyable way. His eyes no longer struggled to remain open, and as he climbed to his feet, he was happy to find they no longer wobbled under the effort to support his weight. After taking a few tentative test steps, he was confident he could stand with no issue. He took some solace from the fact that at least this time he would be able to address the general on more equal footing.

He made his way over to the small table in the center of the tent; the army had laid out a decent assortment of food for them to enjoy. He worked his way through bread and a few pieces of fruit and cheese. Surprisingly, he was not hungry; however, he knew he must eat. It was crucial to bring his body back to full strength in case he was required to summon the power of the Rawl without warning once more.

The sound of several heavy sets of boots outside the tent signaled the arrival of the general several minutes later. Adel turned toward the tent entrance, bracing himself for another conversation with the unpleasant General Bern. He was surprised to find it was not Bern who entered, but a much older man.

The man's gray hair and short, well-kept beard framed a face that bore an unmistaken combination of kindness and intelligence, two traits Bern had failed to demonstrate during their encounter. Adel was quick to note that this man had several more stripes adorning his heavy plate armor than General Bern had, leading him to believe this must be an officer of a higher rank. No bodyguards were trailing this man, the confidence of his gait and demeanor giving the impression that bodyguards were not necessary. The man smiled at all of them as he entered, even Ola.

"Good morning, my friends. I hope my men have been treating you well," the general greeted them. "My name is Randall McLeod, and I am the Supreme General of the Thornatan Army. My apologies that I have not been in to see you sooner. I arrived hours after dusk last night and found I had a great many matters which required my attention. It seems I owe all of you my sincerest thanks for your actions these past few days. I may not have had much of an army left if not for you if even half of the stories my men tell me are true."

Adel had heard stories during his years on the barge about Supreme General Randall McLeod, and his mind was quickly put a bit at ease. This was not an arrogant, blundering fool like General Bern; this was a man well-known and respected throughout the province. He had served as the army's highest commander for almost twenty years, and in that time, he had won the respect and love of nearly all of the province's citizens. Adel doubted he could find a man or woman in the province who would have a single negative thing to say about Randall McLeod.

He had earned his rank in a particularly famous battle twenty years earlier. As the stories went, the conflict had taken place in the infamous Ice Fields in the far eastern reaches of the province. It was the middle of an especially brutal winter, and there had been a report of bandits launching attacks and raids on villages south of the city of Kotlik. Fearing the city itself may be the next target, the army had dispatched a small battalion to root out the bandits and put a stop to the raids. Much to their surprise, the bandits had laid a series of intricate traps, triggering mountain avalanches that wiped out nearly the entire contingent of soldiers.

The Path of the Rawl Wielder

As night fell upon them, the bandits had closed in on the small group of soldiers who had survived and fled south into the Ice Fields. Randall McLeod was the sole officer left at that point, and he led the counterattack against the bandits. The soldiers had been hopelessly outnumbered and had no place to flee; they were caught out in the open. Had they been killed, Randall McLeod would have looked like quite the fool, leading his men out into an open plain of ice. However, that was not what happened. No sooner had the bandits set foot onto the ice then they found McLeod had worked swiftly to spring a trap of his own.

The Ice Fields of eastern Thornata stretched far as the eye could see, a seemingly endless sheet of the purest white ice imaginable. It was impossible to move with speed across the layer of slippery ice. The few men who traversed the harsh area would advise you to look straight ahead as you walked. Their theory was that if you looked down at your feet, you were more likely to make a mental error and take a tumble on the treacherously slick surface. Randall McLeod had discovered this for himself as his men fled across the ice, and it inspired his trap.

Theorizing the bandits would also be forced to look straight ahead as they closed in on the outnumbered soldiers, he ordered his men to strike the ice as hard as possible with their heaviest weapons. So they did, creating a perimeter around themselves of minor blemishes and cracks in the ice. Such small defects would not affect men walking across regular solid ground. But on the unsure footing of the ice, even the slightest misstep could cause a man to slip and fall.

McLeod's plan worked, of course. The bandits had advanced to within fifty feet of the soldiers when they stepped into the trap and began to slip and tumble. The soldiers immediately opened fire, killing most of the bandits before they could regain their feet. Not one of the men left under Randall McLeod's command had died that day. The soldiers killed every last one of the bandits while they slipped and slid on the ice, unable to regain their footing. They were unable to reach the men standing right in front of them due to McLeod's simple, yet effective trap. The post of Supreme General opened less than a year later, and the duke requested him specifically, the man who had orchestrated the most improbable of victories in the most challenging of environments. Adel was awestruck to find the same man now standing in their tent.

"It's an honor to meet you, Supreme General. My name is Adel. These are my companions, Alsea and Ola. Alsea was in Kolig when the city fell and discovered the Hoyt plot to drown the army in the river. Ola is the one who fought his way through the men who guarded the dam and closed the floodgates," Adel explained.

"Thank you all for your service. Adel, I notice you have left out your own contributions. If my men tell the truth, you not only stopped the flow of the river from crushing my army, you also single-handedly put out the fire yesterday morning. General Bern tells me you are none too eager to share information of your abilities. Can you explain to me why that is?" General McLeod asked, the faintest hint of disappointment creeping into his voice.

"You must be joking!" Alsea exclaimed before Adel could reply, outraged by the implication. She waved off Adel's attempts to calm her and continued, "General Bern had the nerve to enter our tent, treat us like children, and bandy threats to lock us up like criminals. That was after the first time we saved his ungrateful skin! In spite of this, Adel went out into that fire and saved him yet again. We had no issue with telling him anything he wanted to know. For some reason, he felt the need to behave like a pouty, spoiled child who needed a whipping. He should be grateful I did not give him one!"

Adel glanced back at the general in horror, fearing Alsea had far overstepped, expecting to find General McLeod's face to be filled with rage. To his surprise, he found the faintest trace of a smile crossing Randall McLeod's face. His shock grew when this small grin became a light chuckle. After a few moments, McLeod regained his composure and waved his hands disarmingly toward Alsea.

"My apologies, young lady, please do not think ill of me. Your name is Alsea, correct? Forgive me, Alsea, I am only relaying the message General Bern gave to me. If

I may speak truthfully, your description of him is far from inaccurate."

Alsea seemed a bit taken aback by General McLeod's eloquent and reasonable response. Seemingly at a loss for words, she contented herself with a smile and nod of thanks in his direction. Randall McLeod turned back to Adel.

"Upon my arrival last night, I removed General Bern from command of this force and sent him back to his post in Kobuk. His lips have always moved quicker than his brain works. I could not allow him to remain in command of a force that, at this point, would have been obliterated if not for you and your friends. Frankly, he should have seen the Hoyt trap coming from a mile away. I wish I had been able to command this force myself, but I was in Kotlik at the time word came into the capital. Bern was the most senior officer available, and the duke selected him to lead the attack in my absence. Please accept my deepest apology for his behavior toward you. It is not acceptable. I assure you that I will treat you with nothing but the respect you deserve," General McLeod reassured them.

"Thank you, Supreme General. You are everything we would expect from a man of your reputation," Adel said.

"Now that we have that business out of the way, would you be willing to answer a few questions?" McLeod asked, to which Adel nodded in agreement.

The Path of the Rawl Wielder

"How long have you known that you possess the power of the Rawl?"

All three sat in silence for a moment; it was clear that all of them were shocked the general knew of his power. To their knowledge, the Rawl was not something that was widely known about outside of those who served the Children. Adel glanced at his companions for advice; he was not sure if he should answer this question. Seeing their confusion, McLeod raised a calming hand.

"Allow me to explain, for I can see you are quite taken aback. I do know what your power is called, though I would wager that I am the only man in this camp who does. As you well know by now, it is not something that is known well throughout the Empire. However, the dukes of Thornata have long known that we house the Temple of the Rawl and its Children within our province. The duke informed me of this many years ago. He also briefed me on the power of the Rawl and what it is capable of doing. I never thought to meet a practitioner until I heard the stories my men told of you. I was under the impression that such people are not common. Am I incorrect in my assumption? Do you not possess this power?"

There was another moment of silence as the three companions exchanged uncertain glances. Adel was not sure how the Children would feel about them discussing such matters with outsiders. Still, if he already knew about the Rawl, could much harm be done by talking about it?

Once it was apparent that nobody else would speak, Adel began to respond.

"You are correct, sir. I do possess the power of the Rawl, though I have not known of my power for long. I discovered it by accident some weeks ago while working as a cabin boy on a shipping barge when we came under attack by the Hoyt. I traveled to the Temple of the Rawl and studied under the Children for several weeks. When Alsea brought us word of the fall of Kolig, they suggested I come here and try to use my power in a helpful way," Adel said, deciding it best to be up-front and honest with the general.

"Well, you certainly managed to do that," McLeod quipped. "Remarkable that such a new practitioner can use the power so effectively, very impressive indeed. How many wielders are there in the province, do you know?"

"I am the only Rawl wielder that I know of, sir, and the Children seemed to think so as well," Adel replied.

McLeod pulled out a chair and took a seat, apparently gathering his thoughts. As they waited for him to speak, Adel's thoughts turned to another question, one he had wanted to ask General Bern. Unfortunately, the man had proven himself to be nothing more than a blustering oaf before Adel had the opportunity.

"Sir, may I ask you a question? Did the army manage to defeat all of the Hoyt left within the city? Has

Idanox been found?" he asked.

General McLeod let out a long sigh, his eyes betraying the answer that Adel had feared he would give. "I am afraid we found only scattered remnants of the Hoyt force inside the city walls. It would appear the bulk of their men fled the city a day or two before the army arrived, leaving behind a token force to open the dam and keep order in the streets. Idanox was nowhere to be found. I suspect he fled to a new hiding place as soon as he felt confident that his preparations in Kolig were adequate. We do not know where he is now."

Adel did not try to hide his disappointment. He knew it was not the fault of the army, knew Idanox had never planned to engage them in battle. The Hoyt leader's plan had always been to kill as many of them as possible from a safe distance and then flee like the coward he was. He did manage to take some comfort in the fact that he and his companions had thwarted that particular plan.

"It would appear Idanox's plan was merely to strike the Thornatan Army as grievous a blow as possible while taking as few casualties as possible himself. His endgame was obviously never to control Kolig, so it leaves us to speculate on exactly what his final plan was," McLeod continued.

"What is your theory, General?" Ola asked.

"The fact that he planned to massacre a large portion of the army tells me he has far more ambitious plans, plans that would be easier for him to achieve if the army were significantly weakened," General McLeod mused.

"You think his plan is not to rule one city, but the entire province, that Kolig was the first step in a grander scheme," Alsea surmised.

General McLeod nodded, confirming that his suspicions matched Adel's. In his handful of encounters with the Hoyt, his perception of the group had changed drastically. He had initially believed them to be nothing more than a ragtag group of outlaws and thieves. Like most, he had thought them capable only of robbing trading caravans and shipping barges. He had seen them as merely the lowest form of scum who enjoyed preying on the weak. It was an opinion everyone he had spoken with across the province had shared. It appeared now that they had far more lofty goals than subsisting as a gang of outlaws.

Adel wondered now if that was an image the Hoyt and Idanox had purposefully cultivated, not wanting the people of Thornata to view them as a serious threat. Their numbers alone vastly exceeded the concept that most people had of them, their strategic skills even more so. Adel would never have thought them capable of seizing control of a major city, yet they had done so with relative ease. The fact that such a group had come so close to wiping out the bulk of the Thornatan Army sent a chill down Adel's spine. If they had succeeded, the Thornatan people would be in grave peril right now.

Unfortunately, he knew Idanox was unlikely to let go of his lofty aspirations so easily.

"General, how were the Hoyt able to take control of Kolig? I was inside the city at the fall, and there was virtually no battle," Alsea said.

"Now that we have broken the occupation, we have been receiving some information on that. It would seem the Hoyt successfully infiltrated the city watch. This was planned well in advance, maybe for months, or even years. When the time for the attack came, the Hoyt infiltrators killed as many of their unsuspecting fellows as possible and opened the main gates. The rest of their forces were able to walk right in, virtually unchallenged."

"It's hard to believe their numbers have expanded so rapidly," Ola said.

"I'm going to be quite blunt with what I am about to tell you," General McLeod began. "Our efforts to stamp out the Hoyt have not been going well. We outnumber them, yet at every turn they have managed to outmaneuver us, setting traps and ambushes. We have lost hundreds of men, yet at the same time have inflicted relatively little damage to them. Every time we think we have them hemmed in, they manage to slip away. Idanox himself is even worse. He's been little more than a shadow for these past two years, as we have been unable to pin down a location on him. I knew him when he was a wealthy timber seller in Oreanna. I always thought he was a pompous, self-important twat. But I would never have imagined he could be capable of leading so many men in such brutal tactics."

"We have seen their tactics up close quite a few times now," Adel replied. "Were it not for the power of the Rawl, I would likely not be alive to have this conversation with you."

"This brings me to my next question. What are your plans once you leave this camp?" General McLeod asked.

Adel had not given this matter much thought and did not wish to speak for Ola and Alsea. He had been operating on the assumption that once Kolig was secure, they would return to the Temple of the Rawl to continue his training as he and Elim had discussed when they departed. He explained this to the general, who nodded thoughtfully.

"I understand that you are not one of my soldiers, and I have no authority over any of you. If you must return to your temple, perhaps that is what you should do. I will see to it that my men outfit you with whatever food and supplies you require for your journey. We should also be able to spare three horses to speed you on your way if you would like. It's the least we can do for you in thanks for your help. However, I wonder if you would consider hearing out a proposal I have?" the general asked.

This caught Adel a bit off guard. He did not see the harm in hearing the general out, though he did not wish to speak for his friends. After a glance to each of them to confirm their willingness, he nodded his consent.

"I am working on assembling a group of the finest soldiers in the Thornatan Army, several hundred of them. It will be the job of this elite group to hunt down and stamp out the Hoyt wherever they can be found, including Idanox. I believe this will be a more efficient tactic than pursuing them with the bulk of our army. A small force will be far more agile in the ways that we can strike," he explained.

The strategy made sense. Assigning a force of soldiers to concentrate on this one task would give them a focus and mobility an entire army could not possibly have. Adel was still unsure of where he and his friends fit into this plan. He would soon have his answer.

"These men are extremely skilled fighters; however, the Hoyt have proven too resourceful time and time again at turning the odds against us. They often use terrain and guerilla tactics against us in manners that are difficult for my traditionally trained soldiers to defend themselves against, and we have paid the price for it in blood and lives. My thought is that having a powerful Rawl wielder at our side could help level the playing field in this regard," General McLeod said.

So, there it was. General McLeod wanted Adel to come with his soldiers and fight alongside them against the Hoyt. His previous accomplishments aside, it was a task Adel was not confident he was prepared to face. Not so long ago, he had been a deckhand with no knowledge that he even possessed the power of the Rawl. Yet, at the same time, could he refuse this request, allow others to fight this battle and die doing so when his presence could potentially save lives?

"Your friends here would be welcome as well, of course. Alsea has proven herself very resourceful, and that is a quality I value above all others in my men. Having a warrior of Ola's ability at our side would be a welcome boon, as well. The men who followed him onto that dam have yet to stop raving about his skills since the battle ended," General McLeod continued.

"You have certainly given us a lot to consider, General McLeod," Adel said, choosing his words carefully. "I wonder if you could please give us the rest of this day to consider your proposal?"

Adel had worried his reluctance to answer immediately might anger the general; this proved to be a pointless concern. General McLeod smiled his understanding, nodding agreeably. Adel already liked him far more than General Bern.

"Of course, I understand this is a complicated request, one that requires a great deal of careful consideration. Please, take your time and discuss your options amongst yourselves. I will return tonight after you have had time to consider. Please, anything you need, do not hesitate to ask. This army is in your debt, all of you," General McLeod said.

The Path of the Rawl Wielder

Rising from his chair, General Randall McLeod shook hands with each of them, stressing that they should not hesitate to ask his men for anything they required. Promising to return later that evening, he took his leave.

Once the general had departed, Adel turned to his companions, desperate for their input. They had remained relatively silent during the meeting with Randall McLeod, and he was eager to have their input. To his dismay, they seemed much more interested in hearing his own thoughts than they were in sharing theirs.

"Adel, I will remain by your side no matter what decision you make here," Ola began. "Ultimately, you are the one with the best understanding of your power. Therefore, you are the best one to make this decision."

"I agree with Ola, and I will also stay by your side no matter what. However, I would advise you to strongly consider returning to the Temple of the Rawl. You have proven yourself greatly on this mission, but Elim stressed to me before we left that there was still much for you to learn. In the end, though, it is your decision to make," was Alsea's reply.

Frustrated by their lack of more definite opinions, Adel turned his thoughts inward. He knew Alsea was right; it would be best for his own interests to return to the temple and resume his training. However, could he really make this decision based on what was best for him when people were dying at the hands of the Hoyt? He posed this question to his companions, and it was a long moment before Ola finally responded.

"Nothing you say is wrong, Adel. It is true that by joining these men and using your power, you could potentially save lives and help end the threat of the Hoyt sooner than the army may be able to without you. However, it is also true that by not completing your training, you are potentially leaving yourself vulnerable in the battles ahead. I will fight by your side and shield your life with my own, but understand that may not be enough to save you." Alsea nodded her agreement with the ogre's statement.

Adel knew Ola was right, of course. Getting himself killed would not do anybody any good. Yet he did not doubt that he could help the general and his men. He had already done so twice, and they were unlikely to face another task as challenging as stopping a devastating flood in its tracks. How many lives could potentially be saved by putting an end to Idanox and the Hoyt? Could he live with himself if he turned his back on them now?

"You are right, Ola. The smart thing for me to do is return to the Temple of the Rawl. I can't argue with your reasoning. But I keep thinking back to the first time I encountered these savages on Captain Boyd's barge. I watched as men I knew, men I considered friends, were cut down, their lives stolen from them for no reason at all. I was not able to save them, but now I know enough of my power that I can stop such things from happening again. How could I live with myself if I returned to the

Temple of the Rawl and then found out about the Hoyt murdering innocent people, knowing that maybe I could have stopped it from happening? I can help put an end to this evil. I do not ask either of you to come with me, but I cannot turn my back on this," Adel said, his mind made up.

Ola and Alsea did not appear the least bit surprised by his decision. Waving aside his rapid suggestion that they need not accompany him, both assured him they would stay with him until the end. He was relieved to have them by his side, though he also felt a significant amount of guilt as well. He understood that they were putting themselves in harm's way due to his decision.

***

When General McLeod returned that night, they told him they would fight beside his men on their quest to destroy the Hoyt. He was happy and wholly unsurprised by their decision, stating he had sensed they were not the type of people to turn their backs on those in need. He informed them their company would depart the camp in two days, intending to seek out and destroy any Hoyt they could find. He already had spies working in every city of Thornata, trying to ascertain the current whereabouts of Idanox.

Late that night, long after his companions had

fallen asleep, Adel lay awake in his bed and wondered if he had made the right decision. He had convinced himself that he had; he had told himself he would save countless lives. Was he truly up to this task? What if this decision got his friends killed? Adel knew he could not express these concerns to General McLeod or his companions. He knew he must show no sign of uncertainty or weakness. Steeling himself for what lay ahead, he fought against his self-doubt, struggling to find the rest he knew would prove to be elusive that night.

Chapter Eighteen

From inside the aging warehouse, the various sounds of daily life in the city of Kalstag were slightly muffled, yet still audible nonetheless. Sundown was fast approaching, and many of the people of Kalstag were beginning to make their way toward their homes, their day of work finished. In other cases, they headed to the many taverns that adorned this dock on the northern edge of the city. Once there, they would attempt to drink away their problems along with what little money they had made that day. It was a vicious, depressing cycle that many of the poorer residents of Thornata repeated day in and day out. Adel could hear them milling through the streets outside the warehouse and wondered if they suspected anything about the danger lurking within their city.

This particular warehouse had sat vacant for several years, and it showed. The structure was dilapidated and crumbling, and every surface was buried beneath a thick layer of dust. It had once housed goods that had been brought into the city by the numerous barges passing through Kalstag. Some crossed the Moyie Sea from the north or came up the Moyie River from the provinces that lay to the south. Its former purpose was now filled by newer, larger buildings that had sprung up in recent years. Its days of holding tons of goods in storage were long since forgotten. For the past three nights, however, it had served a much different purpose.

Adel glanced briefly out one of the windows in the warehouse's upper level, stealing a glance at the movement on the street below before slipping out of sight once more. They had arrived in the city several nights earlier, slipping through the gates in small groups well after dark and coming directly to this abandoned warehouse. They were desperate that their presence not be exposed before they were ready to act. If word got out that they were in the city, their quarry might learn of their arrival and flee before they could move against him.

They had been with this company of elite soldiers for just over a month, traveling first to the southwestern city of Kobuk. They had located and put a brutal end to a Hoyt syndicate within that city but had found no sign of

Idanox. General McLeod had initially intended to take them back north toward the capital city of Oreanna. His thought was that if Idanox did indeed intend to seize control of the province, Oreanna would be a likely destination. The morning they were due to depart Kobuk, however, word had arrived that an informant had intelligence indicating the Hoyt leader was here, hiding out in the southern city of Kalstag.

So they had marched hard across the southernmost reaches of Thornata. They had moved at such a desperate pace that they reached the distant city in ten days, determined that Idanox would not have an opportunity to slip through their grasp. For three days now they had hidden in this warehouse, waiting for further intelligence on the exact whereabouts of the Hoyt leader. When that information arrived, they would finally be able to put an end to the Hoyt insurrection once and for all. Idanox and his lofty plans for the conquest of Thornata would perish soon enough.

Adel was growing impatient with the waiting, but General McLeod had assured him the intelligence was good. Idanox was here, and they would have him in their grasp soon enough. The general's spies in the city were hard at work trying to determine the exact location of the Hoyt leader. Impatient though he may be, Adel knew it was critical to get to the Hoyt leader on their first attempt. There was no telling how long it would take to find him again if they failed, and if he caught wind of them, he would vanish again.

Idanox's reasons for choosing Kalstag, one of the more remote cities in the province, as his hiding place were unclear. General McLeod had two theories, both of which seemed plausible to Adel. Kalstag was the southernmost city in Thornata, and the Hoyt leader could be intending to hunker down for the fast-approaching winter. Adel knew from his years on the barge that snows were likely already beginning to fall sporadically in the far northern cities. It would be a challenge for Idanox to maneuver his men in force under such harsh conditions.

The second theory did not seem as likely to Adel, yet he could not dismiss it entirely. It was possible that after his resounding defeat at Kolig, Idanox was planning to use Kalstag as a base from which to flee the province. Kalstag provided relatively easy access to the neighboring province of Verizia. Adel did not think it likely that Idanox would so easily abandon all he had worked for. At the same time, he vowed to himself that the Hoyt leader would not escape Thornata if that were indeed his plan. Idanox would answer for his crimes, hopefully before this night was over.

Moving away from the window, Adel walked over to the edge of the balcony outside their door. He looked down at the soldiers who marched with them, assessing their readiness for what awaited them. Roughly sixty strong, these were the best of the best the Thornatan Army had to offer, according to General McLeod. They had undoubtedly proven themselves capable in Kobuk, putting down the Hoyt hidden there without losing a single man. Idanox would likely be protected heavily, but Adel doubted even the best the Hoyt had to offer could stand against these hardened and battle-tested men. The Hoyt would fight fiercely to defend their leader, but they would lose.

Alsea paced the room from one end to the other; she had been doing so for most of their three days here, every bit as eager as Adel to see this matter finished. As usual, Ola was far more stoic than his companions, usually sitting in silence, his thoughts a mystery to all but himself. The men the general had assembled had been surprisingly accepting of the ogre. There had been unmistakable glances of uncertainty when the general had first announced he would march beside them. Their comfort with the ogre had seemed to improve tenfold after their battle in Kobuk. Ola had been particularly dominant against the Hoyt forces, cutting down countless opponents during the fight.

General McLeod had given the three of them a small room to share that had served as an office in years past. The bulk of the soldiers were sleeping on the warehouse's main floor below. General McLeod had his own private quarters as well, another old office right beside the one in which they slept. It was from this direction that the knock they had been waiting for came.

"We just received word from the informant. It's

even better than we could have hoped. Idanox and about two dozen of his toughest thugs are hiding out in a warehouse not far down the dock from here. We can be there in ten minutes," General McLeod announced as he entered the room.

At last, Adel thought as he began gathering his equipment. He strapped his sword to his belt. His training with Ola had continued over the past month, and his skills were more refined than ever. If forced to fight hand to hand, he was confident he could defend himself against even the best fighters the Hoyt had to throw at him. McLeod began to go over the plan with them as they gathered their equipment.

"We will leave this warehouse a few hours before dawn. There should not be much of a moon tonight; we will take advantage of the cover of darkness. We will split into a dozen smaller groups. This will hopefully help us avoid being spotted by any lookouts they may have posted along the docks. They will be watching for a larger force—groups of five or six won't concern them. If we travel in small groups, any sentries will assume us to be ordinary street patrols. We will regroup one building over from the warehouse and move in. I will lead the attack on the interior, along with thirty of my men. I would like the three of you to be in this group as well if you are willing. The remainder of the men will form a perimeter around the warehouse to ensure Idanox does not escape if he attempts to flee the warehouse. Every alleyway and side street he might try to slip down will be covered. If they throw down their weapons, we'll take them in alive. If not, you are authorized to kill every last one of them, including Idanox, if you're lucky enough to get a crack at him," he explained.

As soon as all three had nodded in agreement, the general left the room, heading downstairs to brief his men.

The plan is a sound one, Adel thought. It would work, and they would finally put an end to the Hoyt on this night. He wished for a moment that they could train in preparation, knowing the physical activity would calm his nerves. But McLeod had made it clear that such noises coming from this warehouse would draw unwanted attention to their presence. Taking note that his hands were trembling in anticipation, he made an effort to hide this, not wanting to show any sign of fear or weakness to his companions. He wondered if they were making similar attempts to hide their nerves from him.

"Are you ready for this?" Ola asked, perhaps taking note of the trembling Adel was trying so hard to hide.

"More than anything, I am ready for this to be over. I am no fighter. I just hope I can fight well enough tonight to help put an end to this," Adel replied.

"You most certainly are a fighter, Adel. Nobody who isn't could have survived everything you have. Being a fighter is not all about your skill with a sword, though yours improves by the day. Being a fighter is more about having the will to survive whatever challenges fate throws your way, the determination to overcome any obstacle placed in front of you. You will survive whatever comes at you this day. We all will," Ola responded as Alsea nodded in agreement.

Several hours later, they made their departure from their hideout, slipping out into the dark streets of Kalstag. The soldiers had been forced to shed their heavy armor and chain mail, their shields bearing the sigil of the Thornatan Army left behind as well. General McLeod had decided on this at the last moment, concerned they would be more easily visible in their armor. If the Hoyt noticed an unusual number of patrols, the plan could go awry before they even reached the warehouse. All of them, including Adel and his friends, were dressed in clothes of darkest black. The dark garb had been chosen to assist them with blending in with the night. The city was quiet at night, far different from the bustling epicenter of life that it was during the day. It felt like it was a lifetime ago that Adel and Captain Boyd had come here to meet Ola for the first time. It was hard to believe, in reality, it had been only a few months.

Adel, Ola, and Alsea made their way along their assigned route along with four Thornatan soldiers. They wound their way through many twisting streets and alleyways, hoping the winding course would throw off anybody watching them. Ola had no choice but to walk while stooped into a hunch. They were concerned the presence of an ogre in their midst might alert the Hoyt that something unusual was happening. They reached the rendezvous point, the far side of a large building adjacent to the warehouse where Idanox and his men were hiding, without incident. Within minutes of their arrival, the rest of the groups had assembled with no issues. The plan was proceeding flawlessly thus far.

General McLeod raised his hand with one finger elevated, the signal for the men remaining outside to begin forming their perimeter. Most of them would be positioned on nearby rooftops with longbows, ready to pick off any Hoyt fleeing the battle. The rest would take up positions in alleyways and side streets that might be used by Idanox or his fighters in an escape attempt. After allowing several minutes for the men to get into position, the general raised a second finger. It was time for the attack to begin.

General McLeod led the way around the perimeter of the warehouse; the entrance was on the far side of the building. Adel had taken a position toward the center of the group with Ola and Alsea flanking him closely. They reached the entrance to the warehouse, a large door wide enough for half of their entire company to enter at once. The door was wide open, the flicker of firelight emanating from within a clear indicator that this supposedly abandoned warehouse was not what it appeared to be. Idanox was so arrogant that he had allowed the door to be left open, never suspecting one of his men would betray his trust. Holding short, everybody waited for the general's signal. Once it came, they rushed forward, surging through the opening and into the warehouse, cutting off any hope of escape.

There they were, as the informant had promised them, roughly two dozen men gathered around a campfire they had built near the center of the warehouse floor. They turned toward the approaching soldiers, drawing weapons, though Adel noted they did not seem particularly surprised at the soldiers' sudden appearance. A few of them were even smiling. What was going on? General McLeod led the way, raising an arm to stop his men about a dozen yards shy of the Hoyt fighters.

"It is over, gentlemen. We outnumber you, and we have you surrounded. Where is Idanox? If he surrenders now, we will spare your lives, and you will have an opportunity to stand trial for your crimes. You have my word," McLeod cried out.

The Hoyt did not respond initially, at least not with words, but rather with broad-lipped smiles, followed by chuckles that grew into raucous laughter. A profoundly unsettling feeling was growing in the pit of Adel's stomach; something was not right. The Hoyt were not reacting in the way he would have expected beaten men to behave. At last, one of the Hoyt began to speak, revealing that something had gone horribly wrong indeed.

"I do regret to inform you, Supreme General

McLeod, that Idanox is not here and never was. We have infiltrated your channels of communication, and you, brave general, have walked into a trap. Idanox sends his regards, but he could not be here to greet you in person. He asked us to give you a proper welcome on his behalf. Since you were kind enough to make such an offer, I will extend you the same courtesy. If you would like to beg for the lives of your men, we are willing to hear you out." The Hoyt's voice was filled with elation. His delight was unlike any Adel had ever heard, his glee at their successful deception unmistakable.

General McLeod was silent for a moment, obviously wondering the same thing as Adel. How had they been misled? How could the Hoyt have gotten deep enough into the army to pass false information all the way up to General McLeod? Perhaps they had been deceived, but it was a poorly laid trap if they still outnumbered the Hoyt by as many men as they did. Even if Idanox was not here, they still had more than enough men to stamp out this rabble of Hoyt fighters. Why did the Hoyt seem so confident?

A loud scraping noise began to rise up around him, the sound of wood rubbing against wood. Adel looked about the room and saw, to his horror, that small panels along the walls were sliding out of place. Hands inside the walls were shifting the panels aside, revealing dozens of small openings. Not large enough for a man to step through, but large enough for the Hoyt fighters safely tucked away within the walls of the warehouse to take aim with the longbows straight toward them. There was no longer any doubt the information had been false. The informant was likely a Hoyt infiltrator placed in the ranks of the army to lead them into this trap. He became aware of more noise behind him and turned to find the doors of the warehouse slamming shut behind them. A moment later, a loud crashing noise on the other side led him to believe the Hoyt were barricading them inside.

"Attack!" General McLeod cried out, shattering the long silence. It was the correct decision; of course, there was no other option. They could stand there and wait for the arrows to cut them down, or they could fight back with every breath they had left.

Adel ripped his sword from its sheath, aware of Ola and Alsea doing the same on either side. There was not much wind in the warehouse, but what little breeze there was flowing through the windows high above them he immediately reached out to with the Rawl. He began desperately trying to form a barrier between the soldiers and the arrows that were now mercilessly flying toward them.

The confined space of the warehouse limited the effectiveness of the wind shield. While it was able to deflect many of the Hoyt arrows, it did not blast them away with the same force as it had in the past. In the enclosed warehouse, he could not produce as much power as he would have been able to generate in an open field with an endless amount of air available to him. Some of the arrows still found their way through the shield. They were sinking into the men who had shed their armor in exchange for secrecy and thereby left themselves more vulnerable to the razor-sharp arrowheads. The Hoyt had successfully found a way to lessen the impact his power could have on the battle.

General McLeod had charged forward into the Hoyt men on the floor of the warehouse, several of his men behind him. Two of the Hoyt fell to his blade before they could react, no match for the general's exceptional skill. More of the soldiers joined the attack, desperate to kill as many of the Hoyt as possible. All the while, the arrows from the walls continued to fly toward them.

Adel was terrified, and he had no idea what to do. His wind shield was not as effective as it needed to be to shield the soldiers; at least six of them had fallen already, wounded or dead. He had not felt so helpless since the Hoyt had attacked the barge, back before he knew he possessed the power of the Rawl. Ola's hand was on his shoulder, pushing him toward a nearby wall as he tried to shield Adel's body with his own. Alsea was nowhere to be found, sending Adel into a brief panic until he spotted her at last. The girl was racing along the outer walls of the warehouse, thrusting her long knives into the small gaps where the Hoyt archers hid. She was trying to kill the archers hidden inside the warehouse walls, realizing this was their only hope for survival.

Upon seeing Alsea's method, several soldiers followed her lead, charging the walls with spears and swords, desperately trying to kill the archers who were massacring them. Some succeeded, but most were cut down by arrows before they could reach their target.

The wind barrier is useless, Adel thought in frustration. If the door were still open, he would be able to generate more power and protect them more effectively.

Several Hoyt had broken away from the general and his men and were now charging toward Adel. He assumed a defensive pose, his sword held in front of them, ready to fight until they cut the last breath from his body. Ola met them before they could reach him. Adel had never seen the ogre in such a fury, his massive sword hacking and hammering the Hoyt until those who remained backed away in sheer terror, wanting no part of Ola's sword. They fled backward, tripping over their own feet, only to be intercepted from behind by McLeod and his men.

Adel stepped away from the wall Ola had shoved him against. It was no use sitting back and waiting for the Hoyt to kill his companions one by one; he had to act. He had taken two steps when a Hoyt fighter rushed him from the left. The man had slipped around Ola while the ogre was occupied with attackers on the other side. His sword slashed at Adel's chest. Adel parried the man's attack with ease. He launched a counter that came within inches of taking the Hoyt's scalp off. The Hoyt attacked again, a wild swing that Adel caught with his sword. He twisted, wrenching his opponent's blade from his hand just as Ola had done to him so many times. Were their situation not so dire, he probably would have taken quite a bit of satisfaction from properly executing such a maneuver.

Adel took a step toward the Hoyt to finish him, but the man would not allow himself to be defeated so easily. He rushed recklessly toward Adel once more, this time with no weapon in his hand. Adel was so caught off guard by the brazenness of the move that he did not get his sword up in time to find the man with a killing thrust. The man wrapped his arms around Adel's torso, pinning his sword to his side. A split second later, he lashed out with a headbutt, catching Adel full in the face.

The force of the blow sent Adel falling backward, but his opponent did not let go, falling to the ground with him. The pain of the blow radiated through his head, but Adel knew he had to set it aside if he wanted to survive. From the ground, Adel could not get his sword into position to strike, and the next thing he knew, the Hoyt's fist crashed into his nose. His eyes immediately began to water, and the faint metallic taste of blood began to fill his mouth. His nose must've been broken. The Hoyt did not let up, swinging at him with punch after punch. Adel got one arm up to deflect most of the damage, but some still landed, and Adel did not know how many more he could absorb.

It was Ola who saved him, as he had so many times before. One moment the Hoyt was there, his weight bearing down on Adel as he drove blow after blow toward his head. The next, the pressure on his chest was gone, the strikes ceasing. Adel blinked upward through his swelling eyes to find Ola standing over him, the now terrified Hoyt gripped firmly by the throat in one massive hand. The greatsword plunged into the Hoyt's gut before Ola dropped him, sending his dying body tumbling to the ground like a discarded piece of garbage. Adel clambered to his feet, blood running down his face, his eyes scanning the still-raging battle. He vowed to himself as he did so that he would ask Ola for advice on fighting with no weapons if they were fortunate enough to survive this. That Hoyt's brazen attack had nearly been the end of him.

Most of the Hoyt on the floor of the warehouse were dead, but the soldiers were losing the battle. The arrows from the Hoyt hidden within the walls were wreaking havoc. In the chaos, it was hard to discern how many soldiers the Hoyt had killed. Several men were trying to force open the doors of the warehouse, but they were struggling mightily. The Hoyt must have barred the door on the other side, and the arrows mercilessly found their way to every man who tried to force their way through. Alsea was still working her way from archer to archer when Adel saw her take an arrow to the side and slump over against the wall, droplets of blood beginning to pool beneath her as soon as she hit the ground. Another arrow followed it a moment later, missing her head by inches and sending Adel entirely over the edge.

Breaking the wind shield, he sent every last bit of wind he could channel toward the outer walls. He knew this would not stop the archers, but if he were lucky, it might stun them for the split second he needed. He knew there was no way they would be able to kill all of the hidden Hoyt archers, not conventionally anyway, before every last one of them was dead. The only thing left to do was destroy their cover, take away their barrier. In other words, take away the warehouse in which they were standing.

He was thinking back to one of his lessons with Elim. Under the old man's guidance, he had shifted the course of a lightning bolt in a thunderstorm. Elim had told him that, in time, he might even master the art of manipulating the weather conditions to create lightning of his own. He had not tried to do this, Elim having explained it was an advanced technique and not to be attempted by an inexperienced Rawl wielder. This was what he must do now, and he must not allow himself to entertain the possibility that he could fail. He reached out with his power, his mind reaching for the skies high above the warehouse, concentrating with all his might on what he needed.

I need to destroy this warehouse. I need to kill the enemies hidden inside the walls.

From inside the warehouse, he could not see the lightning strike, but the sound it made as it hit the roof of the warehouse was both unmistakable and unimaginable.

The force of the blast knocked him from his feet, along with everyone else—even the massive, immovable Ola. The explosion was louder than anything Adel had ever heard. His ears were ringing in a high-pitched shriek that he was unsure would ever stop, his vision dazed and blurry. The one sense that seemed unaffected was his sense of smell, which was now registering a heavy smell of smoke along with burning wood and charred metal. The attack had happened as he had intended, but now the full consequences were setting in.

He had fully intended to light the building ablaze; however, he had been unprepared for the speed with which the flames began to race along the walls. The ringing in his ears shielded him from the worst of the horrified screams of the Hoyt men trapped within those walls, unable to get out before the flames overtook them. He was vaguely aware that Ola had a tight hold on his arm and was dragging him to his feet. The attack had worked, but they would have to move fast if they were to escape this burning warehouse themselves.

Adel understood this, yet ripped his arm from the ogre's grip nonetheless. He raced toward the wall where Alsea had fallen, fighting through fleeing soldiers to reach her side. The arrow had struck her a few inches above the waist, and she was bleeding profusely. The bottom of her black tunic was already soaked through, with a small puddle forming underneath her. Looking into her eyes, she seemed to be drifting in and out of consciousness; there was no way she would be able to walk out of the warehouse on her own.

Still staggered from his fall, Adel wrapped his arms around Alsea's shoulders, heaving her to her feet, careful not to drive the arrow deeper as he did. He had made it a few feet when he stumbled back to his knees, the smoke beginning to overpower his ability to breathe. The heat from the flames was becoming too much to bear. Adel knew he was not going to make it to the exit. He was going to die in this inferno he had created, and Alsea would die with him. It was all his fault; if he could have defended them more effectively, they would not have needed the lightning strike.

Ola saved him once more, appearing at his side in the blink of an eye. The massive ogre dragged him to his feet, then stooped over and lifted Alsea in one arm as if she weighed no more than a feather. With a hard shove, the ogre propelled Adel toward the warehouse doors, the debris which the Hoyt had placed behind them blasted away by the force of the lightning strike. They rushed through the door as the building's structure began to give out, flaming timber falling all around them.

The soldiers stationed outside to maintain a

perimeter were surrounding them now, reaching out to help them make their way clear of the collapsing warehouse. The high-pitched ringing in his ears still would not stop. His vision was blurry as ever, and each breath a struggle to force through his lungs. Despite the pain, Adel fought to continue placing one foot in front of the other. Slowly but surely, he staggered away from the burning inferno that had come so close to being their grave.

Chapter Nineteen

The inn was as silent as a crypt as the hours crept toward the early morning. The patrons of the tavern downstairs had departed to their homes at last. Those staying in the rooms above were fast asleep, save one. Adel sat in the dim candlelight beside Alsea's bedside, hoping that any moment would be the moment she came awake. He also feared, despite the many reassurances, that the moment would never come. Sitting there, looking down at his wounded friend, he still could not help but feel her injury was his fault, despite Ola and General McLeod insisting otherwise.

They had brought her here to this inn as dawn broke, the surviving members of the company breaking once more into smaller groups and scattering across the city. General McLeod, who had also been wounded in the battle, had warned their former hideout may not be safe. He feared the Hoyt would pursue them there to finish what they had started. It was a near certainty the informant who had betrayed them had also told the Hoyt where they had been hiding in the city. Of the thirty soldiers who had entered the warehouse, only nine of them had emerged alive, and two of those may not survive their injuries much longer. The others had been killed by the relentless arrows flying from the hollowed-out walls, unable to escape the ruthless Hoyt trap.

General McLeod had expressed extreme gratitude to Adel as he had led them to this inn. He had stated in no uncertain terms that his men would all be dead if not for Adel and his exceptional powers. But the thanks rang hollow, no matter how profusely McLeod heaped them upon him. If he had been able to act sooner, more men might still be alive, and Alsea might not be lying here injured. General McLeod had paid for rooms for the three of them and then taken his leave. He assured them that he would send a healer for Alsea and get word to them when the time came for them to leave the city.

The healer had arrived within the hour and removed the arrow from Alsea's side, also finding and mending several other wounds as well. The healer told them he had arrived just in time; the girl may not have survived another hour with the arrow lodged inside her body. Fortunately, the wound had not punctured any critical internal body parts. After tending to Alsea, the healer had also mended Adel's broken nose, allowing him to breathe without pain once more, though his own pain had been all but forgotten in his desperation to get help for Alsea. Assuring them that Alsea would survive, the healer had taken his leave in the early afternoon, leaving a salve that would need to be applied to the arrow wound daily until it had completely healed. Since then, Adel had sat by her bedside, waiting for her to wake up. The healer had stressed it could take some time, but Adel did not care. He would wait for however long was necessary.

Her mouth opened before her eyes did. It sounded as though she was trying to speak, but a faint rasping was all that came out. Recognizing the problem, Adel moved to the table where he had set a pitcher of water, pouring a glass and returning to her side as her eyes flickered open for the first time.

Putting a hand under her back, he gently helped her sit up in the bed, lifting the cup of water to her lips. She drained the water, gasping a bit as she finally pushed the cup away and fell back to the pillows. For a moment, Adel thought back to their positions being reversed after the Battle of Kolig. Alsea had done an excellent job caring for him, and he vowed to himself to do every bit as good for her.

"What happened, Adel? The last thing I remember, things were going very badly for us in that warehouse," Alsea rasped, her voice helped by the water but still not fully returned to normal.

Adel recounted the story of everything that had happened, beginning with her being shot and ending with the healer tending to her wounds at the inn. She grimaced a bit throughout his telling; it was clear the injury from the arrow was still paining her, though she tried her best to conceal it from him. He suspected the pain was far more severe than her faint grimaces were letting on and vowed to ensure she rested, no matter how hard she might try to resist it.

"The healer swears your wound will heal clean. Ola left a short time ago to sweep the nearby streets; he wants to make sure there aren't any Hoyt trying to sneak up on us. I don't think they managed to follow us, but there is no harm in being cautious. General McLeod will come back for us when it is time to leave the city; he feels we should stay separated in case the Hoyt come for us again," Adel said.

"Hopefully he is reevaluating the sources he trusts for his intelligence. We would all be dead in that warehouse if not for you," Alsea said, her displeasure with the general catching Adel somewhat off guard. McLeod had treated them well, but Alsea was not wrong; his intelligence had been poor, to say the least.

Looking down at her, Adel's eyes fell to the floor in shame. The statement she had made bothered him, bringing up feelings of guilt that he had spent most of the last day trying to suppress. He knew in his heart that he was every bit as responsible for her wounds as General McLeod was, and she was too intelligent not to see it as well. His efforts to hide his guilt did not fool her.

"Adel, what is bothering you? You are terrible at hiding your emotions; something is on your mind," she pressed him.

"I was wrong, Alsea. I was wrong back in Kolig when I decided I could help these soldiers. It's my fault you and Ola are a part of this mess. I have no business being here, and you nearly paid for my foolishness with your life. I was unable to shield any of you from those arrows in the warehouse. For all the faith I placed in the Rawl, it was useless in there. Once again, I would be dead if Ola had not been there to save my life. Many soldiers paid the price for my arrogance, and you could have as well," he said.

Alsea sat up a little taller in bed, not saying anything for a moment. At last, she beckoned for him to move closer. Thinking she intended to hug him or whisper something reassuring in his ear, he leaned in expectantly. The hard slap she delivered to the side of his face was the last thing he would have expected. He rubbed the spot she had slapped, amazed that she was able to strike him with such force less than a full day after being dangerously close to death. She had fortunately missed his recently broken nose, but the blow stung nonetheless.

"Adel, you are the reason there were any survivors of that ambush, so please cut that nonsense right now. Keep it up, and I'll hit you again. You created a lightning bolt? I didn't know that was something you were even capable of," Alsea said.

"Neither did I, not until I did it," he replied tentatively, not wanting to be slapped again, his face still stinging from the bite of the last one.

"You're making my point for me. You sit here and feel sorry for yourself and wax on about how you have failed us all. The truth is that even you do not yet know the full extent of what you are capable of doing. You saved Ola and me during that Hoyt attack after we left the temple. Then you saved the people of Kolig when the floodgates opened. After that, you saved the army during the fire in their encampment. Now you have saved the surviving soldiers of McLeod's unit, and yet all you see in yourself is failure. You are your own worst critic, and that will always be the case. But you need to learn to see the good in yourself, Adel. You have done things since leaving the Temple of the Rawl that no other man could dream of doing."

She was right, of course, as she always was. She had a knack for seeing the way things truly were, a way of seeing past the surface. This must be why she was such a valued servant for the Children. Once again, he wondered how she had ended up in this role, a question she had been close to answering a few weeks earlier before their encounter with General Bern. He decided this was as good a time as any to try again.

"You never did tell me, Alsea, why you serve the Children. General Bern interrupted us the last time I asked. You told me you had no place else to go; why is that?"

She lay back in the bed, closing her eyes for a brief moment, and he was sure his answer would have to wait. To his surprise, they opened a moment later, the slightest hint of tears in the corners. Adel had seen many shocking things over the past few months, but the sight of Alsea, who had been as strong as iron throughout their time together, with tears in her eyes was disconcerting. He knew instinctively that the pain she was feeling had nothing to do with her injuries.

"I never knew my mother; she died giving birth to me. My father was a traveling merchant, and he would drive his wagon from city to city, buying and selling whatever he could find to interest people. I spent my childhood traveling all across the province with him. He was not a rich man, but he made enough for us to survive. We had a good life. I learned how to talk to people, how to sell them things. Mostly I learned how to watch and listen. He would always say that a great salesman spent more time looking and listening than they did talking. Your clients will always show you what they need if you let them. It's been a useful set of skills to have," she said.

She took another long pause and glanced toward the empty water cup. Adel hurried to fill it again, and she drank it down as quickly as she had the last cup. Once she had finished, she began to speak again.

"When I was ten years old, we were leaving Kolig to travel to Oreanna. We were a few days on our way when we crossed paths with a gang of thieves in the wild. They were armed and threatened to kill me if my father did not surrender his wares. So he gave them everything we had, told them to take the wagon and mule as well. As they rolled away in our wagon, with everything we owned inside it, one of them put an arrow through my father's skull. They laughed as they drove away with everything we had to our names."

Adel fought down the horror-stricken gasp that had nearly escaped his mouth. To endure such misery at ten years old was unfathomable to him. He had lost his own mother at a young age, of course, but the violent manner in which Alsea had been ripped from her father was unimaginable. The fact she had survived such an ordeal spoke to her resilience.

"The thieves had no interest in me. They left me there next to my father's body, left me there to die alone in the wild. But I didn't die; I would not let them have that. So I started walking north, going toward Oreanna as my father had planned for us. I don't know what I intended to do when I arrived, I only knew I wanted to complete our journey, that it was important to me. I don't think I knew what else I could do." She was having difficulty speaking again, a challenge Adel knew had nothing to do with needing more water.

The tears in her eyes were no longer small and hidden but were flowing freely. Adel hurriedly brought her a cloth with which to wipe them away. For a moment she seemed unable to continue, yet she found a way to do so, strong as ever.

"I walked for about two days, drinking from streams and eating wild berries. I wouldn't have survived much longer on my own. I was lost in the foothills of the Bonners, and I no idea what to do. I would have starved or frozen to death if I had been out there a few more days. I must have stumbled close to the Temple of the Rawl without realizing it. That's when Klaweck found me and took me up to the temple. I told Elim and the rest of the Children what had happened. They took me in and gave me food and clothing and shelter. Ola went out and found my father's body and gave him a proper burial. He even tried to find the men responsible as well, but I was a child, and my memory was not good enough to describe them in detail. They probably ended up joining the Hoyt when Idanox formed them; they were the sort he would like to have on his side. Great, stupid brutes with no conscience would fit in well with the Hoyt," Alsea continued.

She had seemingly regained control of her emotions. The tears had stopped flowing, and her voice was more robust as she continued again. Adel admired her more than ever, listening to all she had overcome.

"The Children of the Rawl never asked for anything in return for their kindness. I was welcome to stay until I was old enough to care for myself and then leave if I wished. But I wanted to repay them. So now I travel across the province, searching for people like you or listening for information they may find useful. Ola taught me how to fight and how to survive in the wild. I'm a better shot than he is now, but he is still my better with the sword. If the temple ever comes under attack, I will fight to defend it. Anything I can give them in payment of the debt I owe will still never come close to repaying what they did for me," she finished.

It made sense now, her reasons for serving the Children. Adel doubted he would be able to accept the kindness of the Children without wanting to repay them himself. He felt closer to her now; she had shown more emotion and humanity in this brief conversation then she had in the entire time they had traveled together. He felt a bond with her. They had both lost their family at a young age, though her experience had been far more traumatic than his.

"I'm sorry for what happened to you, and I'm sorry I asked you to relive it," he said, wishing all the while that he had more comforting words to offer.

"Do not apologize. If you are to be the leader of the Children as Elim thinks you will be, then you deserve to know. For what it is worth, I agree with him; we would be lucky to have you as a leader. But leader or not, I will follow you now. You have earned that much from me," Alsea declared, smiling through her tears.

This declaration took Adel quite aback. After their initial conversation, Elim had not again mentioned the prospect of Adel becoming the leader of the Children, yet he had seen fit to tell Alsea of this notion, and now she was pledging him her service. He felt a great swell of appreciation, but it did not feel right.

"Very well, Alsea," he said. "If you have chosen me as your leader, that is your choice to make. My first act as your leader is to release you from my service."

The girl looked shocked, then slightly angry. His responding smile only seemed to anger her further. He placed a calming hand on her arm as she began to cry out in protest, fearing she may slap him again if he did not explain himself.

"I would love nothing more than for you to continue to travel at my side, but not as some kind of service. You do not owe me a thing. I want you with me because you are my friend and want you with me as my friend, not as a servant. The same goes for Ola; you have both saved my life more times than I can count since we have left the temple. Obviously, I am not going to ask you to leave. After all, I rather enjoy living, and I feel the chances of that continuing will be improved with you along," Adel explained.

Alsea's expression was unreadable as it usually was, so Adel had to content himself with sitting back and waiting for her response. He leaned back in his chair, trying to make sure he was beyond the range of her slap. He was delighted when a broad, shockingly stunning smile crossed her face. She reached out, this time to wrap him in an embrace.

"Adel, I do not deserve you as a friend after the way I treated you when we left the temple, yet here you are asking me for friendship. It will be my pleasure," she replied.

Happy to hear this, Adel brought her another cup of water, following the healer's instructions that she must drink a lot once she came awake. She drank it down dutifully before lying back once more; it was apparent she would not be able to stay awake for much longer. Before fading off, she managed one last question.

"What are we going to do now, Adel?"

It was not something he had given much thought since the night before, but somehow he knew the answer. It came to him more naturally than any thought had since the first Hoyt attack on the barge.

"We are going to stay here until your wounds have had time to heal and General McLeod has regrouped his men. We are going to find out where Idanox is hiding. No matter how far he has run, no matter how deep of a hole he has dug for himself, we are going to find him and put an end to him and the Hoyt.

We can't let them keep hurting and killing innocent people. Their days are numbered."

Chapter Twenty

Many miles to the northwest of where Adel and Alsea were discussing their resolve for the future, Idanox was feeling a similar steely resolve. He had come north to the city of Kolsvard, the most remote city in the province of Thornata, set alone in the middle of hundreds of miles of dense pine forests. Winter would be closing in soon, and he had decided that this was where he would make his home for the cold season. Unlike the other major cities, there were no large waterways that passed through Kolsvard, meaning any information coming or going would need to travel on foot. This made it easier for the Hoyt to keep a firm grip on every piece of information that entered or left the city.

The Path of the Rawl Wielder

The army was hunting him relentlessly, and this location gave him his best hope of avoiding discovery.

He had acquired an old factory on the outskirts of the city to set up as his winter abode. It was a massive facility, once used to process timber from the surrounding pine forests, but the owners had long since moved to a larger facility. This left this building deserted and ready for his use. The owner was a wealthy man, an old friend who shared his distaste for the Thornatan government and was happy to turn a blind eye to the presence of the Hoyt. It was more than spacious enough to house the sizeable contingent of men he had brought to the city with him. Idanox wanted to be sure he was well-protected. He was, after all, the heart, soul, and brains of the Hoyt. Without him, there would be no more quest to forge a better life for the ordinary people of Thornata. Or so he told his followers.

General McLeod and his task force had fallen into the trap he had planned so perfectly in Kalstag. His men had executed the treachery to perfection, only for the cursed Rawl wielder to save them, killing many more Hoyt fighters in the process. The fact that his men had failed to capture or kill the boy was disturbing enough. But hearing tales of him fighting alongside the army, delivering them victory from the jaws of defeat, intensified his rage even further. After the incident on the Moyie River, the boy had been a curiosity, one Idanox wished to learn more about and perhaps use to his advantage. Now he was a thorn in his side that needed to be removed. It was clear he could not count on his men to execute tasks of such importance, and so it was that he paced his quarters this night, waiting for a visitor.

He had tasked several of his men with finding this man and requesting that he visit Idanox here in Kolsvard. His name was Srenpe, and he was a man with a nasty reputation. It was the type of reputation Idanox felt could prove useful in putting an end to the young Rawl wielder, for Idanox had made up his mind that it must be done. He had hoped at one point to meet with the boy, perhaps even persuade him to join their cause. Now that the boy was working with McLeod, Idanox knew such hopes would bear him no fruit. Better to see the boy dead and be done with it. He could not afford to allow the boy to do more damage to his plans; it was time to cut his losses.

It was evident his men were not up to the task of killing the boy, and so he had sent for Srenpe, a man with a skill set not possessed by any Hoyt fighter. Srenpe was a mage, but not just any mage would do. The Order of Mages had expelled him from their order, and though the reasons had never been made public, there were rumors, the type of stories Idanox hoped were true. A powerful mage with a moral compass that could be swayed by gold could be a valuable asset to the Hoyt indeed.

Still, any asset's value was decreased if it was not reliable, and here he was still awaiting the mage's arrival, almost an hour after the agreed-upon time. Idanox was not a man who liked to be kept waiting by anyone; he was used to things happening at his convenience. He had found throughout his life that having wealth and power tended to ensure things happened the way you wanted at the time you wanted. At last, there was a sharp tap at his door, and one of his men appeared to inform him that Srenpe had arrived.

Idanox made his way through the abandoned factory to a dusty old room he had set aside as a small office for himself. He entered to find Srenpe waiting for him, along with two Hoyt men who had escorted him into the facility. Idanox had not met many mages in his time, yet he could tell at once that Srenpe was unique, even among the eccentric group of magic wielders. The robes he wore were similar to those of the rest of his order, yet Idanox had never seen any mage garbed in the bloodred color that Srenpe had chosen. He carried a staff, as all mages did, a long, twisted rod of an unrecognizable, jet-black wood.

Yet it was his face that set Srenpe apart. While most of his features were unremarkable, his eyes betrayed the cunning mind behind them as they scanned the room continuously. Idanox surmised this was a man who was usually the smartest in any room and immediately resolved this would not be the case here. He thanked his men for escorting Srenpe and asked them to wait outside. Once they were alone, he greeted the mage, setting aside his displeasure at the other's tardiness. There was no point in chastising the man and potentially jeopardizing their working relationship. Better if he begin their relationship cordially, for this could prove to be a valuable ally.

"Thank you for agreeing to meet with me, Srenpe. I hope this can be the beginning of a long and fruitful working relationship for both of us," Idanox greeted. He motioned that Srenpe should feel free to sit, a gesture the mage ignored.

"Thank you for the gold you sent to persuade me to take this appointment. I don't make a habit of meeting with wanted criminals, Idanox. I prefer to keep a lower profile; it helps keep the army and the government out of my affairs. I'm sure a man such as yourself can sympathize," Srenpe replied, his voice that of a well-practiced orator. This was a man who likely never opened his mouth without choosing each word leaving it with great care.

"I am a wanted man, no mistake about that. As for criminal, I would argue that part is up for debate. At least when I steal, I have the decency to call it what it is. I don't attempt to dignify it as taxation like those bloated nobles in Oreanna," Idanox replied, knowing he would need to take a measured approach with this man. He should make an effort to appear relatable. It was an approach, after all, that had worked with thousands of Hoyt fighters.

"If you have asked me here to have a political

discussion, I am afraid I must take my leave. I have many far more pressing matters that require my attention. Understand one thing, Idanox. I do not care about you, or the Hoyt, or your little revolution. I am interested in being paid, something your messengers assured me would happen if I agreed to help you. That will be the full extent of our working relationship, and I want to make that abundantly clear now. So why don't you quit wasting my time and tell me what you want?" Srenpe said, his voice never changing from the polite, even friendly tone despite his harsh words.

Perhaps this is a mistake, Idanox thought. Srenpe was powerful, no doubt about that, but he was not sure if he could have a partnership with a man who showed him so little respect. He had paid this mage two hundred gold coins for this meeting, and he was beginning to fear it had been money wasted. He had spent his entire adult life surrounding himself with men who could follow orders, and this was not likely to be the case with Srenpe. An overly independent mind had no place within the ranks of the Hoyt. Still, he had hoped this man could help him resolve the Rawl wielder problem, and it was still worth a try to reason with him.

"Tell me, Srenpe, are you familiar with a power called the Rawl?" he asked.

"I know a bit about it, yes. The Order of Mages is familiar with the power and its abilities, though their records show there are not many people left in the world who possess it. The Order's records indicate most of its wielders belong to a race called the Thrawll. A brutal people, fortunately not found within the Empire," Srenpe replied.

"True, for the most part. Unfortunately, not all of its wielders are fantastical demons living in far-off lands. We have become aware of a young boy who does possess it, right here in Thornata. He has been making life quite difficult for my men across the province. A few days ago, he demolished a warehouse with a lightning bolt he conjured from thin air. You asked me not to waste your time, so I won't. I want this boy dead, and I want to know if you can help me do this," Idanox said, deciding it best to lay it all out at once for the impatient mage.

Srenpe did not respond immediately. Idanox could see his mind at work behind the cunning eyes, though the mage was a difficult man to read. Based on reputation, he had pegged Srenpe as the type of man who would bear no qualms over the murder of a young man, at least as long as the price was right. He hoped he had not made a mistake with this assumption. After a few long seconds, Srenpe responded at last.

"I believe I can do what you have asked. I know of magic I can use that would be sufficiently deadly to kill the boy. It is a complex process, but I can do it. I would need you and your men to acquire certain supplies for me before I would be able to begin. I also need time to make my own preparations, at least two months. Magic this complicated takes time to prepare. Trust me when I say you do not want this to go wrong," the mage declared.

Two months? Idanox had hoped Srenpe would have a solution that could be put into place immediately. Two months was a long time to allow the Rawl wielder to run free. However, the first days of winter were already upon them, and the harsh Thornatan snows would soon limit even the army's ability to move around the province in large numbers. The boy might be powerful, but even he could not overcome the raw power of nature. Perhaps a delay of two months would not be such a bad thing after all. It would give him time to regroup and refocus his strategy for after the boy's interference was no longer an issue.

"I accept your terms, Srenpe. Please make a written list of all the supplies you need us to gather, and I will have my men get to work on it. As long as your plan is ready to be put into effect before the end of winter, I think that will be fine," Idanox said.

"Very good; I will begin my preparations at once. Do you have a place in this building where I can work when needed? I need a large amount of space, more than I have access to elsewhere in this city. It appears space is a resource you have in abundance here," the mage said.

"My men will clear out a large room for your use. Once they have, you can let them know any adjustments you need, and I will see to it they get it done."

"That will be fine. There is also the matter of my

payment. While I am sure the justness of your cause is all the payment some of your men require, I will need a more tangible form of payment for my services."

"How much do you want?" Idanox asked, impatient to be done with this.

"Fifty thousand should do it."

"Fifty thousand? Are you insane? You expect me to pay you fifty thousand gold for a plan that you have yet to tell me anything about?" Idanox cried out, outraged.

"Calm down, Idanox. Such an outburst does not befit a man of your stature. If it makes you feel better, I only expect half up front. You are welcome to pay me the second half once I have produced that which you have asked me to provide. If this is too much to ask, I can leave. I wish you luck in finding another way to rid yourself of this Rawl wielder. I hear they can be quite formidable, but I suppose that is no longer my concern." Srenpe began to move toward the door, forcing Idanox to make up his mind in an instant.

"You have a deal: fifty thousand, half up front. Consider it as a security deposit for your services. But you had better be able to deliver what you are promising," Idanox warned.

"I don't recall promising anything. I simply told you I had a plan to deliver the service you require. Do not bandy your threats at me, Idanox. I am not one of the naive fools you have suckered into believing you are going to build a new world where peasants like them will be equal to rich men such as yourself. You asked me for a service, and I will provide it for the proper payment. That is where this relationship ends. Are we clear on that?" Srenpe hissed, the friendliness evaporating from his voice, his tone low and menacing.

Idanox was not one to allow any man to speak to him in such a manner, but he could not bring himself to talk back to the mage. This was a person he could sense was extremely dangerous, and not a man he wished to anger. He merely nodded his agreement and called for his men to find a room for Srenpe to begin his work. He assured the mage the first half of his payment would be received by the end of the week. Srenpe took his leave without further comment, leaving Idanox feeling more doubtful about the alliance by the second.

He retired to his private quarters after the meeting with Srenpe, unable to shake the feeling that he had made a mistake by bringing in the mage. He had entered the meeting feeling he had little choice. If his own men could not deal with the boy, he had to find someone who could. However, he had not anticipated the volatile temper and unpredictable nature of the mage. Introducing such an unstable element into his meticulously controlled organization was a considerable risk. It gave him the feeling that he may end up needing to have Srenpe killed by the time their partnership ended.

Still, there was a certain comfort at having a plan in place, even if he was not entirely clear on what that plan was. He may not be confident in Srenpe's loyalty, but he was optimistic about the mage's ability to put an end to the Rawl wielder. One meeting had left him satisfied the mage possessed both the power and questionable moral compass to get the job done. Perhaps that was sufficient. After all, with the Rawl wielder out of the way, there would be little standing between him and total control of Thornata. McLeod and the army would try their best, but they were already beaten; they just didn't know it yet. He would soon be sitting in the duke's chair, the rightful ruler of Thornata. It was just as he had seen in his head for years. Nobody could stand in his way.

Adel's story will

continue in the next

installment of the

Rawl Wielder trilogy.

Acknowledgments

It's hard to believe it has been about six years since I first sat down to write the initial outline for this book. It's been a long road and a fulfilling journey, one I could never have completed alone.

First, to my dear wife, Mercedes. She encouraged me that the time had come to follow my dream and never let me give up on it. There were times I questioned my abilities, or whether this endeavor was worth the time I was investing in it. She was there every time to shout down those doubts. She was also the first to read this book and provide valuable feedback and encouragement. Thank you, my love, for your never-ending love and support.

I also must thank my editor, Natalia Leigh of Enchanted Ink Publishing. I can assure you this book would not exist in its current form without her invaluable feedback and meticulous attention to detail. Thank you for your hard work in helping me bring this first part of Adel's story to life.

Thanks are also in order for my cover/map artist, and good friend, Joseph Gruber. I don't doubt many of you are reading this due to his beautiful artwork catching your eye. I can't possibly thank him enough for it. Joe, I can't wait to see what you come up with for Book 2!

Last of all, thank you to anyone who took a chance and spent your hard-earned money on this book. I hope you feel it was a good investment, and know I am hard at work on delivering the next installment!

~Pete Biehl

About the Author

Pete Biehl has been an aspiring author for as long as he can remember. This is his debut novel. When not writing, he enjoys reading and traveling. He lives in Idaho with his wife, dog, and way too many cats that she keeps bringing home, but that he wouldn't trade for anything.

Please visit:

www.petebiehl.com

www.instagram.com/petebiehlauthor

www.facebook.com/petebiehlauthor

CPSIA information can be obtained
at www.ICGtesting.com
Printed in the USA
BVHW071409210921
617189BV00004B/144

9 781736 528617